THE SILENT DIRECTORATE

A. G. Soares

Gypsy Press LLC

eBook ISBN: 978-1-966785-02-6
Paperback ISBN: 978-1-966785-03-3
Hardcover ISBN:978-1-966785-04-0

Cover design by: A. G. Soares
Library of Congress Control Number: 2018675309
Printed in the United States of America

For G.S.

Prologue

February 2002
Afghanistan

The shocks were long dead in the truck.

Every dip in the mountain road sent a jolt up Victoria's spine, the rusted bench seat giving no cushion against the battered terrain. Her back ached from the hours of jostling. Dust poured in through the open slats in the truck bed, coating her scarf, her eyes, her throat. She tasted aluminum and heat. The young gunner standing above them, his thin arms wrapped around the mounted PKM, stared down the road with an empty focus that made her uneasy. He couldn't have been older than sixteen.

Alex was to her left, one knee drawn up, arms folded loosely. His expression hadn't changed since they'd left the last checkpoint—unreadable, detached. He hadn't spoken for over an hour. Just watched.

Doc sat across from them, legs braced wide, camera case at his feet. He chewed on a stick of gum like it was keeping him alive. His eyes flicked from the boy gunner to the mountain switchbacks ahead, then to the convoy's lead vehicle, a Hilux with a .50 cal bolted into the bed.

Five trucks in all. A rolling cliché of a warzone.

The wind picked up, carrying the smell of diesel, urea, and dry earth, sharp and sour, like sweat on metal. The furrowed fields stretched out below, the soil dusting the air like powder shaken from a sack. Tight green buds of poppies just beginning to stir, evidence of the opium cultivation that kept Karim Al-Rashid's little empire afloat. She'd read the briefings. What she hadn't expected was how vast it all felt. How indifferent.

The isolation here was total. There was no signal, no base, no checkpoint after the last one. Just rocks and air and the distant chuff of engines grinding up inclines.

It thrilled her.

This was it, she told herself. Not round tables in Manhattan. No editors, makeup artists, or greenrooms. Here. Dust in her teeth, boys with guns, a warlord waiting at the end of the road. This was where the world turned, where history lived.

She shifted, brushing the dust from the collar of her tailored utility jacket. It was Ralph Lauren Purple Label, chosen as much for the cut as for the message it sent: she was not some amateur with a website. She was here on assignment for a major network. And she was going to get the story of the decade.

Alex leaned closer, his voice low. “We’re twenty clicks out.”

She nodded, brushing hair from her face. “You’re tense.”

He didn’t reply.

Victoria smiled to herself and looked away. She didn’t know why he was sulking; this whole expedition had been his idea. He joined the network in October and pitched the idea almost immediately. She instantly recognized the opportunity and jumped on it, making the pitch her own.

She opened her canteen and took a sip. Lukewarm water. She thought about Montauk, her father’s gin and tonic sweating on the porch railing. She thought about the last phone call with her mother, the clipped silences, the disbelief.

“You’re really going?” she said. “I thought this Afghanistan assignment was just a bluff for attention. Are you punishing me?” For a moment, the implacable façade fell away, and something raw and almost human showed at the edges of her voice.

The truck slowed. The gunner banged the side of the vehicle with his palm and signaled the driver. They were approaching a bottleneck, a narrow ridge flanked by cliffs on either side. Victoria felt a flicker of doubt. She glanced at Alex. He was scanning the ridge line.

Doc muttered, “Jesus.”

Two fighters stepped into view at the ridge’s peak. RPGs slung across their backs. The convoy didn’t stop.

Victoria swallowed and forced her gaze forward. She would not show fear. Not to Alex, not to these boys with weapons and bored expressions. She was a professional. She had been to Gaza, to Caracas, to Yemen, the week of the bombing.

But something in the silence now unnerved her.

The boy gunner shifted his grip on the machine gun. The barrel angled slightly down. Just a twitch of the wrist, a second of nerves, and the whole truck bed would be painted red.

She pulled her scarf tighter, closed her eyes against the dust. When she opened them again, the ridge was behind them. Victoria’s spine ached from the jostling, but she refused to show discomfort. Not to Alex. Not to Doc. Not to the stone-faced boy gripping the PKM beside her like it was part of his body. She kept her chin high, back straight, scarf pulled tight against the grit in the air. Somewhere behind the next ridge waited Karim Al-Rashid, the banker turned warlord, who would make her famous.

The convoy slowed to crawl speed to cross a shallow riverbed. The tires dipped into muck, and Victoria felt her boots dampen from the floor panel beneath her.

“They said we’d be at the compound before sunset,” she said, turning to Alex.

He didn’t answer right away. His eyes were on the hills.

"Road’s longer than expected," he said, scanning the ridgelines. “Too quiet for my taste.”

“Too quiet,” she repeated. “Noted, Colonel Kurtz.”

Doc grunted discontentedly from the opposite side of the truck bed, where he was wedged next to their satellite case. He hadn’t spoken much all day; he wasn’t happy either. Victoria wasn't going to let either of them spoil the adventure.

Victoria turned back to the terrain, unimpressed. Another switchback, another dry valley littered with ancient rusting Soviet wreckage and grazing goats. Afghanistan had a way of repeating itself.

She pulled her sunglasses down and let herself drift for a moment—Bar Harbor, early October. The air smelled of salt and woodsmoke. Her father sat in deck shoes on the wide cedar porch, studying the Times as if it were scripture. Her mother fussed over a platter of smoked bluefish and Lebanese mezze as though it were haute cuisine. They'd begged her not to take the assignment.

"Afghanistan, dahling? Isn't there a piece you could do from Geneva? What about Davos?"

But she hadn't spent four years at Columbia to play hostess at fundraisers. She was here to matter. To make history. And Karim Al-Rashid was going to give her the quote that echoed from every nightly news desk in the Western world.

She adjusted her scarf again, ignoring the gnawing pit in her stomach.

The sun dropped low and blood-red over the horizon when the first guard post came into view: a sandbagged ledge above a narrow gorge, manned by a trio of fighters with scopes and scarves. One leaned on a Soviet RPG as if it were a walking stick.

Alex's posture changed almost imperceptibly. He tilted his chin toward the ridge and lowered his voice so only Victoria could hear, "Two DShKs. Sandbag placements. Good visibility downrange."

Victoria frowned. "Making notes for your travel blog?"

He looked at her. His eyes gave nothing back.

"I pay attention," he said. "You should try it sometime."

She rolled her eyes and sat back. The trucks pushed on, climbing now. The terrain shifted from dust to shale to near-vertical walls of rock. The little convoy rounded a final hairpin, and there it was.

Qala-ye Khun.

Cut into a craggy hilltop like a scar, half-ancient and half-improvised. Mudbrick towers reinforced with rebar. Gates made from scavenged armor plate. Machine gun nests. Barbed wire looped along the edges of terraces where teenage sentries lounged with binoculars and rifles. And behind it all, jagged snow-covered peaks rose like teeth into the sky.

Victoria's breath caught in her throat, and for the first time all day, she said nothing.

Alex was already watching her. “Welcome to Qala-ye Khun, the Fortress of Blood.”

The gates groaned open without ceremony. No sentry challenged them. No orders barked. Just a low mechanical whine and the dry scrape of metal on stone as the convoy slipped inside.

The interior of the compound hummed with activity. Fighters, boys, mostly, lounged on canvas mats or squatted beside tin cooking pots, weapons slung loose over their backs. Piles of spent shell casings, jugs of water, and crates of ammunition sat beneath torn tarps. There was no order, but somehow, no chaos either. It was a place where time bent around purpose.

They were led across the compound, passing barracks, fortifications, and old Soviet mobile satellite arrays. Children flashed across their path like startled birds; gunmen lingered at every turn. A couple of ornately dressed androgynous boys furtively peered out of dark doorways; their colorful silk garments and kohl-lined eyes seemed otherworldly and out of place in the grubby citadel. Victoria wondered if these were the infamous bacha bazi boys she had heard about.

Machine gun nests towered over shanties and makeshift structures, steel-reinforced bunkers gave way to cobbled-together buildings that appeared ready to fall in on themselves. Karim's men and their families occupied a jumbled mass of these hovels at the edges of the compound.

It reminded Victoria of Haiti, of the war zones she'd visited with her mother's non-profit when her parents were trying to instill some humanity in her, before they realized the effort was futile. But it was also different here, and the presence of children wasn't enough to disguise how deliberate and lethal everything seemed. These men were not random, were not wandering rebels or stateless soldiers. They had a discipline and direction that made her uneasy.

Finally, they came to the hulking centerpiece of the compound. It resembled a medieval castle keep, but if it had been constructed in the East, bombed into rubble, and then rebuilt using whatever was available at hand. Victoria shuddered slightly as they walked up the ramp, wondering what horrors must lie inside such a building.

She braced herself as they approached an archway leading to the inner courtyard. As they passed through, her stride faltered and her breath caught as she found herself in a tranquil, shaded courtyard, lined with polished stone and citrus trees.

She felt as though she had been transported to another century, another world.

Karim waited in the center of the courtyard, barefoot on a carpet so finely woven that Victoria instinctively checked her boots for mud. He wore traditional Afghan garb; pale linen, meticulously clean. A gold Patek Philippe gleamed from his wrist. His salt-and-pepper beard was long yet immaculate, and his dark hair was slicked neatly back.

"Miss Ashworth," he said, bowing slightly at the waist. "A pleasure I have anticipated for many weeks."

His voice was richer than she expected, velvet dipped in steel, and his English held the unmistakable lilt of Cambridge polish.

Victoria forced a warm smile. "Mr. Al-Rashid. It's an honor."

"Please. Karim," he said with a generous smile. "And you must be the producer."

Alex extended a hand. "Sterling. We spoke by phone."

"Yes, of course. You were efficient. I like efficiency." His gaze lingered, weighing Alex with something close to curiosity before he turned to Doc.

"And this... is your technician?"

"Doc," the cameraman said. He didn't offer a hand.

Karim didn't seem to mind. "Welcome. All of you. I know the journey is harsh. Come. Let us cleanse it from your bones."

He clapped twice, and two boys appeared from the shadowed portico at his clap, pitchers and towels in hand. The scent of rose and cardamom drifted in their wake, an almost dreamlike breath of luxury against the raw, unforgiving landscape beyond the walls.

Victoria allowed herself to be led up an ancient stairwell into the cool of a stone hall. Inside, everything gleamed. Mosaic tiles. Brass lanterns. Silken drapes moving with the desert wind. She caught sight of a carved wooden door inlaid with mother-of-pearl, ajar just long enough to glimpse bookshelves. Real ones.

Karim walked between them, hands clasped behind his back, posture immaculate.

"I apologize for the security," he said. "It's necessary. Foreign journalists attract attention, and my enemies are many."

Victoria played her part. "We're grateful for your protection. And your hospitality."

White teeth flashed. "You will find, Miss Ashworth, that I am always a gracious host."

They were ushered into a long dining chamber lit by lanterns. The table was already set—lavish by any standard. Grilled lamb, saffron rice, figs, pistachios, and flatbread, still steaming. A feast in the middle of a warzone.

"This place," Victoria said, watching Karim as he poured her tea himself, "It's remarkable. More fortified than I expected."

Karim's eyes gleamed. "Isn't every king entitled to a castle?" A pause. "But really, I consider myself a farmer more than anything else."

Alex's lips pursed, but he said nothing.

They ate. Victoria asked Karim a few pleasantries—his thoughts on the upcoming Loya Jirga, whether he considered himself aligned with the Northern Alliance. He deflected with grace, turning the conversation to poetry, the failures of Western diplomacy, and the weight of history. Always eloquent. Always too controlled.

As the meal ended and the shadows deepened, Karim stood. "First a tour, then I shall show you your quarters," he said. "Then tomorrow, Miss Ashworth, the world shall see us speak together."

The night air turned cooler as he led them into a stone passageway behind the keep that led deep into the center of the mountain. The floor underfoot was worn smooth in places, gouged rough in others, evidence of centuries of use under different regimes. Victoria could smell the age of the place. Dust and rock. Old fire.

"This is the original heart of the fortress," he said. "Bactrian, perhaps older. One of my men discovered coins with Greek inscriptions in the eastern foundation wall last winter. Some say Alexander himself built the first walls. Others say he merely added to what was already here. This is the oldest part of the complex; whether it was a dungeon or merely used for storage is hard to say."

The stairwell led to a broad, vaulted corridor. Ancient stone arches framed the space, their keystones etched with worn, indecipherable markings. Victoria's gaze followed a crack that ran from the floor to the ceiling like a vein. Overhead, a single bulb cast a weak cone of light from a rusted Soviet fixture bolted into centuries-old stone.

"It has served many masters," Karim continued, gesturing toward the heavy wooden doors flanking the corridor. "Bactrian princes. Mongol khans. British surveyors. Russian engineers. Each left something behind."

Alex walked in silence, eyes sweeping the walls. He brushed his fingers along a scorched brick.

They reemerged into the sunlight and walked around the keep to the front entrance. "This section," Karim said, "was reinforced by Soviet advisors in the '80s. Airstrikes damaged the upper levels. We repaired what mattered."

As they returned to the gate, a thick wooden door bound with iron, its ancient hinges newly oiled, Victoria caught sight of a large anti-aircraft gun mounted on a platform across the compound.

Alex stared at the defenses, lost in thought. His voice dropped low, almost to a whisper, "It's a stronghold, not a hideout."

Karim responded cheerfully, with an undertone of condescension, "Yes. That is the point."

He brought them up to the battlements of the keep. Below them, the valley stretched out in moonlit silence. The outer perimeter was clearly visible now: pillboxes set into switchbacks, overlapping arcs of fire—a medieval layout with modern firepower.

Victoria took it in with a kind of reverence, "It truly is like a castle."

Karim nodded. "We are building something that will last a generation."

Doc exhaled softly behind her, more a grunt than a word. He hadn't spoken for nearly half an hour. His camera stayed low, cradled in one hand, lens cap on.

"Hell of a place to do a live shot," he said.

Victoria didn't answer.

Alex drifted closer and gave a taut smile. "I wonder, Karim, if you and I might speak privately later. About the... regional picture."

Karim stopped, turning slightly. "The picture changes hourly, Mr. Sterling. What's the point in painting it?"

Alex smiled. "Sometimes the sketch is more revealing than the finished canvas."

It was a good line. Smooth. Karim didn't bite.

"I'm afraid I have many demands on my time," he said, already walking again. "And besides, Ms. Ashworth is the one who gets the exclusive. Isn't that how the West does things? All business must now be filtered through broadcast."

Alex didn't press. But Victoria saw it: the tiny tightening of his jaw, the flick of his eyes to the compound's walls, bristling with armaments. He knew he was being managed.

Karim led them into the upper level of the gatehouse. It was lit with bare bulbs strung along a single wire. As they descended, Karim gestured through a slit in the wall.

"The old defenders would pour hot oil from up here. Now, we prefer belt-fed systems. More efficient."

Doc stopped, leaning against the stone. He looked down through the slit and shook his head. "Jesus."

Victoria turned. "What?"

"See the antenna cluster on the roof?"

She gave him a blank look.

"Tactical SATCOM. NATO-issue communications equipment. That kind of gear? These guys aren't supposed to have it."

Karim was already moving again, speaking to no one in particular. "Victory does not come from the strength of arms alone. But it helps."

They reached a broad landing and a set of double doors carved from ancient cedar. Two young men stood on either side, Kalashnikovs across their chests. They didn't smile.

Karim turned, gesturing.

"My quarters. You'll be staying in the guest rooms across the hall. Warm water, good beds. I imagine you're tired."

Alex didn't respond. He was watching the guards.

Doc's fingers tapped his lens cap once, then stopped.

Victoria nodded stiffly. "It's an impressive place."

Karim's face was smooth and unreadable. "Yes. And very difficult to leave."

The guest room was cleaner than she expected. Stone walls, but smooth, sealed against the dust. A brass lantern flickered in the corner, its soft light catching on an old Soviet radiator that wheezed as the evening chill descended. There was a narrow bed, a cracked mirror, and a pitcher of boiled water still steaming. Someone had made an effort. Or wanted them to believe so.

Victoria shrugged off her scarf, letting it fall onto the cot. She stared at herself in the mirror, wiping away a line of mascara that had smudged in the heat. Her eyeliner was too dramatic. Amateurish, almost. She looked like she was trying to be brave.

Alex stood by the window slit, arms crossed. He hadn't taken off his jacket.

"That was a show," he said.

Victoria didn't turn. "Which part?"

"All of it. The antiques, the boys with guns, the charm offensive. He wanted us to see just enough to feel small."

She met his reflection in the mirror. "You're upset he didn't want to talk to you alone."

He didn't answer right away. Just looked out the narrow slit toward the black horizon. "Karim Al-Rashid doesn't waste time. If he wanted something from me, I'd have it by now. He's not improvising, Vic. This place is fortified like a NATO base. He's building something."

Victoria turned, hands on her hips. "You don't think I noticed that?"

"I think you noticed the lighting angles and whether your hair would hold in the wind. You didn't see the comms tower behind the west parapet. You didn't clock the storage bunkers under the north wing. I did."

He was keeping his voice low, but the heat behind it was real. It wasn't jealousy, it was fear.

Victoria didn't like that. It felt too close to condescension.

"Just say it, Alex. You think I'm being reckless. That I'm in over my head."

"I think you're being used." He stepped toward her now, voice dropping. "I think this was all staged: the warmth, the hospitality, the security we're pretending not to see. I think Karim wants the West to see this place. And I think he doesn't give a damn about your interview."

Victoria narrowed her eyes. "You pushed for this story. You vouched for him."

"I vouched for the opportunity. Not for the man."

There was a long pause. The old radiator ticked like a metronome.

Then softer, almost pleading: “Vic, something’s off. I tried to make contact. I used the right language. He shut it down.”

Victoria’s expression flickered. “Contact?”

He held her gaze.

“This is more than just media. There are... other interests. Back home.”

Victoria’s breath caught. “You’re running an op.”

He didn’t deny it. Back at the office in New York, there had been whispers that he was still working for the government. He arrived at the network in October, after the towers fell, claiming a State Department past—or so his résumé said. The mystery had drawn her in; their affair had been fast, passionate. Until now.

She turned away, pressing her hands to the edge of the bed. Her voice dropped. “Christ, Alex.”

“He’s done some work for us in the past, going back to the Soviet days. We’re hoping he’ll help us against the Taliban.”

“I just want the story.”

He stepped behind her. “And I just want to keep us alive.”

There was silence between them. Long and bitter.

Eventually, she sat down. Her spine was rigid, arms crossed. She wouldn’t look at him.

He sat beside her, hands clasped. Neither touched.

“I can’t protect you if you won’t listen,” he said.

Victoria’s voice, when it came, was low and tired. “You think he’s going to kill us?”

“I think he hasn’t decided yet.”

The lantern flickered again. Somewhere below, a shout echoed across the courtyard, then silence.

They didn't speak again that night.

The next morning, Victoria stepped out onto the balcony of Karim's tower and drew a deep breath of the sharp, cold air.

The valley opened beneath her in layers, a vast, desolate sprawl of rock and wind and distant fields, the poppies now faint in the morning haze. To the west, the compound stretched like a scar across the slope, its outer walls half-devoured by the centuries. In the far distance, where the mountain shadows curled like ink, the faint glint of movement, men, perhaps. Or ghosts.

She turned from the view. Doc was already at work.

He moved with the same quiet efficiency he always did, setting up the tripod, checking levels on the battered monitor, adjusting the feed. No wasted motion. But his expression was locked in a familiar mask: calm, blank, disapproving. The camera had always been his shield, and now he stood behind it like a man bracing for incoming fire.

"You good?" she asked.

He didn't look up. "Signal's holding. Might degrade after ten minutes. Don't dawdle."

"I never do."

Doc grunted, not quite a laugh.

Alex stood by the far wall, pacing. He kept looking toward the archway that led back into the tower. Waiting for Karim. Or something worse.

Victoria adjusted her dark navy, tailored blazer, then checked her reflection in the small hand mirror tucked into her bag. Her face looked pale against the light. The altitude, maybe. Or the weight of what was coming. She reapplied her lipstick with a precision that felt absurdly comforting.

"You sure he won't back out?" she asked, mostly to break the silence.

Alex didn't answer. Just kept scanning the lower levels. Tension radiated from his body. He hadn't slept.

Victoria walked to the camera and studied the frame Doc had lined up for her, where she'd sit, testing angles and the backdrop. Behind her: sheer drop, then valley. To her left, the edge of a spired tower topped with a black flag bearing no clear emblem. Just a white scrawl of calligraphy that twisted in the wind.

Doc leaned in close, adjusting the boom mic. Voice low, eyes on hers, "This doesn't feel right."

She met his gaze, then nodded.

"I know."

Before she could say more, footsteps echoed from within the tower. Deliberate. Slow. The sound of someone making an entrance.

Karim emerged in full regalia. A tailored black tunic over sand-colored trousers, a silk scarf draped neatly across his shoulder. His beard was oiled, his expression warm. Performative. Behind him trailed two of his armed boys, Kalashnikovs slung lazily over their shoulders.

Karim grinned, all teeth. "Miss Ashworth, you honor me with your presence this morning."

Victoria forced a smile. "The honor is mine, Karim."

He took his seat with theatrical ease, folding his hands in his lap. The early light cast long shadows over the table between them. Alex stood off-camera now, eyes fixed and unreadable. Doc made final adjustments. Karim looked straight into the lens and gave a slight nod.

Victoria took a breath, counted three beats.

Then: "We're live in five, four, three..."

She mouthed the final two silently. The red light blinked on.

"Good morning," she said, "I'm Victoria Ashworth, reporting live from the Hindu Kush, where I'm joined by a man who's been called many things: financier, warrior, revolutionary. Today, we meet the man behind the myth, Karim Al-Rashid."

Karim smiled. "The pleasure is mine."

The interview began the way Victoria had imagined it: calm, composed, with the soft hiss of wind filling the pauses between questions. Her voice was warm but precise, her posture impeccable. She didn't flinch when the camera's red light blinked on. This was her domain. The framing was perfect: the ancient valley spilling out behind them, the sun catching the stone tower just enough to give the scene an air of gravitas. Like something from a war documentary. Or history in the making.

Karim answered her opening questions with smooth, almost weary grace. His Oxonian accent was nearly too perfect.

"I was born in Manchester," he said, "My parents worked in textiles. Immigrants, like so many others. I grew up watching them try to belong."

Victoria nodded, kept her gaze steady. "You excelled academically. Cambridge. Finance. You could have stayed in the City."

"I could have." A small smile. "But money is not purpose."

Off to her left, just outside the frame, she caught movement: another of Karim's boys stepping onto the balcony, rifle slung low. He stood against the wall, eyes scanning the horizon. Then another joined him, wordless. No one had signaled them. They just appeared.

Doc adjusted the zoom. She saw the faintest twitch in his arm, like a breath held too long. He didn't say anything, but he looked toward Alex, who now stood with arms crossed, his weight subtly shifted, as if he were ready to move without moving. They exchanged a glance. Not panic. But something just short of it.

Victoria pressed on.

"You joined the Mujahideen to fight the Soviets," she said. "What made you leave behind your life in London?"

Karim looked past her, toward the valley. "I watched the West prop up tyrants and call it diplomacy. I watched my faith reduced to soundbites. I had no desire to become another banker rearranging zeroes. I came here to matter."

Behind him, the four young guards were now joined by a fifth, this one older, wearing a vest bristling with grenades and a belt of spare ammunition. Still outside the camera's frame. But not by much.

Victoria kept her face neutral. "And now you lead a vast network. What began as resistance has become... a movement."

Karim tilted his head. "You say that like it's a criticism."

"I say that like it's a fact."

His eyes glittered. "Good. Let's speak plainly, then."

Alex stepped forward a half pace. Doc reached out subtly and touched his arm, not to stop him but to remind him they were being watched. Alex didn't react. Just looked at Karim, then at Victoria, then back again.

Victoria caught the exchange out of the corner of her eye. She didn't acknowledge it. She didn't have to.

Karim leaned in, the performative warmth in his voice thinning slightly. "The West calls us terrorists. But they trained us. Armed us. *Lied* to us. And when it suited them, left us to burn. You want to talk about corruption?" He smiled tightly. "Let's."

Victoria kept her tone steady. "This is a live interview, Karim."

"I know." His voice dropped, conspiratorial. "And I want your audience to hear every word."

Behind him, a sixth man stepped onto the balcony.

Something was shifting. The air was getting thinner, not just from altitude.

Victoria glanced toward Alex. He met her gaze, and this time, didn't hide the alarm behind his eyes.

She turned back to Karim, speaking more quickly now, trying to regain pace. "You've been accused of heroin trafficking, of sheltering extremists—"

Karim waved a hand. "Accusations made by frightened men. I am building something stronger than they can imagine."

Victoria pressed. "At what cost?"

Karim smiled again, wider, darker. "All things worth building require sacrifice."

A beat.

Then he turned his gaze not to her, but to the camera.

Karim's gaze locked on the lens. He leaned forward slightly, hands folded, as if addressing a boardroom.

"My brothers in the West, you've sent your armies. You've dropped your bombs. You are building your bases. And yet, here I stand."

Victoria blinked, caught off guard by the shift in tone. This wasn't a response. It was a speech.

"I was educated in your universities. I walked your streets. I wore your suits. I spoke your language. I made your money. And then I saw the truth... that peace in the West means war everywhere else."

Off to the side, Doc adjusted the camera slightly. Victoria saw the fear in his eyes, the way his fingers trembled against the pan handle. Alex took a single step toward them.

Karim continued, voice still smooth, still measured. "We will not be your colony. We will not sell our blood for your stability. And today, you will witness the price of your arrogance."

Victoria's throat tightened. "Karim—"

He stood. Slowly, deliberately. His eyes didn't leave the camera.

"I have prepared a *gift* for your viewers."

Two of his men surged forward toward Doc and Alex. One dragged Doc backward by his camera harness, the other grabbed Alex, wrenching his arms behind his back. Victoria shot to her feet.

"What the hell are you doing?" she shouted.

The camera stayed live. Doc was forced down to his knees, Victoria recoiled at the dull crunch of bone as his shoulder twisted under the guard's grip. He didn't cry out. Just hissed through his teeth and stared daggers at Karim.

Alex fought harder. Elbows and kicks. Trained. Efficient. But there were three on him now. They slammed him against the stone wall. One drove a rifle butt into his gut. He doubled over.

Karim stepped calmly into the center of the frame, like a stage actor hitting his mark.

Victoria tried to move forward. A hand shot out and grabbed her arm, and she was dragged back, roughly, but not out of frame.

Karim spoke again, now louder, his voice edged with righteous fury. "This is the first lesson. The occupiers will fall. The invaders will bleed. And the West will know what it means to be made powerless."

One of his men handed him something wrapped in silk. He unwrapped it with care: a long, curved knife, the steel old and dark.

Victoria began to scream.

"This is insane—he's an *American*! He's press!"

Karim didn't look at her.

He stepped behind Doc first, but paused, then moved instead

toward Alex, now on his knees, bloody and breathing hard, his eyes locked on Victoria. Not pleading. Not angry. Just focused. Ready.

Karim reached down, grabbed Alex roughly by the hair, and dragged his head back.

He raised the knife.

Victoria twisted in her captor's grip, shrieking now, a raw, panicked sound. "Stop! You can't—Jesus, stop!"

Karim said nothing.

The blade descended slowly, methodically. Not quick. Not clean.

Doc shouted something unintelligible.

Alex didn't make a sound.

Victoria sobbed, turning her face, but they held her there, forced her eyes open. She felt her stomach lurch. The heat of the sun, the cold stone beneath her knees, the coppery smell rising into her throat.

Then: stillness.

Karim held the severed head in both hands. His voice rang out.

"We will not be conquered. We will not be silenced. We are the beginning."

He turned to the camera and held the head aloft.

And for a moment, the satellite feed held. The red light still blinked. The transmission still live.

Then, mercifully, it cut.

Victoria collapsed in sobs as the balcony erupted in cheers behind her. The camera clattered to the floor, its final image a smear of blood against ancient stone.

PART I

"The public must be put in its place... so that each of us may live free of the trampling and roar of a bewildered herd."
— Walter Lippmann

CHAPTER 1

September 21, 2003, North Yorkshire, UK

The road kept changing under the tires, loose gravel, then packed dirt, then gravel again. The van rattled with each shift, metal shivering somewhere in the panels. Geoff sat in the passenger seat, arms crossed, boots planted wide on the floor to keep steady. The new kid, Danny, was in the back and hadn't shut his gob since they had left the main guardhouse.

Out past the beams, nothing. The hedges were just hints, flickers of outline as they passed. Trees leaned over the road here and there, their branches close enough to feel like they might reach in. The old, ruined stone farmhouse should be coming up soon, Geoff thought absently, trying to keep his mind off Danny's endless chirping.

The driver, Mac, hadn't spoken in miles. Just a grunt when they hit the turnoff, then silence. *Silence.* That was part of the routine, or it was supposed to be. 0500, check in at the guardhouse. 0515, Mac drives them to the facility (in silence). 0545, arrive at the facility and start security procedures. 0600, relieve the watch. 1800, oncoming shift relieves the watch.

Up ahead, movement. Sharp and fast. A flash of feathers. A pheasant darted across the road, gangly and panicked, wings flapping hard enough that he could hear them over the engine. Another followed, then two more. A whole mess of them, scattered like marbles. He flinched, hand bracing on the dashboard. Mac didn't slow.

Danny was undeterred by the pheasants. "Bloody hell, she was something to see. Mini skirt, see through mesh top, pierced tongue, tattoo of a demon on her chest! She was marvelous, just bloody marvelous." Danny sighed as if he had seen Aphrodite in the flesh. He had spent the weekend in Leeds with some mates and wouldn't shut up about it.

Mac grunted again, eyes locked ahead. The road dipped, and the van tilted slightly before leveling out. The gravel sounded different here, thinner, like they were moving over bones instead of stone. Geoff rolled the window down an inch, more out of habit than anything, and caught the smell of cold earth and damp wood.

"She gets up on the bloody bar, right—no knickers, I swear—and starts dancing like she's on telly..."

Geoff's head started to throb. "*Enough* about the damn bird Danny!" he erupted.

"Sorry Geoff."

Silence, blessed silence.

They were close now. No signs. No lights. Just a right turn after the broken fence, and the road would rise a little before it dropped toward the compound. The headlights caught something up ahead, stone, maybe an old boundary wall, collapsed in places. Geoff leaned forward slightly. It was the old farmhouse, just a shell, half-eaten by ivy.

"It's just, well, it was a helluva night, Geoff. Slags everywhere, the one with the tattoo, she wasn't even the fittest bird." He exploded into a guttural laugh, "Wait till you hear about the Welshman with the ferret—swore it could sniff out cocaine, and by God, it nearly started a fight with a bouncer."

Geoff groaned and sank lower in his seat. He missed Mitch. Quiet, steady Mitch, who read Melville on breaks and never talked about strippers. Mitch retired two weeks ago. Now Geoff was stuck with Danny, possibly for two more years. The van rolled on, slower now, tires crunching with a softer rhythm. The road narrowed.

How had the kid even gotten this job? Geoff vaguely recalled someone mentioning that his mother worked for someone important. Whitehall? An MP? Didn't matter. What mattered was that the place had gone soft. Facility Echo-7 used to mean something. The place clearly wasn't deemed important enough to warrant strict hiring procedures anymore. They had once only considered former military police or retired cops. Since the Cold War ended, the facility had gotten progressively quieter. Some of the other guards fretted that it might even close as they hadn't had a 'guest' in months. Until a few weeks ago, that is.

The van crunched to a stop on the cracked tarmac outside what looked like a deserted radar station: squat concrete buildings ringed by rusted fencing and long-dead satellite dishes. A dented sign, half swallowed by brambles, still bore the faded crest of the Royal Air Force. The place appeared to have been abandoned after the war and left to decay for decades.

Geoff stepped out first, boots grinding against gravel, breath fogging faintly in the morning air. A sharp morning wind carried the bite and scent of wet moorland. Danny hopped out behind him, still chattering about the club in Leeds until Geoff silenced him with a look.

The main building's steel door groaned as Mac pulled it open. Inside, the air changed: dank and close. Decades of neglect had left layers of smell. Mildew, old concrete, and metal steeped in stale cigarette smoke.

To the left, an eye-level retinal scanner buzzed to life with a low electronic whine. Geoff leaned in, letting the thing read him. A green light blinked. *Access granted.*

He punched in a six-digit code on the keypad beneath. A hiss of hydraulics followed, and a narrow elevator door shuddered open in the wall. They stepped in. The interior was painted battleship grey, walls dented and scratched. Fluorescent lights flickered overhead with a nervous hum.

Danny shifted his weight, whistling nervously.

Geoff broke the silence. "You stop whistling, or I'll break your bloody nose."

The elevator lurched downward.

"This place is creepy, Geoff, feels like a horror movie or something. You see that one about..."

The doors opened to a low-ceilinged corridor, lined with green-painted steel. The air was cooler here, with a bite of something chemical and sterile. At the far end, two guards stood behind a bulletproof window beside a reinforced turnstile.

"Name and clearance," barked one of them, not looking up from his clipboard.

"Blackwood and Walsh, Level Two. New kid," he jerked his head at Danny, who seemed impressed enough by the security to interrupt the endless chattering.

The guard grunted, glanced at a monitor, then buzzed them through. Geoff and Danny stepped past the checkpoint, their boots echoing on the floor—a grooved metal mesh laid over poured concrete. The next elevator waited, humming faintly.

Again, the descent. The corridor was tighter, more claustrophobic. Condensation ran in slow lines down the walls, collecting at the edges of rust-stained floor plates. Another checkpoint, this one with two guards holding compact carbines. More scrutiny. More protocol. Geoff went through it all robotically. Danny fumbled with his badge.

Geoff leaned in. "Try not to look like you're fresh out of bloody nursery."

They passed through.

The final elevator was older, slower. This one rattled as it sank into the earth.

The door opened with a reluctant clunk. The air was heavy, with the acrid sting of ammonia lingering just beneath the silence. Overhead, tungsten lights spread a dull yellow haze along the corridor.

Along the walls, dusty framed black-and-white photos showed the facility's Cold War heyday: technicians in headsets, grainy shots of Soviet satellites, a proud Ministry of Defence crest over the year *1948*. A pipe hissed in the ceiling. Somewhere far off, a buzzer echoed.

They passed a thick door marked *Holding Cells: Restricted Access*, then another: *Interrogation Wing: Authorized Personnel Only*. Neither of them looked at those doors for long.

Finally, they reached the control room, tucked behind a reinforced hatch labeled *Operations*. Inside, two guards looked up from their screens.

"You're late," one said.

"Blame the pheasants," Geoff said.

He hung his coat on the same peg Mitch used to, took his seat, and stared at the flickering monitors. The day shift had begun.

The control room hadn't changed since he had first set foot in it 28 years ago, Geoff reflected. Fluorescent tubes buzzed in the ceiling panels. The tea station in the corner still smelled faintly of mold and old milk. On the far wall, twelve CRT monitors sat stacked in three rows of four, framed in metal and dust. Eleven were dark.

Only one screen glowed.

Geoff settled into the chair with a grunt, eyes already fixed on the lit monitor. He nodded at Stu and Malcolm, the night shift. Both men looked tired. Malcolm was slouched with a paper tucked under his arm, and Stu stood, arms folded, eyes on the screen like he didn't trust what it was showing.

Geoff didn't either.

The image was grainy, washed out in harsh white light. The cell was square, sterile, white walls, white floor, no bed, no toilet, no fixtures. Just a man. Cross-legged on the floor. Still.

"Still hasn't moved?" Geoff asked, already knowing the answer.

"Not an inch," Stu said. "You'll love this. Hasn't blinked since we came on shift. Not once."

Geoff leaned forward slightly. The prisoner was young, mid-twenties maybe, with wiry, athletic limbs and a pale, unwashed face. Hair a tangled mess of copper-red, beard creeping wild over his jaw like bramble. His eyes, too wide, too fixed, were locked on the far wall. No, not the wall. The camera. Hidden behind a pinhole, high in the corner. But somehow, impossibly, the man looked like he was staring right through the lens and into Geoff's eyes.

Danny lurked behind him, shifting his weight nervously from one foot to the other. "Jesus," he said, "It's like he knows we're watching."

Geoff didn't answer. The prisoner didn't move.

"Light hits every corner of the room," Malcolm said. "Bright enough to give you migraines. The alarm goes off every fifteen minutes to keep him from sleeping. Loud as a bloody airhorn."

"Doesn't react to that either," Stu added. "Eats in silence. Shits in silence. Never closes his eyes."

Geoff exhaled. Back in the old days, every screen used to glow. All twelve cells full—Soviet defectors, East German spies, maybe even the odd double agent that MI5 wanted to disappear. Facility Echo-7 had once been a pressure cooker of secrets. Now it was a ghost.

Except this one.

Danny kept staring at the screen. "What the hell's he looking at?"

Malcolm smirked. "You."

Danny blinked and stepped back.

Stu chuckled. "Give it a week. You'll stop gawking. Or you'll quit."

Geoff stood and stretched. "Come on. I'll show you where the tea lives."

They crossed to the corner, where a rusted vending machine offered outdated crisps and warm cola. Next to it sat a squat electric kettle and an assortment of mismatched mugs left behind by the long-retired. Geoff dropped a tea bag into two cups and nodded for Danny to pour the water.

"He always sits like that?" Danny asked uneasily.

"Always," Geoff said. "Like a bloody monk."

"Do we even know who he is?"

"Somebody important," Stu said, his voice lowered just enough to make it feel like gossip. "Two VIPs flying in. Helicopter. Oh-nine hundred. You lot are to make sure he's showered, shaved, and manacled in interrogation."

"First time we've had that in fifteen years," Malcolm put in. "Last time someone flew in, they wore suits that cost more than my house. Took a man out in shackles, face covered."

"MI6?" Danny guessed.

"Special Branch?" Malcolm offered.

"Aliens," Stu said. "You laugh, but I wouldn't be shocked."

The banter circled like that, speculating who would be on the helicopter. MI5? MOD? Section D? Americans? Maybe even the PM himself! Then the voice came.

Calm. British. Clipped. Not from the room. Not from the hallway. Not from any of the guards.

"Tell them I'm ready to talk."

The voice echoed through the speaker system monitoring the cells. Crisp. Precise. No distortion. No background noise. It felt like it was spoken directly into the back of Geoff's skull.

Danny dropped his mug. It shattered on the floor. Tea spread across the concrete in a brown puddle.

Everyone froze. The monitor still showed the prisoner. Same posture. Same blank stare. He hadn't moved.

Geoff's mouth felt dry. He cleared his throat. "Was that—"

Danny leaned in, whispering.

"Was that *him*?"

No one answered.

The screen flickered slightly, then steadied. The man in the cell continued to stare. Unblinking.

Watching.

CHAPTER 2

The prisoner sat alone in a square room that had been dreary when the Queen had her coronation. Over the years, dreary had been replaced by bleak, and bleak by desolate. Stone walls painted institutional grey were peeling, mildew that had defied years of bleach-fueled assaults crawled obstinately up the walls. A single fluorescent tube buzzed faintly overhead, casting a sterile glow on the metal table bolted to the floor. His wrists were shackled to the tabletop—polished steel cuffs, reinforced chain, no slack.

The door opened, and two men entered.

The first was lean, silver-haired, and immaculate in a charcoal suit. A thick leather briefcase hung from his hand. He moved with the clipped efficiency of someone who expected others to make room for him.

The second man was broader, heavier, a bit older, draped in a long black overcoat that hung past his knees. His thick glasses caught the overhead light, magnifying pale blue eyes that blinked slowly, almost lazily, as he studied the prisoner. His movements were unhurried. Deliberate. He said nothing.

The lean man approached the table, pulled a key from his pocket, and unlocked the manacles with two crisp turns. The cuffs clicked open and clattered against the tabletop. The prisoner flexed his wrists once, then lowered his hands to his lap.

The briefcase was set on the table. Unsnapped. Opened.

From it emerged a crumpled paper bag stained with grease. It was pushed across the table, and the smell that followed was unmistakable: beef, salt, old fryer oil.

"Cheeseburger" was the curt explanation.

Next came a bottle of Balvenie. Three glasses. A soft pack of cigarettes. A lighter. An ashtray. Each item was placed with precision, aligned neatly, like offerings.

The man in the coat took a seat, soft, pudgy hands resting lightly on the table, expression unreadable.

The silver-haired man remained standing. He adjusted the cuffs of his shirt, glanced at the prisoner.

"We're here," he said, "to pass around the peace pipe."

The prisoner said nothing.

The man tapped the table once, lightly, then lowered himself into the chair opposite.

"I'm Arthur Creighton," he said. "Permanent Secretary in the Foreign Office, among other joys."

He gestured vaguely toward his companion. "This is..." he began and hesitated. A pause hung in the air as if he were unsure if he should reveal the man's name.

The man in the coat smiled faintly. "You can call me Mr. Churchill."

His voice was soft, exacting, patient.

The prisoner leaned back in his chair and studied the two men, his expression calm.

"I'm happy to tell you, gentlemen, anything you want to know." His accent was classic upper-class British. Refined and aristocratic.

Creighton reached into the briefcase again and pulled out a thick file. "You needn't put on the accent on *our* account, Mr. Harrington."

The prisoner shrugged, "Feels more natural these days, Sir. Haven't had to do American in years."

Creighton opened the file, "You've become quite the linguist, haven't you? Fluent in all the Romance languages, Arabic, Pashto, and passable Russian. Able to mimic dialects and accents, too. Quite impressive, Tom... may I call you Tom?"

Tom smiled, "Languages seem to come naturally to me, Sir. Funny that. I almost flunked Spanish in school. I suppose I'm more focused now. It's like working out a puzzle."

Creighton continued to thumb through the file, "Yes, you nearly failed out of university—Harry Fletcher's wayward American college student."

"You don't approve of OGI, do you?"

Creighton's face twisted with disdain, "*Overseas Growth Institute,* an intelligence agency masquerading as an international aid charity. Run by Harry Fletcher, a former organized crime associate." He shook his head. "It's reckless, irresponsible. Believe it or not, Mr. Harrington, British Intelligence does not make a habit of hiring foreign students with personality disorders and a penchant for breaking and entering. So, yes, I disapprove of Harry's little fiefdom. He's been given too much latitude and far too large a budget."

Creighton pressed on, eyes flicking down the file, voice sharp. "Discipline problems in high school. Violent outbursts. In 1995, hospitalized four students. Charged with aggravated battery, four counts. Pled guilty to disturbing the peace. One-month juvenile detention. Court-ordered psych evaluation." He looked up at Tom then, a trace of relish creeping in, and continued:

"*Diagnoses:* Conduct Disorder. Likely trauma from his father's death. Severe depression. Aggression toward authority. Lies with ease. Superiority complex. Risk of Antisocial Personality Disorder. Ongoing treatment strongly recommended." Creighton snapped the folder once for emphasis. "Expelled. Boarding school for senior year. And wouldn't you know it? A string of burglaries in wealthy neighborhoods surrounding the school. Which stopped, quite miraculously, the moment you graduated."

He scowled, letting the silence stretch.

Tom grabbed the pack of cigarettes, removed the cellophane, and lit one, inhaling the smoke deeply, savoring it. "Harry liked that bit, too, when he brought me on."

He leaned forward on his elbows, shoulders coiling, eyes boring into Creighton's, "You know *damn* well that the Service doesn't recruit choir boys, Mr. Creighton."

Creighton shifted uncomfortably.

Mr. Churchill broke in, his voice smooth and unflustered. "You acquitted yourself well in the Phoenix affair—and since. I doubt an Oxford or Cambridge man would have fared any better, wouldn't you agree, Creighton?"

Creighton scowled, undeterred. "After Phoenix, Harry had you formally trained. SAS selection, new identity, your past erased. Even your family thinks you are dead. That about the long and short of it?"

Tom shrugged, disinterested.

"Why don't you tell us your story, how you came to be in here," Churchill said. "Take your time, start at the very beginning. We want every detail. Be *precise*." He poured three tall glasses of scotch and pushed one to Tom.

Tom took the glass and slumped back in his chair.

"I suppose we should start in Italy. Harry sent me there to recover after I was injured on assignment..."

CHAPTER 3

It was an old villa, ochre plaster, flaking shutters, cracked tiles that still held the day's heat by dusk, surrounded by vineyards that curled into the hills like green smoke. Stefano said it had once belonged to a bishop, then a banker, then a fascist. Now it belonged to no one in particular, which suited everyone involved. Stefano looked sixty, moved like fifty, and had the eyes of a man who'd done unpleasant things at thirty. He didn't say much, just pointed to the gravel path that wound up into the hills and said, "Again." Every morning. Run. Carry rocks. Lift crates. Kneel, stand, kneel, again. I'd been out of surgery for three weeks. The stitches in my side were fresh enough to tug when I turned wrong. The blade had gone in low, under the ribs, through the meat, and out again. If she'd twisted it, I might've bled out in that courtyard in Cairo.

I hadn't seen her until it was too late. Hijab, eyes downcast, walking with groceries. She pulled the blade from a plastic bag like it was nothing, like she was plucking fruit. I hesitated. That was the mistake. That half-second. If it had been a man, I'd have seen it coming. Stefano never asked for details. Just watched how I moved and decided how much punishment I could take. In the evenings, his wife would make pasta by hand and serve wine from unlabeled bottles.

We ate in the garden, always in silence for the first course. He talked more once the second bottle came out. Nothing direct. Just stories. Fables, really. Smuggling the family of a scientist out of East Germany. A mole who spent ten years undercover and fell in love with his target. An old friend who drowned in the Black Sea while trying to tap underwater communications cables.

"There are no clean wars," he said once. "Only clean uniforms."

Another night: "You fight long enough, you either forget why, or you remember too clearly. Neither helps."

He never asked when I was leaving. But when the call came, he was waiting with espresso and a train schedule. At the platform, I asked him if he ever missed it. The job. The work. He looked at the hills, then quoted something about the sorrow of remembering happiness in misery. Typical Stefano.

Churchill broke in, smiling faintly. "Dante. Italians often exhibit theatrical tendencies."

Creighton didn't look up. "Egypt was the mission?

"Sinai job. Western weapons turning up in the wrong hands: American, French, Brit kit. Somebody was laundering stockpiles. We were meant to follow the trail."

"And you were compromised."

"I got soft."

Churchill leaned forward. "You hesitated because it was a woman."

Tom didn't answer.

"Understandable," he said. "But not excusable."

Creighton flipped a page in the file. "So, Harry brought you home."

Tom leaned back in his chair. "He didn't say why. Just that he needed a conversation..."

London was damp and mean as ever. OGI headquarters was the same respectable stone facade behind the brass plaque. Up the service elevator in the back, past the analysts and tea ladies, and into Harry's office. Same rug. Same smell of Cohiba's.

Harry wasn't slumped behind his desk this time. He was standing by the mirror, halfway into a tuxedo jacket, muttering at a stubborn cufflink. Bow tie hanging loose, shirt untucked, cigar wedged behind his ear like a carpenter.

He caught my reflection and grunted. "About bloody time."

I leaned against the doorframe. "What's with the monkey suit? You joining the Bolshoi?"

He snorted, tugging at the lapel. "Black-tie charity thing. NovaTerra's annual gala. Big do. All the great and good sniffing their own virtue."

I raised an eyebrow. "NovaTerra? Konstantin Varga's lot?"

"Mm." He finally got the cufflink through and inspected it with suspicion. "You heard of him?"

"Who hasn't?" I said. "Do they know you used to be in the mob?"

Harry grinned. "Why d'you think they invite me? My accent makes 'em feel like they're slumming it. Adds grit to the brand."

He shoved the lapels into place and finally waved me toward the chair. The tux was immaculate, as always. Harry dressed like a man who'd fought his way into the world he now inhabited, but the eyes were wrong. Red-rimmed, exhausted.

"You heard about the Yank journo?"

"Victoria Ashworth. Yeah."

"Her old man was a bloody ambassador under Carter. Well-connected. One of those Brookings types." He fished for his lighter, didn't find it, patted his pockets. "One of those families who think diplomacy is hereditary."

"I figured."

"We've got a mess," he said, lighting the cigar off a candle on the credenza. The radio behind him warbled some syrupy

1950s ballad. “Americans want to go in and pull her out. Our lot want to take the lead—it’s a Brit what’s knicked her, after all. But the Yanks won’t let it go without stickin’ their noses in.”

“So what’s our angle?”

He took three deep puffs until he vanished behind a cloud. When he emerged, his face was set. “I think the CIA’s up to something. Quiet-like. They’ve been sniffin’ round this warlord for months, long before the news crew got in the middle of it. Now they claim they’ve got someone on the inside. Too much interest for my taste.”

“And you want me to play watchdog.”

“You’ll be Captain Thomas Avery, SAS,” he said, as though reading it off an internal memo. “Military Intelligence liaison. Credentials already sorted.”

“That cover still clean?”

“You passed selection, didn’t you?” He jabbed the cigar at me. “You earned the stripes and technically hold the rank of Captain in the regiment. Most lads would kill for a posting like this.”

I shook my head. “You know I don’t do well playing soldier for the cameras. I like working alone. Quiet. No formations. No briefings with blokes who iron their socks.”

Harry sighed through his teeth. “Tom, you’ve done covert ops before. Phoenix ring any bells?”

“That was different.”

“It won’t be much different this time,” he said, though the flicker in his eyes said otherwise.

“And the mission?” I asked.

“Madness,” he said flatly. “Karim’s hole makes Tora Bora look like an open house. Rugged terrain, fortified approaches. And he’s got his own army.”

"Sounds like Mogadishu."

Harry winced. "Exactly."

There was a silence. Rain ticked against the window like tiny knives.

"You're nervous," I said.

"I don't like mysteries," he said. "And this one stinks of spooks. Yank ones."

"What's the brief?"

"Her cameraman got out. CIA's debriefin' him. You're sittin' in on it."

"Where?"

"Whitehall. Tomorrow."

"That's fast."

"That's pressure."

I stood. "I'll get ready."

Harry nodded, flicking ash into a tray shaped like Gibraltar. He tightened his bow tie with a grunt. "Keep your eyes open. Ears sharper. And Tom—"

"Yeah?"

"Don't let the Yanks get you killed." He straightened his jacket, suddenly every inch the reluctant statesman. "They're not as sentimental about ghosts as we are."

CHAPTER 4

“Let’s move on to the debriefing,” Creighton snapped. "The cameraman. The fortress."

Tom exhaled slowly, fingering his glass thoughtfully.

"Right," he said. "Whitehall. That’s where it really started." His voice softened, and his mind drifted to a memory of a colder morning, the weight of a borrowed uniform.

The black cab let me out at the Horse Guards’ entrance; it was one of those real bone-chilling London mornings that make me desperately miss California. I crossed the square, past the Household Cav in their finery, dolled up in my two’s. The uniform felt wrong—too crisp, too theatrical. I carried it with confidence, but the lie still itched beneath the collar.

Whitehall was all hush and varnish, dripping with centuries of history. I’m not used to going in the front entrance of these grand government buildings. I always feel like a tourist or an impostor, the American kid from a small town on a tour of the old country. A young MOD corporal escorted me to a briefing room deep below ground, proper British Empire stuff, with wood paneling and paintings of old generals. Inside, I was introduced to Major Edmund Hooper, gung-ho Army through and through. He was the Commander of the Joint Rescue Planning Group and led the raid.

His eyes took the measure of me: medals, posture, cadence. He seemed skeptical. The CIA entered next. The woman, Kate Prescott, had East Coast money written all over her: tall, brown hair, athletic, stylish, yet conservative in her attire, and about thirty years old. Remembering Harry's brief, I went straight into my act, but didn't lay it on too thick. I wanted to give her an opening, see if she would pursue me. I made little jokes about American charm, travel fatigue, London weather, and the like.

The girl took the bait. She offered a jibe about English food being as good as the weather (she emphasized this by describing the soggy naan and appalling curry she had eaten the night before at a smelly dive by her airport hotel). I parried with an offer to solve all her problems: I could buy her a good meal, show her a proper pub, *and* keep her warm. Her boss, Dick Hawthorne, ruined the fun by demanding to know if we were planning a hostage rescue or running a matchmaking service. I pretended to be suitably admonished and winked at Kate, who pretended to blush. Everyone was acting out their part in the script. Hawthorne was chilly, with silver hair and an expensive suit; no handshake was offered. The kind of man who reads loyalty reports before breakfast. The Brigadier and his aide entered, had everyone introduce themselves, then bade everyone to sit."

Two guards led in a man who looked like he'd walked through hell. Marcus "Doc" Washington. Late fifties, dark skin, grey peppered into his hair and mustache. His borrowed clothes were loose, and so was his skin, evidence of significant weight loss. His eyes moved slowly, carefully, haunted.

The Brigadier thanked Doc and asked him to tell his story. He was quiet for a while and sat with a stiff sort of dignity. Finally, in a Georgia drawl, he agreed to tell the tale.

"You want to understand that place, you start with him. With Karim."

He described Karim's charisma, the eerie hospitality, the fortified compound masquerading as an opulent relic. Karim brought them up to his tower, to the top floor. Real showpiece. Balconies, silk rugs, mint tea in crystal glasses. But it wasn't a palace. It was a throne room. He knew exactly what he was doing, showing them around. Doc could sense tension building between Alex, the producer, and Victoria. They had been having an affair, so it could have been related to that, but Doc didn't think so. Alex seemed to get nervous during the tour. Ever since Alex came to the network from the State Department after the 9/11 attacks, there had been rumors among staff members that he still worked for the government, maybe even the CIA. Doc stopped here and gave Dick and Kate a hard look. They just stared back at him, expressionless.

The morning of the interview, Alex told Doc he was worried. Victoria, on the other hand, looked like she'd been born for the job. Hair perfect, voice clear, calm. She didn't see what Alex and Doc saw. Karim shifted in that interview. Started out like a scholar. Ended like a madman. Doc paused... started to get emotional, had to compose himself. Karim said he had a gift. A message for the West. Four of his men came out with ropes. Grabbed Alex and Doc. Victoria screaming. Doc forced to kneel. Alex too. Karim stood behind him, made a speech about imperialism, injustice. Then pulled his head back. Long knife in hand, well, you've seen the video.

Afterward, Doc was dragged to a cell. He talked about all the war zones he'd been to: Vietnam, Cambodia, Sarajevo, and Rwanda. He had seen nothing like this.

Creighton cut in, "Mr. Washington was in the US Army, wasn't he?"

Tom nodded, "Infantry in Vietnam in '68, then came back as a combat photographer embedded with Special Forces in '71."

Churchill stirred. "His cell. Where exactly was it?"

"East wing, lower level, deep inside the ancient part of the fortress. Stone chamber. No window. One guard posted day and night. I think he said they rotated every six hours. Doc said he could hear voices down the corridor. There were other rooms, maybe storage, maybe cells."

Creighton shuffled more papers. "Tell us about the escape."

"A week later, someone came to his cell. Young, local. He had no English but kept saying '*America. Freedom. Follow.*' Gave Doc a map, native clothing, water, and some flatbread. He took Doc outside, then back down into an underground room where they were keeping goats. There was a hole high up in the wall that led into some tunnels, part of an old irrigation system, maybe Hellenistic, maybe older. Doc got out, and the boy disappeared. Doc followed the trail marked on the map; he hiked for thirteen days. Nights were freezing. Days worse. Drank from streams, ate what he could. Slept in caves when he found them. His feet looked like raw meat by the time he finally ran into an American patrol on the eastern edge of Jalalabad."

"Doc got real upset here, he said, 'I left her behind. Victoria. She was still alive when I escaped. I don't know what they did to her after. I think about that every damn night.'"

Churchill exhaled, "That poor man."

Even Creighton looked sympathetic.

Tom pressed on.

Kate and Hawthorne said the kid who helped Doc was theirs. Vetted, reliable. 'You can trust him,' she said. Then the Major got down to business. Details. Defenses. Fortifications. Doc's time in the military and as a war journalist served him well. "Walls are thick, two meters in the old parts. Newer stuff's reinforced concrete. Two gates: south main, then a second at the inner curtain wall."

"Manpower?" the Major asked.

"Around 200 at full strength. AKs, RPGs, PKMs. Two snipers I know of. One ZU-23 anti-air emplacement, northeast ridge. MANPADS inside —SA-7s."

“Communications?”

“Sophisticated. Military-grade, American-made satellite dish on the west roof. Every team has radios. There’s a command post inside the tower near the kitchens. Reinforced.”

I asked, “Access to the cells where you were kept?”

“Staircase on the north side of the tower.”

Kate told us Victoria was being held in a heavily guarded cell in Karim’s tower, at least according to their contact. That was the end of Doc’s story. We thanked him, and I think he was glad to be done with the telling of it.

Kate took over the briefing. She opened a folder and slid a satellite image across the table. “Karim’s headed to a compound near Maimana, northern Afghanistan. A tribal leadership summit about resisting coalition forces in the north. Narcotics routes, Gulf money, it’s a power grab.”

Hawthorne added, “We believe Karim is consolidating his influence. It’s not just about Afghanistan anymore. This is about laying the foundations for something regional, perhaps even global. He’s already hosting pre-negotiations for access to new overland heroin corridors through Turkmenistan. The summit will lock in new alliances.”

I watched the two Americans closely. They looked too rehearsed, too pat, too perfect. It felt like a play, and their audience was eating it up.

“While he's away,” Kate said, “Security will be down. Twenty men left, tops. He trusts his lieutenants, but they’re lazy. This is our window.”

The Brigadier and the Major were enthusiastic.

"How convenient, Mr. Harrington, that your friends in Langley found a window just wide enough for us to risk a team. Did that not strike you as... contrived?" Creighton cut in.

Tom glanced at him in irritation, "Of course. My gut told me we were walking into a play where the final act was already written."

Churchill leaned forward slightly. “And yet you played your part.”

“I always do.”

CHAPTER 5

Creighton's pen tapped sharply against the table, eyes locked on Tom.

"Did you dine with Agent Prescott, Harrington?"

"Harry wanted me to keep an eye on the CIA, sniff out ulterior motives, so I got as close as possible."

Churchill's silent contemplative gaze felt heavier than Creighton's words. Tom leaned back, letting the past pull him under.

"We met at Veeraswamy, a posh Indian place frequented by hip, prosperous locals. Craft cocktails, polished wood, silk drapes, and sitar remixes. Oh, and top-flight curry. I reckoned it was her kind of place, that it would set the right tone. I scanned the exits, wondering if she had a minder. Her demeanor was guarded, but so was mine."

Tom hesitated, "We had a lot of small talk at the restaurant, I'm not sure all of it is relevant."

Mr. Churchill smiled placidly and cleaned his glasses with a handkerchief, "Details, Tom, my boy, details. Everything you can remember, if you please."

Tom shrugged and continued.

Kate leaned back, twirling her martini glass. "Gotta say, Captain, I had you pegged for a greasy Army pub type of guy, warm beer, darts, maybe a fight in the back. This place is... civilized." She was fashionably dressed, understated but sexy, showing just enough skin to get my attention.

I grinned and loosened my tie. "What, you think I'm all brawn and no taste? I'm full of surprises, Kate. Besides, after that airport curry you bitched about, I figured you deserved a proper meal."

She laughed, quick, genuine. "Proper? That hotel slop was a crime. You're setting a high bar here, Tom."

"Trust me, I deliver," I raised my gimlet. "To better nights than Heathrow dives."

We clinked glasses, her eyes locking on mine, "I'll drink to that. So, what's the deal with Hereford? I've heard it's a grinder. You ever miss normal life, or is the Army your whole deal?"

I sidestepped. "The training and the schedule can be brutal, but it sharpens you. Long runs, bad food, worse weather…" I directed the conversation back to her, probed her backstory. Where was she from? Did she have family baggage, all that rubbish. She gave me the usual prep-school-Connecticut résumé: yachts, Smith College, daddy in finance. Too polished by half. She said her father had worked near the World Trade Center at the time of the attack in '93, which got her interested in intelligence and counter terrorism. So, she got a job at Booz Allen, where she worked on threat reports until the Cole bombing. Claimed she had a friend on the ship, that the attack shook her. She wanted something operational, something that would make a difference.

It was my turn to get interrogated. She asked if I'd ever been to Tora Bora. "Our Delta boys said it was a mess…"

"Missed that party," I deflected. "Chasing ghosts elsewhere. Your lot pull anything useful from it?"

She said they got what they needed. Then she asked if I had ever run with Delta or worked on her side of the pond.

"Once or twice," I said. "Too many burgers, not enough tea."

She tested my legend. It was a solid cover, and I knew it like the back of my hand. I told her I grew up in the Home Counties, summers in Wales, winters in the south of France, public school, pretty standard stuff. She wondered if I had ever worked with MI6 since I was in military intelligence. I just told her that they were suits with big mouths.

I moved to the mission and asked her what she thought of Doc's story. Her expression softened, almost too perfect. She got serious and said, "We *must* get her out."

I studied her, kept pushing. "Your kid in the tunnels, how do you know he's not playing both sides?"

"We vet our people. He's solid," she said, but her fingers tightened on her glass.

"Got more sources like him?"

"One's enough," she said. "You got any SAS tricks to share?"

"How would you hit that fortress?"

"Helos insert a team, snipers provide cover, night op," she said, voice crisp. "Fast, no heroics. You?"

"Sounds like you've run ops, not just read about 'em," I told her pointedly.

"Reports teach you plenty," she parried. She was more guarded now.

Something about the way she said it… she was too seasoned to have been on the job for only a couple of years. In fact, the timeline of her career didn't really make sense. The Cole bombing was in the fall of 2000, then she's recruited by the CIA, gets through her training, and is running high-profile ops in early 2002? Unlikely.

The chill bit us as we stepped onto Regent Street. The typical crowd was out. Clubbers trying to look posh and yuppies going to upscale pubs. I took Kate's hand and guided her toward Carnaby Street. I briefly clocked a figure in a doorway, subtle, but something was off. A hesitation, an unnatural movement, too still for Soho's chaos. Whoever it was had disappeared;

they were good.

"Soho's nosy tonight. You bring company?"

Kate's laugh was sharp. Too sharp. "Ghosts, Captain? Or just bad spies?"

My instincts were flaring, and the hair on the back of my neck stood up. I wanted to finger the team that was working us, but I couldn't use tradecraft with her there; couldn't risk her knowing I wasn't an Army Captain who kicked in doors for a living. We kept walking, but I kept scanning.

I took her to the Clachan, an old upscale pub by Carnaby: oak beams, frosted glass, warm air, Coldplay on the juke. Yuppies in chunky sweaters and blazers chatted over pints. I scanned the crowd while I got our drinks, and Kate chose our seats, facing the door. She sipped her wine, her smile teasing, her knee brushed mine. "You're too smooth for a soldier. Sure, you're not a spy?"

"And you're too sharp for a desk jockey. What's Langley hiding?"

She laughed, leaned closer. Her foot worked its way up my calf. "This pub's charming, Tom, but I'm not ready to call it a night. Your place nearby, or are you all talk?"

You know when there's real chemistry with a woman? The air changes, there's electricity, it's tangible. This wasn't like that. It was too rehearsed, too contrived, but I still wanted her; maybe I convinced myself that she wanted me. Besides, Harry said to get close… I took the bait. "You're trouble, Kate. My place is close. Let's see if you can keep up."

She seemed triumphant, "Lead the way, Captain. I don't salute, but I'll follow."

Across the bar, a man's gaze lingered, his pint untouched.

"Friend of yours?"

"Probably just a drunk," she laughed, but her glance at the

stranger was too quick. “You’re paranoid, soldier.”

“Victoria’s out there,” her tone softening, redirecting me, “Are your boys ready for that fortress?”

“We’re always ready,” I said.

I took her home… to Captain Avery’s home. I’ll spare you the spicy bits. While I played dead, she gave the place a thorough rummage. Drawers, papers, even the bloody photo frames. Logistics did their job. The cover held.”

Creighton’s sharp voice sliced through the memory. “You bought her story about the source, Harrington? Or was the wine too good?”

“I never buy anyone’s story. I gather facts and put them in my reports. But she played a good game.”

Churchill stirred, “Good enough to cloud your instincts?”

Tom stared into the glass, “Maybe.”

CHAPTER 6

March 02, 2002, Credenhill, UK, SAS Headquarters

The briefing room was standard issue, and the atmosphere was electric. The only hint of the substance of the briefing to come was on a long table at the front of the room: a 3D replica of Qala-ye Khun, complete with its mudbrick towers, concrete gates, and gun emplacements. Anticipation was high. Rumors had run rampant that the mission would be high-profile. The lads were rowdy, talking trash, boasting about past and future feats of bravery, accusing each other of a variety of venal sins, and already planning the victory parties once the mission was done and dusted.

Corporal "Baz" Baxter eyed the model of the fortress. "Sarge, don't worry about your bad knees. I'll get ya over the walls. Plus, I hear they have ramps to get in and out of the helos now." Baz glowed in triumph, grinning like a Cheshire cat. He was the youngster of the unit, cocky, brash, and desperate for the respect of the veterans.

"I'd worry less about those walls and more about getting to the clinic to get tested Baz, that barmaid I saw you with last weekend has been with half the base." The Sergeant, Mick Riley, an experienced soldier from Northern Ireland, crossed his arms and leaned back, pleased with himself. Baz's grin faltered, replaced with a scowl as the words hit home. His eyes darted around the room, looking for a quick way to recover, but the laughter had already started. Corporal Carter, seated one row behind them, leaned forward, his voice laced with false sympathy, "It's true, Bazzie, Prosser from Supply got the clap from her last month. Nearly lost his... well, you get the idea."

My mind drifted back towards the previous day, spent finalizing the mission plan with Major Hooper, Lieutenant Wells, Sergeant Major Donovan, and, sadly, the CIA. The Lieutenant was green and was a stickler for regulations and proper uniforms. He had only been in the regiment for a year, had seen no combat, and was a proper officer and a gentleman. I didn't have to read his file to know that his parents had an old country pile within a couple of hours of London and that there was an OBE or a Peerage within a generation or two. The Sergeant Major had taken up the challenge of knocking Wells down a peg or two. He frequently chided the Lieutenant for speaking out of turn or not understanding the tactical situation: "Steady on, *Sir*, we'll let you know when your opinion is needed..." or "Oh good, I was *hoping* the Lieutenant would grace us with his knowledge." Sergeant Major Donovan had served for 27 years. He maintained a flawless uniform, possessed a withering glare, and had experienced combat on multiple continents.

Kate and her boss, Dick Hawthorne, hadn't come alone. They brought along the two CIA operators who rounded out their four-person team. Voss and Maddox were more like thugs or mob enforcers than soldiers. Voss was a giant man with a big, bushy, dark beard, a shaved head, and nearly black eyes. Despite the cold and wet weather in the UK, he wore a tank top, ball cap, shorts, and flip-flops. Maddox was shorter, thicker around the middle, barrel-chested, and had a short, greying beard.

The meeting started amicably enough. We debated how many helos we needed, weapons, communications, and contingencies. I argued for caution, for more assets held in reserve, and for more time. We would only have about two weeks to run rehearsals. Major Hooper and Donovan were inclined to agree. The CIA had stayed silent until this point, Dick sitting erect in his Brooks Brothers suit, his dead eyes staring at us with barely contained contempt. Kate was tapping buttons on her secure laptop, seemingly uninterested in our plans. Voss was silent, had a massive wad of chewing tobacco in his lip, and spat loudly into a cup. On the other hand, Maddox had laughing eyes and wore a smirk—as if our plans amused him.

Finally, Dick rose, his voice clipped, American confidence dripping. "Your caution is touching, Major, but our HUMINT source, corroborated by signals from Maimana, says it's a cakewalk. Twenty fighters, stoned on opium, no discipline. The hostage is a political prize, but the real objective is the servers." He tapped the replica's command post. "Maps, hard drives, Karim's network—that's what wins wars. With the intel we gather on this mission, we can dismantle Karim's entire network of warlords."

Voss grinned menacingly and spat again.

Kate finally looked up from her computer. Her tone was firm, her jaw set, eyes blazing, daring us to disagree. "The servers are time sensitive. We must enter hard and fast to secure them before they're wiped. There *is* no other window of time, gentlemen; this is our only opportunity. Debating any other scenario is a waste of time." She shot me a malicious look, a warning. We had been together every night since The Clachan. She was vulnerable and open while we ate take-out noodles in my apartment, tender, yet passionate in bed. She confided her anxiety about measuring up at work, meeting her family's expectations, and her desire to settle down and start a family someday. I confess, this sudden shift in her personality caught me off guard. Only a few hours before that meeting, she had been nibbling my earlobe, whispering shockingly suggestive ideas about what she would do to me that night.

Maddox whispered something to Voss, and the pair started laughing uproariously.

Seeing our resolve weaken, Hawthorne pressed his advantage. "Staging any significant conventional Army resources for contingencies will tip our hand to the enemy. Prescott is right, we go in with a small force, hard and fast, or we don't go in at all." They kept on in this manner, chipping away at our counterarguments, until they largely got their way. I began to suspect that I had been managed and steered while I thought I was keeping an eye on Kate. I knew I had let my guard down and was ashamed and angry. Voss and Maddox magnified my humiliation; they became my Greek chorus, sneering, whispering, mocking.

"*Attention*," a Sergeant roared. Major Hooper and Sergeant Major Donovan entered the briefing room, snapping my attention back to the briefing.

"Seats," the Major ordered. "I know you gentlemen have been eager to get in the fight in Afghanistan," he said, "we can't let our cousins have all the fun, can we?" The room started to buzz, and a few excited whoops were released.

The Sergeant Major restored order with a thundering "*Silence*." The lights were dimmed, and a projector spun to life, displaying satellite pictures. Major Hooper continued, explaining the background of the mission, about Victoria and Doc, the tunnel, and how we were going in with a CIA team to rescue Victoria and gather intel.

"Qala-ye Khun's a bastard of a target," Hooper continued, his voice sharp, cutting through the buzz. "It predates Alexander the Great's incursion into the area. Ancient mudbrick, modern defenses: rebar, concrete gates, a ZU-23 anti-aircraft gun that'll chew our helos to scrap. Karim's off at Maimana, chasing warlord clout, leaving twenty fighters. Sloppy, but armed with RPGs, snipers, and enough ammo to make a mess. Our source says the hostage is in the lower levels of the fortress, a kind of ancient dungeon, worse for wear but kicking. She's our primary objective."

"Twenty blokes? Piece of piss, sir. I'll have that tower cleared before Specs finishes his Harry Potter book." Baz grinned widely, his Newcastle swagger begging for a laugh.

Lance Corporal Ollie "Specs" Morgan retorted, "Oi, Baz, it's

Dune, not that kiddy wizard trash. It's about a war in the desert, maybe you should check it out instead of reading comic books and listening to the Spice Girls."

The room chuckled. Lieutenant Wells glared at them. "Focus, lads," the Sergeant Major growled.

Hooper tapped the replica's tunnel grate, unfazed. "Mission's simple: get the journo, secure any intel, get out—four teams, coordinated to the second. Infil team: Captain Avery, Baxter, Riley, hits the tunnel at 0200 to knock out defenses, secure the girl. Sniper team: Carter, Morgan, takes the northeast ridge, 800 meters out, to clear threats. Helo teams fast-rope into the north gate at 0315, secure the courtyard. Clear the barracks and command post, grab maps and drives."

Corporal Danny "Red" Carter, a quiet sort of lad, spoke up, "Ridge is ours, sir. Their sentries won't see daylight." He glanced at his spotter, Specs, who gave him a fist bump and a grin.

Baz piped up, undeterred by his earlier roast. "Tunnel's gonna be a doddle, sir. I'll blow that ZU-23 to Newcastle and back, maybe nick some goat curry for the lads." He winked at Sergeant Riley.

"Keep dreaming, Baz," said Riley in an Irish lilt, "That tunnel's tighter than your boyfriend's arsehole. One wrong move, and we're goat food."

Hooper pointed to the replica's north gate. "Helo teams are the hammer. We'll be kitted with new helmet cams. Prototype live feeds, video grainy as hell, but command in London and Jalalabad will see every move. Signal's dicey in the Hindu Kush, so don't count on them holding your hand. Otherwise, we'll have a standard loadout: suppressors, breaching charges, and night vision.

Sergeant Major Donovan and Lieutenant Wells lead Fire Team 1; I lead Fire Team 2. Team 1 holds the outer courtyard and rendezvous with the tunnel team. Team 2 and the spooks grab the intel from the tower. As you can see, the tower is a bit like a medieval keep. Heavy wooden doors, inner courtyard, 4 levels. The command post is on the first level. We blow the doors with C4, clear the inner courtyard, my squad secures the CP, Sergeant Rai's squad holds the courtyard, CIA takes the upper levels. Once we have the intel, we move back to the outer courtyard and exfil."

On a satellite image, Hooper pointed to the cluster of ramshackle dwellings between the courtyard and the tower. "These dwellings are a primary threat; we'll post a machine gun in the courtyard to keep the path to and from the tower clear."

Donovan summarized, "We fast-rope in, secure the outer courtyard, spooks and Team 2 gather intel from the tower, the tunnel team secures the hostage. No heroics, no faffing. Primary exfil's the helos, 0340, same courtyard. We'll have air support from an American AC-130 Spectre gunship. Secondary exfil's a 3-mile hump west to a wadi, QRF waiting. Tertiary, survivors scatter to caves 8 miles southwest, cache for 48 hours."

He nodded at Lieutenant Wells. "Stay sharp, son, you're with me." Wells swallowed, trying his best not to look nervous, his pen scratching notes in a green field notebook. "Yes, Sergeant Major."

Major Hooper gestured to me, "Captain Avery, why don't you provide details of your team's part in this?"

I nodded and gave them the rundown. We would infiltrate 20 clicks from the fortress 48 hours before the mission, wearing local garb, and then proceed to our checkpoint, where we would lie low. At 0100 on D-Day, we scramble to the tunnel and make entry. The original builder of the fortress installed an irrigation system that pumped water from the river into a cistern adjacent to the tower, which was now used as a goat pen. Our access tunnel's original purpose was to allow excess cistern water to flow back into the river. The tunnel was tight, and we'd need to move fast, so we would only carry pistols and submachine guns and scavenge anything else we needed. It should take us at least half an hour to get to the goat pen; I gave us a 30-minute buffer just in case. We would emerge from the cistern, place a C4 charge on the anti-aircraft gun, then gain access to the underground chambers where Victoria was being held (the CIA source said she had been moved down there while Karim was gone), through an entrance behind the tower. Once she was secured, we would rendezvous with the other teams in the courtyard and exfil.

As the briefing came to a close, the room erupted in a flurry of excitement. The boys were enthralled, their eyes gleaming with anticipation, but a heavy weight settled in my chest. A gnawing unease settled in my gut, whispering that the plan was overly complicated, the rehearsal timeline far too tight, and we needed more assets. Yet here we were, past the point of no return: there was no backup, and time was slipping through our fingers.

Mr. Churchill maintained his inscrutable demeanor. His posture was relaxed, and his pudgy hands rested on his ample stomach. Had his eyes not been open, one would have assumed he was napping. Perhaps this is why he startled Tom when he asked, "You said you didn't trust the CIA's intel. Why didn't you push back harder?"

"I thought I could handle Kate," Tom admitted. "I thought I could play their game, I should've fought harder."

CHAPTER 7

March 05, 2002, RAF Base Brize Norton

The RAF hangar was frigid. Fluorescents hummed overhead, washing everything in a pale, institutional glare. Rows of kit stretched across the concrete in perfect grids: plate carriers, helmets, rifles, bergen packs, radio batteries, med pouches. A regimented sea of olive and tan.

The lads were sprawled across it like dogs sunning on a pavement.

Riley was lying on his back, boots crossed, flipping through a dog-eared Penthouse Magazine with scholarly interest. Carter checked over a PRC-148 radio with practiced irritation, as if expecting it to fail out of spite. Wells's breaths came short and shallow as his trembling fingers checked and rechecked every pouch on his carrier.

Baz was buzzing around his own kit like a puppy, too much energy and nowhere to put it. He was gushing about his latest crush, an Italian girl who worked at the on-base pub.

"Right, *leesten*," Baz said, slipping into the terrible accent he'd adopted since meeting the barmaid.

"Thees *bambina*... she love me!"

A chorus of groans rolled across the kit line.

"She only smiled at you because you tipped her a fiver you couldn't afford, for Christ's sake," Carter said without looking up.

"And because she wanted you to leave the bar," Riley added as he examined the centerfold of his magazine.

Wells tried not to laugh, making a choking sound.

"No, no... that was amore, lads. Pure *amore*."

"Christ. If that was amore, I'm the bloody Pope." Riley said.

Baz turned to me, "Tell them, *Capitano*. Back me up."

The name hung in the air. Riley started chuckling immediately. Carter gave Baz a mock salute. Wells tried to hide a smile behind his collar.

I crouched by my pile of kit and checked a buckle, pretending not to hear.

Proper mates, the lot of them. I tightened a strap. Kept my eyes down. Belonging was something I'd traded away years ago.

The banter rolled on until it was cut clean by the sharp echo of boots.

Major Hooper and Sergeant Major Donovan stepped into the hangar, and every conversation died instantly. Kit rustled; backs straightened. Wells popped tall and nervously shifted his weight from foot to foot.

Riley shut his magazine and slid it—smooth as a card trick—into an open pouch on Wells's ruck. I suppressed a laugh.

Hooper held a clipboard. Donovan's face was grim.

"Right," Hooper said. "Let's see if any of you remembered how to pack a rucksack."

They started at the far end. Carter got the first inspection. Hooper flipped his carrier, muttered "barely acceptable," and moved on. Riley earned a raised eyebrow for the contraband packet of mints tucked into his admin pouch.

Hooper flipped open the side pocket on Wells's ruck and held up Riley's dirty magazine.

Wells turned bright red. His mouth gaping, he shot Riley a baleful look.

Riley struggled to keep a straight face. "*Shameful*, Sir, just shameful," he said.

Hooper pursed his lips and eyed Wells. "Really, Corporal?"

"Morale, Sir!" Wells blurted out.

Hooper stared at him for a moment, then shoved it back into the pouch and moved on.

When they reached Baz, the temperature dropped a full ten degrees.

Hooper knelt and began to examine Baz's layout.

"Where's your spare tourniquet, Baxter?"

Baz froze. "Sir, I—uh—I had it earlier, must've—"

Hooper's voice became surgical. "The spare, Corporal. Not the one on your chest. The *spare*."

Baz swallowed. "It might be in my pack—"

"*Wrong answer.*"

The hangar went pin-drop silent.

Donovan, without comment, lifted Baz's NVG pouch, thumbed open the compartment, and held up a pair of AA batteries between two fingers like damning evidence.

"You planning to power night vision with these?"

Baz blinked. "Sir... I thought—"

Donovan cut him off sharply. "You didn't think at all."

Hooper stood, face taut. "Two failures before we've even boarded the aircraft. Forget your med kit, and you bleed out. Pack the wrong batteries, and you go blind. You want to die on some hillside? Fine. Do it on your own time. But you do not *ever* risk your team because you're too bloody careless to pack your kit like a professional."

Baz's face had gone the color of chalk.

Donovan leaned in, quiet enough that it hit harder than shouting. "Sort yourself out. And the rest of you—check your mate's kit. If he dies because you didn't, that's on you."

Then they moved on.

The lads didn't speak until the officers were thirty paces down the line.

Riley let out a long breath. "Smooth one, Baz."

Carter shook his head. "Brilliant. Might as well have brought glow sticks for night ops."

Wells, trying to be kind, managed a wobbly smile. "Could've been worse."

Baz didn't reply. He just stared at his kit like it had betrayed him.

I knelt beside him.

From my own pouch, I pulled a spare tourniquet and a pack of CR123 batteries and handed them to him.

Baz said quietly, "Cheers, Capitano. Didn't think anyone—"

"Then start thinking," I said sharply.

He nodded, swallowing the last of his humiliation.

"Form up! Movement order in five!" Donovan's voice echoed through the hangar.

The team snapped into motion. Kit hauled up, helmets clipped, straps tugged into place. The low hum of the C-130K Hercules outside deepened as the crew spun up the engines.

Baz, still rattled, tried to make a joke about the weight of his rucksack. Riley shoved him lightly. Carter clapped him on the shoulder. Wells hurried to keep up.

I watched them go.

Good men. Real soldiers. I prayed they would make it back home.

I slung my pack, fell into step, and didn't look back.

CHAPTER 8

March 12, 2002

Forward Operating Base Sphinx, Northern Afghanistan

The training compound was hot as a furnace and stank like diesel. The SAS and CIA teams had arrived a week earlier, and since then, we'd spent every waking moment rehearsing the assault on Qala-ye Khun. The mock-up of the fortress, hastily assembled from shipping containers, Hesco barriers, plywood cutouts, and chalked outlines on concrete, was crude but functional. A towering goat pen made of rebar and sandbags stood in for the cistern entry point. After each drill, the command staff rearranged paper targets, some showing armed 'Tangos,' others unarmed civilians. Each one was placed with surgical precision to keep us guessing. We would identify and appropriately engage each target we encountered, using paint bullets. The courtyard, the barracks, and the tower all accounted for.

Helmet cams and comms units were already live. Rehearsals ran on a tight loop: infil, breach, room clearance, hostage recovery, exfil. Every misstep was replayed in the debriefing tent, projected on grainy monitors, dissected by the Joint Rescue Planning Group like a postmortem.

I led my team through the fourth and final dry run of the day, Baz on point, Riley close behind. We'd hit our ingress timing, crawled through the simulated tunnel in good order, rigged the antiaircraft gun with C4, hit the dungeons, got the hostage (played by a 'loggie' corporal), and were linking up with Fire Team 2 and the CIA at the tower.

"On time for once," Maddox muttered, chewing a toothpick. I ignored him. Relations with our “cousins” were at an all-time low, and nerves were frayed. Kate studiously avoided eye contact with me. Since we left the UK, she had frozen me out. Hell, Voss was more personable at this point. Her face was dripping with sweat and caked with dust. She looked almost absurd, like a child dressed up for war. The helmet, plate carrier, and rifle seemed to swallow her petite frame. And yet, she hadn’t collapsed. She tried to give the outward appearance of being unaffected by the heat and strain of carrying the heavy combat loadout, but I could see the exhaustion in her eyes.

We moved down the main thoroughfare in bounding overwatch. My team took the right flank, the CIA mirrored us on the left, and Fire Team 2 covered our six from the rear—tight wedge, clean lines.

Baz was wired. He'd been too fast all day, trying to prove himself after Riley gave him a chewing out that morning. This time, as we passed through a bottleneck between two buildings, Baz broke formation and surged ahead.

"Baz, hold up," Riley snapped.

But Baz didn’t hear. Or didn’t care. Weapon up and focused on a pile of sandbags in front of him, he pushed past a gap between two buildings without checking the red zone.

A target of Bin Laden with an AK swung from behind a barrel. Baz had already moved past. In a real op, he’d be dead. Worse, so would most of the team and the hostage. Riley and I each delivered two shots to the target, center mass. Hearing the gunfire behind him Baz froze. An instructor shouted, “Training time out! You just lost your team, Corporal."

Baz's face flushed red beneath his helmet, and he began stammering with embarrassment. Riley cursed under his breath. Voss exploded.

"You stupid fucking child! You don't clear your sector, you

don't check your angles, you endanger the entire mission. You just got everyone in this damn courtyard killed!"

Baz turned, eyes wide. "It was a drill. I just missed it—"

Voss grabbed Baz by the vest and slammed him against a plywood wall, eyes blazing with fury. "You missed it? That's the difference between a medal and a fucking body bag, shit for brains. You want to impress someone? Learn to crawl before you try to run with the adults."

I stepped in, "Voss! That's enough."

Voss didn't let go. Maddox moved in, but didn't stop him; he just watched with an impish smile.

"Back *off*," I said again, louder.

Riley helped pull Voss back. "It's a training run, mate."

Voss shook free, spat on the ground, and stormed off, still cursing. I watched Voss disappear behind the shipping containers. If this was just training, what the hell would the real thing look like?

Kate intercepted me before the debriefing, offering a bottle of water. "Voss is wound tight," she said.

"I hate to say it, but he's right. I'm not sure Baz is ready," I said.

Kate nodded. "He did counter-cartel work in Colombia before this. One of his guys bled out because an indigenous fighter didn't check his angle. That's not the kind of thing you forget."

"I expect not."

We stood in silence for a moment; I studied her face carefully.

"You've been avoiding me," she said finally.

I laughed in disbelief, "That's not how it looks from my angle, you haven't even made eye contact with me since we got here."

"Because you've been acting like a petulant child since the briefing. Don't tell me it's because I embarrassed you in front of your team."

"It's because your intel doesn't add up," I said. "Because your story shifts. Because this 'cakewalk' looks more like a trap every time I see the map."

She looked away, toward the mountains beyond the FOB. "We don't get to wait for perfect intel, Tom. Not in this job."

"Maybe. But you came into this op with too many holes."

"We have a shot at stopping Karim. Maybe the only one. That woman is still alive. Doesn't that count for something?"

I stared at her. She was lying or desperate—I couldn't tell which.

“You look exhausted. How are you holding up?” I changed the subject.

Her face softened, “Everything hurts. This fucking plate carrier is like a torture device.”

I couldn't argue, she must have had 80 pounds of gear on, and it looked like it was eating her alive. I smiled sympathetically, “We're done for the day, go take that thing off.”

She touched my arm gently, "Be careful in that tunnel."

I watched her go, then turned toward the debriefing tent.

Voss was already inside, thick arms crossed, jaw locked.

The debrief began with muted grumbling. The team crowded around a makeshift conference table under a dim canvas canopy, a space barely large enough for two dozen men and the playback equipment. The grainy helmet-cam footage lit the tent walls with flickering grey shadows. Sergeant Major Donovan leaned over a laptop, his expression fixed in a stern scowl.

Major Hooper stood at the front, laser pointer in hand, red dot darting across still frames of Baz's misstep.

“Here's where it went wrong,” Hooper said. “Failure to clear. Failure to communicate.”

Baz kept his eyes down.

Hooper continued, "Now, we all know training is meant to iron out errors. But this isn't just a screw-up. It's a pattern. You're too fast, Corporal. Too eager. I'd rather have a man half as skilled and twice as patient. We can't afford any more mistakes like these."

Baz swallowed hard. "Yes, sir."

Maddox gave a theatrical yawn from the corner. "Maybe next time we run a bake sale instead of a raid. Safer for everyone."

I turned to Hooper. "We'll sort it internally, Major."

Donovan grunted his approval. "Fix it. Or I will."

I shot Riley a pointed look. The frustration with Baz was evident on his face. "I'll handle it, Sir," he said. "I'll sort him *proper*." Baz stared at his feet, wringing his hands.

The next day, we ran it again. And again. Until muscle replaced thought. Until doubt had no time to bloom. Until it stopped being training and started to feel like fate.

CHAPTER 9

March 14, 2002

Forward Operating Base Sphinx, Northern Afghanistan

With just 48 hours to go until wheels up, the tempo around the FOB shifted. Rehearsals were complete. No more drills, no more helmet-cam playback. Now came the quiet before the storm: gear checks, weapons cleaning, tightening comms protocols, and staring too long at the sat maps. There was an edge to everything; the air was heavy when the laughter faded. Even Baz, who normally couldn't keep his mouth shut, moved with an eerie, subdued focus.

Someone in command, probably Hooper, possibly the Brigadier, had the bright idea to stage a morale night. Fire rings and a makeshift grill appeared by dusk. The supply guys wheeled out coolers stacked with cans of lager, and someone found a boom box. A few classics from The Who and Bowie buzzed across the cracked loudspeakers. Soldiers gathered around fires in little knots, swapping lies and laughing too loudly. The air had that haunted camaraderie peculiar to soldiers who knew they might die together but weren't ready to say it out loud.

I was leaning against a stack of sandbags, sipping from a can of Stella, when Baz approached with a hangdog look painted across his face.

"Sarn't Major says I should square things," he said. "With Voss."

I raised an eyebrow. "You planning on being civil?"

"Gonna try."

Riley joined us. "We'll supervise. If he lunges, I've got your back, Baz."

The three of us walked across the dusty compound toward a blazing fire where Voss, Maddox, and Kate were camped. Maddox spotted us first and raised a can in greeting.

"Evening, gents. Come to join the misfits?"

Baz cleared his throat and shifted his feet around uncomfortably. "I just.. I wanted to say thanks for the other day. I was out of order. You were right to kick off. Shouldn't have taken it so lightly."

Voss stayed silent, his eyes fixed on the embers, a thick plug of tobacco jutting from his lip.

Maddox slapped a hand on a nearby crate. "Sit. Have a beer. We're all friends here, right?"

Baz hesitated for a moment, then dropped down onto the crate beside him. I sat next to Kate; she gave me a smirk and a quick wink.

"It's your first operation, isn't it?" Maddox asked.

Baz nodded somberly—for once, no jokes or false bravado.

Maddox chuckled knowingly. "I remember when I popped my cherry."

"Though I walk through the valley of the shadow of death, I will fear no evil..." he quoted.

"You'll know what to do when the time comes, lad, the training takes over."

"What'd you do before the CIA?" Baz asked Maddox after a long pause.

Maddox slouched back and cracked another can. "SEAL. Until a few years back."

Baz lit up. "No kidding?"

Maddox smirked. "Yeah. Got a story for you, if you're interested. About how we almost stopped this war before it started.

How we almost took out Bin Laden years ago."

Baz was incredulous. "Before 9/11?"

Maddox nodded, taking a slow pull from his beer. "Way before. Nineteen ninety-eight. Nobody knew his name yet—not really. Not the public, anyway. But we knew. CIA had a thread on him, followed it to a compound in the mountains."

He shifted, resting his elbows on his knees, beer dangling from his fingers.

"They dropped us in the desert for six months. Trained the operation like it was Apollo 11. Breaching drills, night jumps, helicopter insertions, the whole damn thing. We planned out and rehearsed every second, every room, down to where the guards would be standing and where the lights would be off. We had a real window. Clean intel. The guy was there."

"Jesus," Baz said.

"We were wheels up, man. Sitting on the tarmac. A whole naval fleet was on standby for air support. I was locking in my NVGs, loading mags. Everyone was calm. Focused. Ready to go into hell and get it done."

Maddox took another drink and contin ued, voice dropping.

"Then the call came. *Abort*. Straight from the fucking White House."

A stillness fell upon us as we absorbed this revelation.

"Why?" Riley demanded.

His nostrils flared in anger; old wounds were being torn open. "Clinton didn't want to spook the Saudis. Didn't want headlines. Didn't want a messy black op going south and hitting the news. You know what they told us? 'Stand down. Mission's off. Pack up.' Just like that."

Maddox threw his empty can into the fire. It hissed and crumpled.

"We were *right there*. We could've taken him out. Before the embassies. Before the Cole. Before the Towers. Before all of this."

Riley let out a low whistle.

"You think about it a lot?" I asked.

No answer at first. The firelight caught his eyes, sharp with suppressed anger.

"Every damn day. We had him. And the suits," he spat into the dirt, "the suits let him walk."

Kate grimaced in frustration. "I fought against that decision," she said, almost to herself, then caught herself, glancing away. My gaze snapped to her. She'd claimed she joined the Agency after the Cole bombing in 2000; her backstory was falling apart.

Maddox stood and grabbed more beers from the crate, passing them around.

"Politicians," Maddox said, turning back toward the fire. "They never bleed for the decisions they make. We do."

I studied Kate's face with suspicion. She quickly broke the silence, "Sergeant Riley, you've been quiet. Got any stories from the old days?"

Riley shifted in his seat. He swirled the liquid in his battered tin mug. Not beer, not for him, he was a whisky man.

Finally, he looked up, "Few," he said. "You lot ever hear of Operation Barras?"

Baz perked up. "Sierra Leone, right?"

Riley nodded. "September 2000. The West Side Boys had grabbed six of ours, Royal Irish, plus a Sierra Leonean officer. They were holed up near Rokel Creek. The whole area was a goddamn nightmare. Jungle so thick you couldn't see five feet. And those bastards... they weren't just militants. They were kids, mostly. Strung out on amphetamines and jungle brew, painted up like devils, waving machetes, AKs, RPGs, the works. Some of 'em wore wedding dresses. No joke. They had no tactics, no discipline, but they had numbers, unpredictability, and no fear. We'd already tried negotiations. Useless. One of our lot was marched out at gunpoint to deliver a message. Came back pale as chalk. Said they were ready to start executing hostages, one at a time."

Taking a sip from his mug, Riley continued.

"We inserted just after first light. Chinooks in low, blades kicking up the jungle like a hurricane. Touchdown zone was no bigger than a tennis court. The second we hit the ground, it was on. Gunfire, tracers, the whole place lit up like Blackpool bloody illuminations."

He grabbed a stick and drew a rough diagram of the compound in the dirt.

"Two-pronged assault. One team hit the main camp. The other, mine, looped through the brush to flank the secondary site. I remember the heat. You couldn't breathe. Sweat in your eyes, adrenaline in your veins. The noise was like standing inside a drum."

Riley's voice dropped a notch, more measured now, as if pacing through it all again.

"We breached the first hut; it was chaos. Muzzle flashes everywhere. Couldn't hear a damn thing except screaming and gunfire. You couldn't tell who was shooting at who—half of them were firing blind, some just waving AKs and pulling the trigger."

The sergeant gripped his mug tightly; his voice was rough.

"I remember kicking in one of the corrugated shacks—tin walls, no windows, just smoke and shadows. Inside was one of our hostages and a guard. The guard had a pistol to the hostage's head. A heartbeat from pulling the trigger. I didn't think. I just moved. Double-tapped him before he could blink. He dropped. So did the hostage. He was covered in blood, couldn't tell whose."

Riley took another drink, not a sip this time, but a large gulp.

"I stepped in to clear the room. And that's when I saw it. There was a girl in the corner. Maybe twelve. Her dress was torn, face swollen, lip split. She wasn't crying. Just staring. Her wrists were tied to a post. One of those bastards had left his belt on the floor next to her. I didn't even need to ask what had happened."

He scanned our faces now, his expression icy and unreadable.

Kate's voice was soft. "What did you do?" She moved closer to me, pressing her weight into me.

"I cut her free, and she bolted. Out into the jungle. Never even looked at me. I still don't know if that was terror or relief. I'll never know. We lost one man, Captain McCarthy. Took a round to the neck, clearing a path to the hostages. We got all six out alive. One of them had broken ribs and malaria, but they all walked out."

Kate nodded, her expression unreadable.

"What was it like, after?"

Riley gave a small, grim smile.

"They pinned medals to our chests. Called it a textbook rescue. Precision chaos, they said. Then, no joke, they packed us off to Kosovo the next week. Still had blood on my boots. No time to polish the tin."

Baz shook his head. "That's mad."

Riley shrugged. "That's soldiering."

All eyes turned to Voss. Even Kate hesitated.

"You got one?" Baz asked, too young to know better.

Voss didn't answer at first. He sat motionless, his broad frame hunched slightly forward, elbows on his knees, a dented can of beer clenched in one calloused hand. His face was blank and unreadable, and for a few moments, it seemed as if he wouldn't respond. Finally, he spoke, his voice emotionless.

"El Mozote. El Salvador. '81. I was twenty-two. Special Forces. We'd been dropped in-country to embed with a Salvadoran battalion. Mission was to train them in counterinsurgency. Keep an eye on their operations. Work hearts and minds, they told us." He snorted softly, a bitter edge to it, like he was mocking the memory of his younger self.

"The Atlacatl Battalion," he continued, his voice steady but heavy. "Freshly trained by us. Top-notch, or so we thought. Proud of 'em, in a way. At first." He paused, his gaze distant, as if they were replaying the scenes he described. "They were disciplined, sharp. Moved like they'd been born with rifles in their hands. We'd drilled them for weeks—night raids, ambushes, how to read the terrain. Felt like we were building something."

Nobody interrupted. Not even Maddox, who usually couldn't resist a sarcastic quip, his thick frame slumped against a crate, his eyes narrowed but attentive.

"Intel came down that the village of El Mozote was sheltering FMLN guerrillas, we'd done some recce flights, low passes over the valley. Saw nothing. No weapons caches, no troop movements, no fighters slipping through the jungle. Just farmers, kids, old women hanging laundry. But orders came straight from San Salvador to support the op. No questions. So we went in. We watched. We were supposed to observe only. Document." His lip twitched, a flicker of disgust. "That's what they called it. Document."

His knuckles whitened around the beer. I slid forward on the edge of my crate and lit a cigarette.

"It started with the men," he said. "They dragged them into the village square: fathers, brothers, old men with bad backs. Accused them of being rebels, of hiding weapons. No proof, no questions. Just shouting. Then they pulled the women and kids out of the houses. Families screaming, clinging to each other. The soldiers claimed they were insurgent families, collaborators. Said they had to be 'cleaned out.'"

Voss tilted his head skyward for a moment, then exhaled sharply and continued.

"They separated them. Shot the men first. Lined them up against a wall, some still begging, some didn't make a sound. Then some of the women. The rest were herded into the church, a little white building with a cracked bell tower. We tried to raise command. Me and my team, we were screaming into the radios, trying to get someone, anyone, to call it off. Comms were jammed. We were cut off. Helpless."

My mind spun into overdrive as I processed Voss's story. Something about it felt off. We had reviewed case studies of special operations that went sideways during my SAS training, and the El Mozote massacre had been one of them. Some details from Voss's story didn't match up with the classified reports I had read. I strained to pinpoint where the discrepancy lay.

He continued, "The rest of the day was..." A dramatic pause. Real emotion? If so, it was the first time I had seen him express anything other than anger, disdain, or animosity. Or was this all performance art? Voss took another sip from the can, his hand steady, but his eyes were unfocused, apparently lost in the past. "They didn't always use bullets. Too loud, I think. Too final. They used knives. Rifle butts. Ropes. I saw a soldier, a kid, younger than Baz, grinning as he swung his rifle like a club. I watched a boy, maybe ten, try to crawl out of a pit full of corpses. His hands were bloody, clawing at the dirt. Someone put a boot on his back and shoved him back down. Then they laughed. Laughed like it was a game."

His face was impenetrable, but I saw a softening in his eyes. No one said a word. My cigarette had burned down to ash, forgotten. Kate's fingernails dug into my knee. Baz's bravado was gone, his mouth slack, eyes darting nervously. Even Maddox sat rigid and quiet.

My racing mind finally identified one of the discrepancies in the story. Voss's claim about comms being jammed didn't add up. Green Berets carried PRC-77s, encrypted with KY-38. FMLN couldn't touch those frequencies. The after-action reports I had read stated that advisors had comms with San Salvador. Why lie? What else was he being dishonest about? My stomach churned, picturing Voss not as a helpless observer but a willing participant, maybe even pulling a trigger.

"Later, I went into the church," Voss said. "Blood everywhere. I slipped, caught myself on a pew. There were bodies piled near the altar, some burned, some not. Men, women. Children. I found a girl, maybe twelve, near the back. She'd been strangled with rosary beads, the kind you'd see old women clutching at Mass. Her fingers were broken, twisted at the wrong angle —she'd tried to fight. Her eyes were still open, staring at nothing."

A long pause stretched out, the only sound the distant laughter of other clusters of soldiers. My mind was still reeling, trying to align his story with the reports I had read.

"We got pulled out two days later," he continued. "Helicopters came at dawn, kicking up dust and ash. A guy in sunglasses debriefed us, some spook from Langley or maybe just a desk jockey with a power trip. Told us we'd seen nothing. That it was a rebel hoax, propaganda to smear the government. We signed NDAs, thick stacks of paper that promised jail or worse if we talked. Then it was on to the next mission. Next war. Like it never happened."

He drained the rest of his beer, the can glinting as he tilted it back. He set it down on the ground with deliberate care, the soft clink of aluminum against gravel louder than it should have been.

"That's my story."

By this time, I was fully convinced that Voss's story had a sheen of bullshit all over it. It was too pat, Voss, the poor victim who could do nothing to stop the killing despite training the soldiers responsible. Officially, most of the relevant documents and intelligence about the operation had been destroyed, and the US denied any involvement. However, the reports I had read in school suggested the Americans knew more than they had let on. If Voss had been present during the massacre, that would blow up the entire official narrative. My mind raced with the implications, and none of them improved my confidence about our mission or our CIA partners. I glanced at Kate, the gears in my mind churning. That slip about the cancelled Bin Laden raid nagged at me; her Cole timeline was fraying. Did she know Voss's truth, or was she hiding her own?

She smiled softly at me and stood, "Come on, Captain. Walk with me."

The embers of our fire were fading, and no one seemed eager to tell more stories, so I nodded and followed her, her arm threaded through mine. Tents cast long shadows, muffling the camp's hum. I churned Voss and Kate's lies over in my mind. I kept it light, grinning. "So, you worked on that Tarnak Farms raid Maddox mentioned? Must've been wild, chasing Bin Laden back then." My eyes flicked to hers, a casual probe hunting for a tell.

Kate's lips curved into a smile, "Curious, aren't you?" She stepped closer, fingers brushing my jacket, her scent—lager, dust, expensive soap—curling around me. "I was… around for that one. Not quite on the front lines." Her voice was soft, evasive, but her gaze held mine. She's dodging, and she knows I'm digging.

She leaned in, lips grazing my ear, breath warm. "Enough shop talk, Captain," she said, tugging my collar, pulling me into a tent's shadow. She kissed me first, sudden and soft, then deeper. Her hands slipped under my shirt, warm against the chill, and my questions faded, though the doubt still flickered in the back of my mind. The raid loomed, forty-eight hours out, but I realized that I wanted, no, I needed a respite from the planning, the drills, the questions, the suspicions. I left Tarnak Farms and El Salvador behind and kissed her back.

CHAPTER 10

The sex didn't change the temperature between us. If anything, it made the air colder.

We were tucked behind the Hesco barriers on the far side of the FOB, half-dressed, boots off, the dust still settling. Kate shivered lightly and pulled her jacket over her shoulders without looking at me. I lit a cigarette. Across the perimeter, the bonfires were still going. Dark figures clustered around them —laughing, shoving, passing bottles around. Proper mates. A real team. I watched them longer than I meant to.

Kate followed my eyes, but not the direction. She was watching me.

"You envy them."

I shrugged. "Straightforward. Loyal. A brotherhood… what's wrong with that?"

I paused. Smoke drifted past.

"In my experience," I said, "the only person you can trust is the man next to you. Planners have their own agendas."

I didn't intend to say it. It just came out, the way words do when you're half tired and the night presses in.

Kate turned a little, the firelight catching the edge of her cheek. "That's how soldiers think, Tom. Not people who shape things."

I gave her a sidelong look. "I'm not one for shaping things. Never have been. Not built for it."

Her expression flickered. Disappointment? Curiosity? Hard to tell with her.

“When I was a kid,” she said, “my father used to take me out to the Hamptons. An old friend of his had a house on the water. The kind of place where the dock’s worth more than a normal person’s mortgage.” A faint smile ghosted across her lips. “He was good to me. The rare adult who actually listened when you spoke. Taught me to sail. Remembered my birthday. One of the few people I—”

She cut herself off.

“When I got older,” she continued, “he asked my father for help. A small thing. An inquiry on the Hill into a contractor he was tied to—nothing major. He just wanted to know how to handle it. Keep his name clean.”

Her voice tightened, almost imperceptibly.

“But later, he refused to return the favor. Wouldn’t make a call. Wouldn’t lean on a staffer. Said it was improper.” She gave a humorless little laugh. “Improper. Like anyone else cared.”

She nudged a pebble with her toe.

“After that? Things started happening. Quiet things. Ethics complaint. Leak to the press. Bank pulled a loan early: routine policy review. His partners distanced themselves. Donations dried up. Stock he held tanked after a conveniently timed rumor. Nothing you could point to. Nothing you could fight. A year later, he shot himself. His family was ruined, destitute.”

Kate looked over at me—searching for judgment, or maybe for agreement.

“He made the mistake of thinking a small refusal wouldn’t matter,” she said. “He didn’t understand that the favor was never optional. Power works a certain way. You move with it, or it moves you out of the way.”

I didn’t say anything.

It sat between us for a long moment. I should have felt sorry for the man in her story. Instead, I pitied Kate. She talked about power as if she could bend it to her will—as if she weren't just another pawn waiting to be sacrificed.

"There are people out there who think bigger, Tom. People who... who aren't afraid to—"

She stopped. Froze.

I waited.

She didn't finish the sentence.

Whatever she'd been about to say, whatever she almost trusted me with, she pulled it back behind her teeth.

Her eyes hardened. "Never mind."

She stood, brushed dust off her trousers, the mask sliding back into place.

"We should get some sleep. Big day tomorrow."

She started to walk away. Took three steps. Stopped.

Didn't turn all the way back. Just enough that I saw the line of her jaw.

"Tom... try not to get killed. Don't ask me why I care," she said.

A small pause. A breath.

"There's a safe house outside Bordeaux. Little stone place with a broken chimney and good wine. If we make it back... maybe we could commandeer it for a weekend."

Before I could answer, or even decide what the hell I would've said—she stepped in hard and fast.

She grabbed me by the front of the shirt and pulled herself against me. Her forehead pressed into my chest. I felt her breath stutter, once. My hand came up before I could stop it, the back of my knuckles grazing her jaw, but she pushed herself away as quickly as she'd come in, like she'd touched fire.

She walked off into the dark.

I stood there with the cigarette burning low between my fingers, watching the last of the bonfires die. The smoke tasted wrong. Or maybe everything else did.

I went back to my cot eventually.

Didn't sleep worth a damn.

CHAPTER 11

March 18, 2002
Qala-ye Khun, Northern Afghanistan, 0030

A sharp, icy wind swept down from the massive peaks that loomed in the distance. We lay flat against the ridgeline above Qala-ye Khun, where the hulking compound loomed large over the expansive valley beneath it. The occasional flicker of a cigarette or lantern revealed enemy movement. As the wind shifted, I caught the sweet scent of the fresh poppy blooms that filled the valley. I tucked my frozen hands under my armpits to warm them; it was still bitterly cold in the Hindu Kush.

Forty-eight hours earlier, we inserted 30 kilometers away. Carefully making our way through the hills, we scrambled over rocks and avoided contact with locals. We had grown out our beards since the briefing three weeks earlier, and native clothing concealed body armor, weapons, and radios beneath. Finally arriving at our perch late the previous afternoon, a miserable night was spent trying to get a few precious hours of sleep. I glanced at the rest of my team. Riley was carefully studying the ramparts of the fortress through a spotting scope, and Baz was working to stretch out a cramp in his thigh, his face scrunched up in pain.

I raised my own scope and traced our path down to the tunnel entrance for the thousandth time. Down the hill, across the river, then a few hundred meters to the tunnel's hidden mouth. Kate's intel said twenty guards inside. I'd already counted eight—so much for her Pushtun contact. I wondered how many battles had been fought here over the millennia; it was called The Fortress of Blood for a reason. How much would be spilled here this morning?

I glanced at the team. Riley checked his magazines. Baz had gone pale and muttered nervously into his hands, maybe a prayer, maybe nerves. He'd been uncharacteristically quiet the whole hump to our checkpoint, which put me on edge. Riley studied him for a moment, then asked, "Sir, do you mind if I say a prayer before we go?" I nodded. "I wrote it after a friend 'got it' in Bosnia," he said. The three of us knelt in a huddle. Riley reached into his kit, pulled out a stack of laminated cards, handed one to each of us, and began:

God our Father, strengthen our hearts and minds so that the weakening instinct of self-preservation, which besets us all in battle, shall not blind me to my duty.

If it be my lot to die, let me do so with courage and honor, in a manner which will bring the greatest harm to my foes and all evil things which threaten our way of life.

With the guiding strength of your hand, lead us to victory.

When Riley finished, he slid his card into his plate carrier. "I always keep one tucked behind my Kevlar," he said. Baz stared at his prayer card thoughtfully, then slid it into his vest. The color had come back into his cheeks, and he gave me a slow, certain nod, as if he had made a decision. I checked my watch.

0100 hours. Showtime.

I checked our route one last time and gave the signal.

The descent off the ridge was slow and brutal. We took a switchback trail carved by goat herders over generations, each step a gamble against loose rock and wind shear. I led, and Riley had our six, his suppressed MP7 sweeping the darkness behind us. We moved silently, each footfall placed with surgical care.

Frost bit at our boots. Somewhere below, a dog barked, and we all froze. A single light blinked on in the valley, then off. We stayed motionless for nearly two minutes before I gestured us forward again.

The river came into view, dark and sluggish, a black ribbon under the moonlight. The current was gentle, but the water was icy. We stripped down and wrapped our weapons and clothing in plastic before wading in. Baz hissed a curse under his breath as the water climbed his thighs. I gritted my teeth. The cold was a physical shock, a clamp around my chest.

Midway across, we hit deeper water. Baz lost his footing, plunging beneath the roiling surface with a splash that shattered the suffocating silence. Riley grabbed his arm, preventing him from getting lost in the current, until I yanked him up with a grunt. We hesitated, our chests heaving, checked for signs of movement on the shore, then pushed forward. Finally, we reached the far bank, stumbled out of the water, and frantically rubbed down our extremities, forcing the blood to circulate.

We pulled on dry layers and checked our weapons. The slope ahead was steep but manageable, a winding path cut through a grove of scrubby trees and boulders. We moved, bounding up the incline, ears straining for voices or footfalls. The fortress loomed closer with every step, its jagged towers silhouetted against the moonlit sky.

At two hundred meters, we dropped to a crawl. There was a shepherd's wall here, broken and half-buried, and we used it for cover. I paused to scan the perimeter of the fortress. Two sentries paced along the southern parapet, located about 800 meters above us. We listened to their faint laughs and carefully moved as they each lit a cigarette.

We followed the path as it curved along a rocky outcropping until finally, there it was: a shallow depression behind a tangle of scrub brush. I knelt and brushed away leaves and gravel, revealing a stone slab. Baz and Riley crouched beside me as I worked the iron ring free and slowly lifted the hatch.

The air that emanated was ancient: stale earth and wet

limestone. I clicked on my red-filtered flashlight and aimed it down the narrow shaft. Stone steps curved away into blackness. Riley slid in first, his boots vanishing into the dark. Baz followed. I took one last look at the sky, then descended and pulled the hatch shut behind me.

The tunnel closed around us like a tomb. The walls were damp and cold, carved by hand centuries ago. No one spoke. The tunnel was about three feet tall by three feet wide. Roots hung from the ceiling like veins, and insects dropped on our heads. We scrambled over the packed mud, weapons raised, watching for sensors, tripwires, anything out of place. A rat darted across Baz's boot, and he startled, then muttered a silent curse.

The passage twisted and climbed. We passed two side channels, one choked with rubble, the other too narrow to crawl through. Ahead, a shaft of pale moonlight spilled from a break in the ceiling. We stopped for a moment to reorient. According to the sketch from Doc, we were less than 40 meters from the fortress's inner foundation.

The final stretch sloped upward. Sweat mingled with cold as we ascended. Then, a hiss from Baz. He pointed to a sliver of stonework, moss-covered and half-concealed—the exit.

I tapped twice, a signal to ready up. Cool air washed over me as I peered out into the old cistern—a sunken pit reinforced with rebar, sandbags, and rusting oil drums. It had once housed goats. Now it stank of feces, stagnant water, and old blood.

A sentry stood on the rim, silhouetted in the dim moonlight filtering through cracks in the ramshackle roof. He leaned on his rifle, half asleep.

Riley and I rose from the pit like wraiths. I clamped a hand over the sentry's mouth while Riley drove his blade under the chin and twisted. The man died with a sigh. We dragged him down and tucked the body into the shadows.

I scanned the area above. The ZU-23 was perched on a crude

platform, flanked by two sentries and bracketed by sandbags and corrugated tin. Its long barrels glinted faintly—if we didn't take it out, it would rip our helicopters apart.

The gun wasn't far, but the route wasn't simple. The tower was just a few hundred meters east of us, looming over the compound. To the south, between us and the gun was a web of alleys and blind corners. We slipped into the narrow lanes, and the scent of spices and unwashed bodies clung to the walls. Somewhere, a radio played a warbled pop song. A dog barked and yelped as it was silenced.

Two men ambled past—fighters, rifles slung lazily. Baz melted into a doorway. Riley flattened against a wall. I ducked beneath a sagging laundry line.

They passed. Baz stepped out behind one, quick and precise. Blade in. Twist. Riley slammed the other against the wall and crushed his windpipe with an elbow. Baz was doing well — I was impressed.

We dragged the bodies into the shadows.

Approaching the courtyard below the gun platform, I saw that it was open ground, lit faintly by moonlight, a perfect killing zone.

I scanned windows and rooftops. No movement. No voices. Just wind.

"We go fast," I said.

We sprinted low, quiet. Halfway across, a door creaked. A figure stepped out onto a second-story balcony.

We froze. Riley dropped to a crouch. Baz ducked behind a stack of barrels. I stood in the crook of a doorway.

The man pissed over the edge, sighed, and wandered back inside.

We moved.

The gun emplacement loomed ahead. Two guards stood chatting, weapons slung, unaware. I signaled—Riley left, Baz right, I'd go center.

Baz stepped on loose gravel—his man turned, eyes wide. I fired once—suppressed pop. The round took him in the sternum. He folded like a curtain.

Meanwhile, Riley was a blur. His garrote slipped around his guard's neck and pulled tight.

Baz swore. "Slippery footing."

"Rig it."

I pulled the charge—C4 block, pre-wired, remote detonator clipped and ready. We pressed it beneath the pivot of the ZU-23, wedged it under a steel support. Baz ran the det cord in a wide arc, tucking it behind the sandbags. Riley kept scanning, tense and silent. It took less than a minute. The adrenaline made my breath come quick and shallow.

Once the timer was set, I gave the word. "We're good. Move."

We vanished into the alleys again, quicker now. Less cautious. Blood up.

But as we passed through a small courtyard choked with sleeping goats and overturned crates, I felt something nagging at the edge of my mind, a whisper of wrongness. The silence was too deep. The shadows too still.

Too easy.

But there was no time to dwell.

The dungeons waited. So did the girl. And the next layer of hell.

CHAPTER 12

March 18, 2002
Qala-ye Khun, Northern Afghanistan, 0300

While we made our way to the dungeons, Red and Specs lay hidden on a ridge high above the fortress. Their helmet cams blinked to life. I'd watched the footage so many times that the images were now etched into my mind until they felt like my own memories.

Red adjusted his position, the cold stone biting through his layers of camo netting and fatigues, damp with early morning dew. The wind up here came in thin, piercing gusts that whipped down from the towering mountains. They were located on the opposite side of the valley from my team's infil position, and they'd been dug in for days.

Specs shifted beside him, peering through his spotting scope. "Bloody hell," he muttered. "This ridge is rougher than my ex-wife's temper. Reminds me of that hill outside Peć. Remember?"

Red didn't look away from his scope. "The one where you fell into a ditch full of sheep shit?"

"That was tactical repositioning."

"Right."

The two men lay prone beneath a sheet of camouflage netting, their hides perfectly blended into the rocky outcrop. Beside Red lay the L115A1—Accuracy International's finest. Chambered in .338 Lapua Magnum, it was a cold-bore killer, fitted with a Schmidt & Bender scope and suppressor. The rifle had reach, power, and reliability. Red played this instrument of war like a maestro, the L115A1 his Stratovarius.

Specs scanned the compound through the lens, fingers adjusting windage by muscle memory. "Three tangos on the upper battlements," he said. "Left to right. That last one's smoking again."

Red exhaled through his nose. "Figures. Always the same ones. Getting predictable."

"Not for long." Specs checked his watch. "0310. Should be getting the signal any moment."

The radio gave a soft crackle.

"Green light. Repeat, green light. Execute."

Specs gave a slow countdown. "Three... two... one... send it."

Red fired. The rifle barked three times in succession, just suppressed thumps in the stillness. Two of the sentries dropped without sound. The third stumbled back, arms flailing toward the parapet. Red adjusted and fired again.

The man folded forward, vanishing behind the wall.

"Close," Specs said. "He almost lit the whole place up."

"Almost doesn't count."

Moments later, a muffled explosion shattered the night. The ground beneath them trembled as fire and smoke belched from the far side of the fortress.

"C4's gone off. That'll be the gun platform."

Radio chatter crackled again, confirmation of detonation.

Specs nodded, shifting position. "Here we go then. Showtime."

They settled into overwatch.

Figures burst from doorways below, shadows scrambling in confusion. The fortress was coming awake. Red began methodically engaging targets: lone runners, sentries trying to man the walls, a fighter attempting to unlimber an RPG.

Each shot was quiet, precise, final.

Specs called corrections between rounds, spotting impacts, and adjusting for wind. The night was alive now: tracers, shouts, alarms.

“Twenty guards my ass,” Specs growled.

“Fucking spooks,” Red said bitterly.

In the distance, rotor blades thundered against the valley walls.

“Helos inbound,” Red said.

Specs grinned. “Time to clean house.”

They kept firing, two executioners on the ridge, carving silence into chaos.

CHAPTER 13

March 18, 2002
Qala-ye Khun, Northern Afghanistan, 0310

The assault team's helmet cams flickered on as the helicopters roared through the valley in formation. Green lights bathed the interiors of both Chinooks—Fire Team 1 in the lead bird, Fire Team 2, and the CIA spooks riding tail. The darkness outside was absolute, save for the starlight glinting off the jagged ridgelines.

Major Hooper crouched by the open hatch, headset clamped tight, eyes locked on the shadowy sprawl of Qala-ye Khun. Beside him, Sgt. Major Donovan checked and rechecked his rifle, jaw set, and a grim, determined look on his face.

Wells, hunched beside the door gunner, looked green but focused. Across from him, the rest of Fire Team 1 sat silent, strapped in, weapons prepped, nods exchanged in lieu of speech.

Behind them, in the third bird, Voss stood as if wired to the fuselage. He bounced slightly on the balls of his feet, tension radiating from every muscle. Maddox lounged beside him, seemingly half-asleep, a black balaclava rolled halfway up his face.

"Still with us, cowboy?" Maddox asked, eyes half-lidded.
Voss didn't respond. He was staring out the hatch window, breathing hard, fists clenched.

The pilots' voices crackled in the command headsets. "One klick out. Weapons hot."

A second later, the night exploded with fire. The door gunners opened up in unison, belt fed 7.62mm ripping into the courtyard and upper levels of the fortress below. Fighters ran in every direction, some diving for cover, others simply crumpling where they stood.

The Chinooks banked hard, adjusting for descent.

"Go! Go! Go!"

Ropes dropped.

Fast-roping under fire was the kind of chaos that training never quite simulated. Dirt, rotor wash, muzzle flashes. Sgt. Major Donovan was the first down, landing hard, discarding his gloves and spinning into a crouch, rifle up and identifying targets. The MG team followed, dragging their kit to the northern wall.

Major Hooper hit the ground next, shouting commands into his radio. "Red Eagle One on deck—perimeter hold. Weapons north-facing. Check sectors."

From the second bird, Voss came down like gravity owed him money—hit the dirt, rolled, and fired three rounds at a scrambling fighter in the same motion.

"Contact left," someone shouted.

The Chinooks peeled off, away from the compound, out of the line of fire.

The firefight lit up the courtyard. Bullets smacked stone. Clay walls shattered. The stench of gunpowder and blood filled the air.

Donovan dragged the MG into place with one of his lads, set up behind an overturned cart. "Get me eyes," he barked. "Radio check-ins, now!"

"Alpha sector clear!"

"Bravo has movement!"

"Contact rear wall!"

Rounds pinged off metal. The defensive nest was barely in place before the next wave of resistance hit. Heavier than expected—AKs, RPGs, more coordinated than anyone liked.

Major Hooper ducked beside the MG team, face calm, weapon resting on his knee. "They knew we were coming."

Voss snarled, shoving another mag into his rifle. "Then we don't disappoint."

The Major barked over the comms: "All teams—adjust formation. Fire Team 2, advance on the tower. Fire Team 1, perimeter lock. No one in, no one out."

The sky above rumbled as the Chinooks flew away to safety.

CHAPTER 14

March 18, 2002
Qala-ye Khun, Northern Afghanistan, 0320

The rear of the tower loomed in the dark like something pulled from another era. We moved fast, the muffled chaos of the firefight echoing behind us. A weathered stone archway marked the entrance to the passages deep below the tower, where Victoria was being held. The narrow stone stairway was just wide enough to squeeze through single-file. Beyond it lay the Bactrian cell blocks—relics from a time when men were chained by candlelight. Kate's asset said Victoria was down here, and I prayed he wasn't lying.

"Stack."

We formed up tight. I took point, Riley second, Baz rear: night-vision goggles on, weapons up.

Riley squeezed my shoulder, giving me the signal that he and Baz were ready, and we moved carefully into the dark bowels of the Qala-ye-Khun. Each step on the stairs was worn smooth from millennia of use. Hewn from granite, the stairs spiraled tightly downward, the curve designed to slow down attackers and give defenders an edge. As we descended, the air thickened, cold and dank, heavy with the scent of earth and rot.

Boots softly scuffing the slick granite, we moved as one, each man's off-hand gripping the shoulder ahead to stay locked in a stack. *Slow is smooth, smooth is fast.* I reminded myself. A drip echoed, steady as a heartbeat, somewhere below. Riley's breath was even, a ghost at my back; Baz's caught once, then leveled. He was learning, but one slip could kill us. Through the green glow of the NVGs, I could make out faint carvings on the walls, faded by time.

The stairwell tightened, forcing a crouch. Roots pierced the ceiling, snagging my clothes like skeletal fingers. A pebble skittered under Baz's boot, clattering down the spiral. We froze, hearts pounding, listening for a response. Nothing but the drip. Too quiet.

I eased forward. A faint scuff echoed below—boots, or imagination? I raised a fist. Hold. Riley's hand gripped my shoulder, firm. Something's waiting. My finger grazed the trigger, every nerve taut. If her asset sold us, we're boxed in this trap.

The stairwell's curve deepened, shadows swallowing us. A light flickered below—torchlight, or a guard's cigarette? It vanished, leaving only the hum of silence. Victoria's close, if Kate's intel holds. My gut churned, the uneasiness I felt in the courtyard clawing louder. Twenty men turned out to be at least fifty so far. What was waiting for us ahead? I signaled, and we inched downward.

Finally, around a last bend, a soft glow of light. I signaled to turn off our NVGs, and we crept forward. The stairwell ended at a stone passage, cells flanked by heavy wooden doors, lit by an oil lamp between two guards. Rifles slung lazily, laughing, deaf to the chaos above. Kate's contact said she was being held one level below this passage.

I dropped to a knee and raised my suppressed MP7. Riley mirrored. Two pops, near simultaneous. Both dropped in place, one twitching as he bled out.

We moved rapidly down the corridor. The walls sweated with condensation. Stale air and human filth filled my mouth and nostrils. We reached the guards and secured their weapons. Riley nudged one with his boot. "He won't bother us." Taking a moment to check our gear, we swapped out magazines and adjusted our body armor under our native robes. Baz was breathing rapidly, and tension radiated from him. I grabbed his arm roughly.

"You okay?"

"Adrenaline, Cap. I'm fuckin' wired."

"Stay focused. Breathe. You're doing fine."

Baz nodded, but his breath still came fast and shallow. I squeezed his arm again.

"Focus, Baz. You're still in the fight. Breathe with me—*now*."

He closed his eyes and took two deep breaths.

"I'm good Cap'n, honest."

We pushed forward. There was another stairwell descending to Victoria's cell. Once again, we moved, spiraling deeper and deeper into the depths of the dungeon, to the next level. This time, the stairwell ended in the center of a passage.

Voices, low.

Riley gave me the squeeze, and I rolled right. Riley left.

Two guards huddled around another lamp on my side. I dumped two rounds center mass into one, but his partner was quick. He fired blindly and moved for cover. The first muzzle flash blinded me; the second cracked like a hammer against my eardrum. The corridor turned into a coffin of ricochets. A round sparked off the stone beside me. Another hit Baz square in the chest, dropping him like a sack of bricks.

Riley and I returned fire—three controlled bursts. The man hit the ground hard, weapon clattering.

"Clear, I've got security, check Baz," I said, weapon sweeping the corridor.

Baz sat up, groaning, "Armor took it, I think."

Riley propped him up against the wall and thoroughly checked him. "He's okay, Captain, just rang his bell a bit. You good, Baz?"

Baz grimaced and struggled to his feet. "Good, Sarge."

"We're on a timeline, let's find the girl and go home," I said.

We cleared chamber after chamber: storage alcoves, rusted cages, old torture pits, boxes of ammunition. At one end of the passage was a thick iron door, rusted and ancient. We stacked, Baz on breach. I gave him the nod, and he unlatched the door. It groaned as Baz shoved it open. We hit the room, sweeping left and right.

Huddled in the corner, barefoot, hair matted with sweat and dirt, there she was. Victoria Ashworth. She looked up, wide-eyed, lips cracked and trembling.

For a second, she didn't move.

Then she lunged forward and collapsed into my arms.

"It's okay," I said. "We're here."

Victoria looked up at me, eyes wide with terror. "He said you'd come, that he has a surprise for you."

"Karim's gone to a clan gathering," I said. "Fortress is lightly guarded."

She shook her head, frantic. "No. He's still here. I heard his voice outside my cell. Yesterday."

I played the stoic. "Don't worry, we can handle anything he throws at us."

However, internally, my mind raced with possibilities. We had to move; we had to get the hell out of here—and fast. I glanced at Riley; his jaw was set, and his eyes blazed with fury. He started muttering curses in Irish about American spies.

Victoria was half-starved. I could feel her ribs through the rags. No shoes. No coat. I passed her a satchel with a keffiyeh, loose robes, and sandals.

"Put these on," I said gently. "We need you to look like one of us."

She nodded numbly.

We gave her space. Riley turned away, scanning down the corridor.

She dressed quickly, hands trembling the whole time.

Riley stepped in and knelt before her. "You good to move?"

She nodded again.

Without another word, he swept her into a fireman's carry, and we started back the way we came. Up the stairwell, through the passage, up again, until we emerged into the shadow of the tower.

Gunfire echoed from the courtyard. Small explosions lit the tower above.

I keyed the radio. "Blackbird One to Anvil—hostage secure. Exfil in progress. Hostage reports Moriarty has not flown the coop. I repeat, Moriarty is *here*."

There wasn't a response for a moment. Finally, Sergeant Major Donovan's voice crackled back, clipped and tense. "Copy that. We're taking heavy fire in the courtyard. Red Eagle is pinned. Watch yourselves."

We double-timed it through the alleys, sticking to the shadows. We moved fast, but the worst surprises almost always come last, I thought.

CHAPTER 15

March 18, 2002
Qala-ye Khun, Northern Afghanistan, 0328

The main gates to the keep stood three meters tall, reinforced cedar strapped with black iron, pitted with age. Fire Team 2 and the CIA team stacked in two columns against the outer wall—Major Hooper's squad—Sgt. Graves, Corporals Walker, Bruce—crouched left, their carbines at the ready. Sgt. Rai's squad—Corporals Carter, Tytler, and Ridgeway—knelt right, carbines steady. The CIA crew—Voss, Hawthorne, Kate, and Maddox—formed up behind Rai's squad, their NVGs glowing green, their faces impassive. Occasional gunfire from Fire Team 1 in the courtyard echoed faintly.

"No sentries," muttered Carter. Sergeant Rai nodded grimly, but said nothing, his eyes fixed upon the heavy gates. Rai was a Gurkha, recruited by the British Army from the jungles of Northern India over two decades earlier. He was the backbone of the regiment; the men believed that any mission Rai was on was destined to succeed.

Hooper signaled, his gloved hand slicing the air. Bruce hurried forward and slapped a C4 strip across the gate's hinges, wires trailing. Hooper signaled again. The team turned, ears plugged, bodies braced. A sharp thump tore the night, iron buckling, dust billowing like a shroud up the ramp that led into the heart of the fortress. Splinters rained down. The team surged forward, over the debris, flooding into the smoke-filled portcullis, sweeping left and right, checking every angle, every nook and cranny that could hide a guard.

Meeting no resistance, they continued up the stone ramp into the central courtyard, a 50-meter expanse ringed by square towers—northeast, northwest, southeast, southwest. Absurdly incongruous to the poverty-stricken exterior of Qala-ye Khun, the courtyard was like something out of the Arabian Nights. Silken drapes rustled in the night breeze, casting eerie shapes among the manicured hedges and bubbling fountains of an opulent pleasure garden, Karim's private oasis. Still no fighters. No movement. Just the creak of a loose shutter. Too empty, Hooper thought, his IR laser cutting left. Rai, Tytler, Ridgeway, and Bruce fanned out and established a perimeter.

Hooper turned back toward the bulk of the keep and gestured to Hawthorne. "We move now. On me."

Together, they breached a heavy door in the southeast tower that was their entry point to the heart of the old castle. Low ceilings forced a slight crouch, the air heavy with dust, lamp oil, and a faint hint of rot. Hooper's squad cleared chambers with surgical precision, stacking at each door. Graves kicked the first, hinges groaning. Walker swept left, Bruce right, lasers crisscrossing. A woman shrieked, clutching two children, their eyes wide in the green glow. Bruce zip-tied her wrists while the rest of the team secured the room: bedrolls, a rusted AK propped in a corner, no threats. It appeared that the first floor of the building was the domain of the guards and their families; no opulent furnishings here.

The next chamber contained two fighters, just inexperienced boys, not even old enough to grow beards. Hooper fired twice, suppressed pops, center mass. Blood sprayed straw, bodies slumping. Their wrists were secured, pulses checked. Hooper glanced at Hawthorne, "I suppose you were right about the resistance being light."

Hawthorne smiled faintly, a rare sight. "The CIA aims to please, Major."

Maddox gestured at the two dead youths, "This op's turning

into a youth outreach program. 'Scared Straight: NATO Edition.'"

Voss grinned and spat a long stream of tobacco onto one of the bodies.

Pushing ahead, they reached the first-floor intersection at the northeast tower. “Command Post is ahead,” Hooper said. Pointing to a stone stairwell, “Hawthorne, I believe that’s your entrance to Karim’s chambers.”

The CIA team peeled off into a stairwell without hesitation. Maddox led, climbing two steps at a time. Voss followed, swapped his chaw of tobacco for a fresh wad, then adjusted his rifle sling. Hawthorne trailed Voss, his face betraying nothing as usual. Kate paused a second, just a flicker, and then vanished up after them. They seemed oddly nonplussed, Hooper thought.

Hooper’s team pressed forward.

The Command Post had been stripped in a hurry. Maps were still pinned to the walls, but key hard drives were gone. Cabinets stood open. Hooper started barking orders.

“Grab what’s left. Bruce, go digital. Pull anything you can from that workstation. Graves, bag maps, paper logs, anything with numbers or ciphers.”

Walker moved to the window. “Still clear,” he reported. “Courtyard’s quiet.”

Hooper didn’t like it.

CHAPTER 16

March 18, 2002
Qala-ye Khun, Northern Afghanistan, 0336

Upstairs, the CIA team climbed toward the private chambers. The layout matched the intel—tight spirals, thick stone steps, narrow murder holes in the wall to allow archers to shoot down. A fortress designed for last stands.

Finally, Maddox reached the top. "Bingo."

Karim's quarters were palatial compared to the rest of the keep—ornate rugs, polished stone, hand-carved furniture. A silver tea set still steamed. A tray of figs sat untouched.

They bypassed it all.

Voss moved to the rear wall, running his fingers along the limestone. "Found it."

He pressed inward. A section clicked. The panel swung open, revealing a passage behind. The room beyond was packed with safes, documents, and a single running laptop.

Maddox grinned. "Merry fuckin' Christmas." He began sweeping documents from a desk into a duffel bag.

Their helmet cam feeds went black.

Cameras back on.

"Focus," Kate snapped at someone. "Just pull what we need."

Black.

Maddox's camera flickered on. Voss was nowhere to be seen, Kate and Hawthorne were huddled in a corner, whispering.

Black for several moments.

Finally, all the feeds came back on.

“Time to go, stack on the door,” Hawthorne said.

Without warning, static filled the entire compound, emanating from old Soviet military PA speakers wired throughout the building. Then, Karim’s voice echoed through every hallway of the fortress.

"Ah, the lion returns to the den with fire in his mane. I trust you brought my retirement package? I am delighted you’ve come to visit. Qala-ye Khun is famous for its hospitality. I hope you enjoy your stay."

His voice was calm. Precise. Confident.

“Kate,” he continued, “I still have your little drawing from Islamabad. The one you left under my teacup. Very sentimental.”

Then to Hawthorne: “And Dick, I regret our last meeting ended with such acrimony. But the CIA has always been an unforgiving family.”

The line went dead.

CHAPTER 17

March 18, 2002
Qala-ye Khun, Northern Afghanistan, 0345 Hours

The courtyard was still. Too still. Dust swirled around the manicured hedges and cracked fountains of the inner square. Sgt. Rai stood at the center of the garden, eyes scanning the ramparts above. He adjusted the sling on his L119A1 carbine, motioning silently to Carter and Ridgeway to take positions at the north and east archways. Tytler remained near the main gate, crouched behind a low stone trough with a PKM mounted on a bipod.

Ridgeway keyed the radio. "Nothing yet."

"Eyes up. Check your corners," Rai ordered.

He moved quietly across the flagstones, stopping beside Carter. The young corporal was sweating despite the cold.

"Sarge," Carter whispered, "you feel it too, right?"

Rai nodded once. "Always watch the quiet."

Above them, a lone wind chime clinked from a balcony, delicate notes jangling against the hard silence. Rai glanced at the northwest tower. Still dark. No muzzle flashes. No movement. He checked his watch. Ten minutes since the breach. Seven since the CIA team split off. Still no enemy contact beyond the two scared kids Hooper cut down.

"Tytler," Rai said, "any movement?"

"Negative. Nothing on thermals. Still scanning."

Rai's fingers tapped once on his kukri's sheath, then stilled. He looked across the courtyard to Ridgeway, who gave him a silent thumbs-up.

Carter leaned closer. "Maybe they cleared out. Ran."

Rai said nothing. The wind picked up. Something shifted behind one of the balconies—just a shadow.

Then came the voice. Karim, over the old PA system. Calm. Taunting. Personal.

Carter: "What the fuck have we stumbled into, Sarge?"

The first shot came a heartbeat later.

A single crack. Then a second. From the upper level of the west tower.

"Contact! West balcony!"

Tytler opened up with the PKM, chewing stone, and plaster. Ridgeway fired a burst. Carter dropped prone and returned fire. Rai sprinted left, firing controlled bursts at the flashes.

From the east archway, four fighters spilled in. Kalashnikovs up. Ridgeway went down, clutching his leg.

Rai slid in behind a planter and took one in the chest with a thud against his plate. He came up firing, dropped two. Carter took down a third with a three-round burst.

Rai turned, eyes tracking movement high above. Another silhouette with an RPG. Too late. The rocket slammed into the far corner of the courtyard, blasting rubble and heat. Tytler screamed but held his ground, spraying upward.

Then they came.

From all sides, fighters poured into the courtyard. Dozens. Too many.

"Hold the line," Rai roared.

His rifle clicked dry. They were too close to risk taking time to reload, so he let the gun dangle from the sling, drew his kukri, and surged forward.

A fighter lunged with a bayonet. Rai sidestepped, hooked the man's wrist, and plunged the kukri under the ribcage. Another swung a rifle like a club. Rai ducked, slashed across the thigh, then spun and buried the blade in the man's collarbone.

Carter went down hard beside the fountain, clutching a gut wound, just below his armor. Rai kicked over the man who had shot him and slit his throat without slowing.

Tytler dragged Ridgeway behind cover. Blood pooled. He fired until the PKM jammed, then pulled his sidearm.

Rai fluidly moved through the chaos. He disarmed one man with a twist and elbowed him unconscious. Another tried to grapple; Rai stabbed him twice in the neck, then threw his body into the next attacker.

Gunfire tore through the haze. AKs blazing. Someone threw a Molotov. Flames arced across the courtyard. A hedge caught fire.

Tytler screamed. His arm jerked violently with every recoil, blood streaming from his side. He didn't stop. Not until the slide locked back and his pistol clicked dry. He looked toward Rai, gave a half-smile, and slumped.

Rai didn't stop. He ducked low, found Carter still breathing. He dragged him behind the trough. Then he turned, blade red and gleaming, as the last wave advanced.

He didn't yell. He didn't curse. He exhaled.

The first man he met died instantly, throat opened. The next, Rai headbutted and stabbed in the belly. Blood soaked the stones.

Only three remained. Two backed away. The third clumsily tried to change magazines, hands trembling. When he couldn't complete the reload, he charged, screaming—half terror, half bravado. Rai parried a wild slash and countered with a brutal overhead strike that split the man's face.

The others fled.

Silence. A choking veil enveloped the courtyard, accompanying the stench of gunpowder and burning silk.

Rai stood alone, breathing hard. A shiver ran through his shoulders before he forced himself still. He scanned the carnage. Carter was alive, just barely. Tytler slumped unconscious over Ridgeway's body. Rai reloaded his rifle, then propped Carter up against a pillar, shoving a rifle into his hands. "Shoot anything that moves." He keyed his mic. "Red Eagle 2 to Red Eagle 1. Courtyard held. Casualties heavy. Immediate support required."

No response. Just static.

He leaned against the stone, blood drying on his face. He could still hear Karim's voice echoing somewhere deep inside the walls.

The fortress was bleeding. So was he.

But he was still on his feet.

And the gate was still his.

CHAPTER 18

March 18, 2002
Qala-ye Khun, Northeast Tower, 0348

The PA system died with a soft pop, the last vestiges of Karim's voice lingering in the chamber. For a beat, there was nothing—just the hush of old fabric swaying, the scent of rosewater and dust.

Kate looked up, voice low. "He's here."

"Good," Maddox said, doing a press check on his carbine. "Saves us the trouble."

Voss peered out of a window. "Let's finish it."

The helmet cams stuttered—brief static, a ripple of digital snow, then cleared.

A ceiling hatch snapped open above them. The door to the chamber burst open. Bodies flooded through both, bristling with weapons.

Maddox reacted first, shoving Kate into the shadowed corner behind a thick tapestry. Bullets ripped through the drapes, showering them with plaster and fabric.

"Multiple," Voss shouted, laying down fire—three-round bursts, controlled and surgical. Two fighters dropped instantly, crumpling to the ground. A third staggered back, gurgling, before collapsing. But more poured in behind them, filling the hallway like a rising tide. His rifle clicked dry. They were just outside Karim's inner chamber now, the gilded rugs and perfumed air giving way to cracked stone and war-era concrete. Without hesitation, Voss drew his sidearm and dropped a fighter charging through a side hallway—then another appeared behind him. Voss pivoted, holstered his empty pistol, and pulled his knife, a brutal recurve blade honed for wet work. He carved through the fighter with two brutal slashes, blood spattering the gold-inlaid tiles. More gunmen surged into the corridor, their boots pounding over shattered mosaics, only to meet Voss head-on in a vortex of gunfire and steel.

He moved like a butcher at closing time.

Hawthorne rotated right and fired down a side corridor—two targets. One fell immediately, the other stumbled into the wall, clutching his gut. Hawthorne put a round through his head before he dropped.

A fighter lunged at Maddox, another close behind him, fear clouding his eyes. Maddox shot the first through the sternum. The second fighter surged forward and grabbed the barrel of Maddox's rifle, forcing it upward. The two collided. Maddox pivoted, slammed the man into a marble pillar, and snapped his neck with a savage twist.

Voss chuckled as he wiped blood off his knife on a velvet curtain. "We could've charged admission for this."

"Kate, on me," Maddox barked.

They broke into the northern wing, sweeping room to room. Maddox pulled a flashbang from his rig and lobbed it around a tight corner. It went off with a thunderclap just as he rushed forward, smashing into the stunned occupants.

He opened up. The recoil thumped into his shoulder as he gunned down two fighters scrambling for cover.

Kate moved in behind him, covering angles. She dropped a man who stumbled out of an antechamber, two to the chest, one to the head, without breaking stride. Her face was expressionless.

In the southern hallway, Voss and Hawthorne cleared methodically. Voss fired in brutal rhythm, muzzle flashes strobing off the stone. He transitioned seamlessly between rifle and blade, dispatching wounded fighters with precise, silent efficiency.

One charged from a side room. Voss sidestepped, hooked him low, then buried the blade beneath his ribs.

Hawthorne checked his corners, slammed home a fresh mag, and moved with efficient speed. They never spoke—they didn't need to.

Back in the northern corridor, Maddox took a round that grazed his upper arm, tearing fabric and flesh. He grunted, more annoyed than injured, and wiped the blood on his sleeve.

They regrouped at a spiral staircase leading down.

Kate eyed the steps. "They've got it locked from below."

"We blow it?" Maddox asked.

Voss was already kneeling, pressing a breaching charge against the wall, facing the stairs. "Not here. Too tight. We'd kill ourselves."

Hawthorne's eyes flicked up the passage. "We're not supposed to get out."

Kate didn't argue. She checked the battery on her satphone.

Footsteps echoed. They piled into the stairwell and closed the heavy door. Voices in the hallway outside. Fighters stacking up at the door.

Maddox began humming "Sympathy for the Devil."

Voss looked up from the breaching charge trigger, "Final act."

The feeds from their helmets steadied.

They were calm.

Maddox slapped in a fresh magazine.

Voss spat onto the stone floor and adjusted his grip, weapon ready.

Kate affixed a second charge to the stairwell doorframe. They backed down the stairwell, weapons up.

"Three seconds on my mark."

Maddox's helmet showed Hawthorne, mouth twisting into a half-smile.

The feed went dead.

CHAPTER 19

March 18, 2002
Qala-ye Khun, Northeast Tower, Command Post, 0348

Half-empty file cabinets, overturned chairs, a clock on the wall was frozen at 0417. Two large duffels by the door were bursting with paper and electronics. Major Hooper stood at the window, grimly processing Karim's broadcast.

"Get what you can and stack up," Hooper barked. "We're moving in two."

Graves crammed a folder into one of the duffels. Bruce yanked a hard drive from a rusted terminal. Walker checked the hallway. No contact. Not yet.

Hooper thumbed the comms: static

"Red Eagle 1 to Anvil. Do you read?" he said again, quieter this time. Nothing. The communications were a disaster, much like this entire mission.

The team stacked up and filed into the hallway, rifles at the ready; tension coiled around them. The exit was only fifty meters away, but it might as well have been miles.

"Movement, north corridor," Walker called, already raising his rifle.

The first wave came fast—a half-dozen fighters, ragged men with AKs, screaming as they pushed in from the western hallway.

"Contact right," Hooper shouted.

Graves dropped to a knee, laying down suppressive fire toward the corridor. Bruce and Walker shifted left, controlling the flank.

Muzzle flashes lit the narrow stone hall. Ricochets sparked off the walls. A flashbang went off, deafening and bright. One insurgent barreled through the smoke, firing wildly. Bruce dropped him at five feet with a burst to the chest.

"Graves! Ammo!" Walker yelled.

"Down to two mags!"

"Red Eagle 2, report," Hooper shouted into the comm.

Only static.

"Fall back, Barricade!" Hooper ordered.

They moved, dragging furniture, desks, metal cabinets, anything they could find. The CP room became a bunker. Chokepoints were set. Doors jammed with shelving. The air thickened with sweat, gunpowder, and fear. Bullets came punching through the door, rapid fire.

Walker cried out. He was hit in the thigh. Bruce pulled him behind cover, slapping on a tourniquet. Walker gritted his teeth, biting down on his glove, and snarled as the pain hit.

Hooper checked his radio again. Still nothing.

"Graves, anything?"

"No word. It's been fifteen minutes. CIA's either gone, or they're not talking."

Hooper swapped out a magazine, his expression impassive. "We hold until we're told otherwise."

Outside the barricade, voices echoed. Different now. More disciplined. Commands, not shouting.

Hooper passed mags to Graves and Bruce. No speech. Just a look. They understood.

The breach came hard.

A grenade hit the door and blew it in. Then a smoke grenade was tossed in, hissing as it flooded the CP.

"NVGs," Hooper snapped. They flipped them down just in time to see shapes rushing through the smoke.

The squad poured gunfire through the door, but the fighters continued to advance, now crawling over the heap of bodies obstructing the entrance.

Bruce clubbed a man in the jaw with the butt of his rifle, then dropped him with a knee. Another fighter jumped the barricade. Hooper caught a blade in the shoulder, screamed, and shoved his pistol into the man's ribs and fired five rounds.

Graves went down, hit in the neck. He kept shooting until he bled out.

Hooper's rifle jammed. He grabbed Walker's sidearm, firing point-blank into a masked fighter charging him.

A grenade rolled across the floor.

"No!"

Bruce dove on it.

The blast slammed through the chamber. Ears ringing, Hooper looked over. Bruce wasn't moving.

Only he and Walker remained. The CP was wrecked. Blood pooled beneath overturned desks.

Hooper dragged Walker into a back room—a narrow chamber lined with Soviet-era radio gear. Dust choked the air. A single doorway.

Hooper sat with his back to the door, pulled a frag grenade, and rested it on his thigh.

Walker groaned, gripping his bleeding leg. "What now?"

Hooper keyed his radio. Static. Then, a faint response:

"Red Eagle, this is Anvil. Exfil window closing. Blackbird secured the hostage. We have heavy contact here. Move if you can."

Hooper said nothing.

Footsteps. Voices. They were coming again.

He stood, slammed home his final mag.

Walker raised his rifle, his offhand holding a second grenade. He grinned through the blood. "Hell of a thing. I guess it's last call, Major." He pulled the pin on the grenade with his teeth.

Hooper keyed the radio one last time. "This is Red Eagle to all units, CP is compromised. Get yourselves out. Hooper over and out."

Walker's helmet feed showed him calmly leveling his weapon. Shadows filled the door.

The cameras went black.

CHAPTER 20

March 18, 2002
Qala-ye Khun, Outer Compound, 0355 hours

Gunfire echoed behind us as we double-timed it through the alleys, sticking to the shadows. The crackle of small arms fire and the dull thump of explosions rolled over the rooftops. Smoke bled from the upper floors of the keep, lit sporadically by muzzle flashes and flares.

I kept one hand tight on Victoria's elbow, steadying her as we wove through the narrow passageways that spiderwebbed between the tower and the outer courtyard. Her breath came shallow and ragged, but she stayed upright. Baz took rear, a scavenged AK up and ready, eyes scanning. Riley moved ahead, his frame low and tense.

Somewhere behind us, a burst of automatic fire erupted. Not aimed at us, not yet. The shouting grew louder.

I slowed at the alley's mouth, raising a hand. Ahead, dozens of armed men flooded from the scattered buildings. Some carried rifles, others just knives and old Soviet pistols. Most were disorganized, moving toward the tower like angry ants. They must have been hiding for several days in preparation for the ambush.

I turned to the others. "Stay close. Let me talk."

Riley adjusted his headscarf, lowering his rifle beneath the folds of his robe. Baz pulled Victoria's scarf tighter over her face. She didn't resist.

I rounded the corner with shoulders slouched and eyes downcast, adopting the gait of a local.

A man in a tan vest stepped into our path, AK slung across his chest. “Who are you?” he barked in Pashto.

I didn’t blink. “My cousin is hurt. She needs a doctor.”

The fighter looked past me to Victoria, who kept her head lowered. “Where are you coming from?”

“The lower kitchens,” I replied. “The foreigners are attacking. We don’t want trouble.”

A burst of gunfire echoed. The fighter hesitated, then waved us through. “Move. Get off the street.”

I nodded and moved quickly. Riley fell in behind me, hand still under his robe.

More fighters streamed past. I nodded to each, exchanging brief words in the local dialect—phrases I’d learned in the south, ones that would peg me as mountain stock.

A figure detached from the shadows behind us, following. I caught it in a reflection—too deliberate, too steady.

We turned a corner, ducking between two collapsed buildings. The follower came closer.

I turned, hands up. “Stay back,” I said in Pashto. “We want no fight.”

The man lifted his rifle.

Baz stepped in, no hesitation. One hand deflected the muzzle, the other buried a blade deep under the man’s ribs. The fighter jerked once, then went limp.

Riley caught the body, dragging it into a ditch. No sound but the breathing of the team.

I adjusted Victoria’s scarf again. Her eyes met mine, glassy and tired.

“Not far now,” I said.

We crossed behind a smoking generator shed, then ducked beneath a broken archway that led into the outer courtyard. The sounds of gunfire were more distant now, focused on the tower. Fighters raced in the opposite direction.

Near the gate, a line of soldiers held a perimeter. I recognized the shape of British kit—Donovan's team.

I raised a hand. "Friendly! Bringing the package!"

Weapons raised, then lowered.

Donovan stepped forward. "Avery?"

I nodded. "We got her."

Victoria stumbled forward. Riley caught her.

Baz covered our rear, rifle up.

Donovan keyed his mic. "Package secure. Repeat, Valkyrie secure."

Donovan wore a grim expression on his face. "Fire Team 2 is in trouble inside the tower. They're not answering," Donovan said. He paused, then added, "We got a transmission from Hooper ten minutes ago, 'CP is compromised.' That's the last we heard. Doesn't look good."

I gritted my teeth. Kate. I wanted to ask, but there wasn't time.

More gunfire now—closer. Fighters were beginning to descend on the courtyard, slipping from the alleys and side passages, weapons up.

Donovan raised his rifle and fired. The rest of his team followed suit.

"We've got incoming!" he shouted. "Raptor One, this is Anvil, we're engaged at the LZ. Not clear. I say again, not clear!" Donovan shouted into his radio.

The response came in through heavy static. A pilot's voice, calm but strained: "Negative, Anvil. We're inbound. Two mikes out. We'll clear the area with the miniguns."

And then we heard it—the thump of rotors building in the distance. The Chinooks were coming.

I raised my rifle; the fight wasn't over yet.

I glanced at the keep.

Just in time to see the top floors erupt in flame. The explosion bloomed upward, a pillar of destruction, raining stone and fire into the sky.

CHAPTER 21

March 18, 2002,
Ridge Above Qala-ye Khun, 0405

Red squeezed the trigger again, the suppressed crack barely audible over the wind. One of the fighters charging toward the outer courtyard crumpled mid-stride.

"One left," Red said, not taking his eye from the scope.

Beside him, Specs was counting ammo. "Five in the mag, three loose. We've still got rounds."

Below, the compound burned like a pyre. Smoke twisted from shattered windows in the tower; gunfire cracked in staccato bursts. In the courtyard, shapes darted and collided—fighters, friendlies, civilians. It was chaos in motion.

Specs swept his scope over the western hills, then froze. "Jesus."

Red looked up.

"Hundreds," Specs said. "No—thousands. Coming down the slopes. Whole hills are crawling."

Red shifted his scope. The ridgelines boiled with movement—robes, weapons, banners. A flood of fighters.

"We're about to be very alone," Red said grimly.

Rotor wash thumped in the distance. Three RAF Chinooks surged in from the east, flying low, nav lights off, their black silhouettes rising against the burning compound.

"Raptors inbound," Specs radioed. "LZ hot. Repeat: LZ hot as hell. There's Tangos everywhere."

"This is Raptor, we're on it."

The Chinooks reached the fortress and hovered just above the southern gates. Then came the miniguns—streams of tracers slicing the night. Entire rows of fighters dropped in seconds. The rear birds joined in, rotary cannons sweeping the hillsides and alleys.

"Jesus," Red whispered.

Then came a flash—not from the compound. From the opposing ridgeline.

"Missile!"

The first Chinook banked, too slow. The explosion tore the tail apart. It spun, caught fire, and crashed into the compound wall.

Specs swore. The second bird lifted, but another missile slammed into its belly. Fireball. Wreckage spiraled into the gully.

The third bird veered off, but it too was struck midair. Metal rained down.

"We just lost all three," Specs said, stunned.

Red grabbed the PRC-117. "Anvil, this is Overwatch. LZ is gone. Massing hostiles, west ridgelines, battalion strength. We need steel on target."

Donovan's voice came back: "What assets do we have?"

"Spooky-1 is loitering."

"Then burn them. Now."

Red keyed up. "Spooky-1, Overwatch. Danger close. Whiskey-four-eight-zero-niner. Ridge line. Massed personnel. Bring the rain. Repeat: bring the rain."

"Copy, Overwatch. Guns hot. Thirty seconds."

Specs deployed the thermal beacon. It pulsed infrared into the sky.

Red loaded his last rounds. "Make them count," Specs said.

"Always."

Red fired. Headshot. Another. He paused.

Then came the thunder.

The AC-130 opened up. 105mm shells tore the ridgelines. Then 40mm Bofors. Then 25mm. The hillside erupted. Fighters flung skyward. The world turned to fire. The flood broke. Survivors ran.

"Spooky-1, good hits," Red radioed. "Adjust ten meters west. Repeat."

More explosions. The hills flattened under steel.

Then silence.

Specs checked his last mag. Red cleaned the scope.

They waited.

CHAPTER 22

March 18, 2002
Qala-ye Khun, Outer Courtyard, 0415

The world was ash and fire.

We crouched behind the fractured remnants of a marble wall, the only cover we had left. The Chinooks were gone, all three torn from the sky like paper toys. Their burning wreckage smoldered near the southern gates, rotor blades twisted like mangled wire. Victoria knelt beside me, her head low, face streaked with soot. Baz stood watch at the corner, rifle ready. The Sergeant Major was already scanning the compound's edges, a vein throbbed on his temple, a radio clutched in his fist.

He keyed up. "Anvil to Overlord Actual. Confirm any air assets inbound. Any air support?"

Nothing. Just static.

Donovan lowered the radio. "That was our ride," he said. His tone was calm, final.

The AC-130's barrage had quieted the hills, but only for a moment. In that stillness, we all realized what came next.

Donovan looked at me. "The tunnel. You can find it again?"

I nodded. "Under the cistern west of the keep."

"Then that's your exfil."

I opened my mouth to argue.

Donovan didn't give me the chance. "You've got the package. You and your team get her out. That's your job now." His voice was low, clipped.

Gunfire popped from the direction of the keep. A shout. Then a scream.

"*Go,*" Donovan ordered, his voice thick. He reloaded his rifle without looking at me.

Baz didn't wait. He moved first, tugging at my sleeve. Victoria followed, silent. I gave Donovan one last look. He was already shouting to his men, directing fire toward the west ramparts.

We slipped into the alleys.

The compound was hell. Smoke from the burning tower made it hard to breathe, thick and acrid in our lungs. The courtyard was strewn with bodies—some torn apart, others moaning in pain, crawling through the blood-slicked dust. A man with no legs screamed for help. Another clutched at his own entrails, eyes wide with shock. The aftermath of the minigun barrage was grotesque and total. Shadows flitted between buildings. Fighters, maybe civilians. It was hard to tell anymore. Every face could be an enemy.

We kept to the walls, cutting between alleys and ruined outbuildings. I led the way, pistol in hand. Baz stayed rear, rifle sweeping. Victoria moved fast, mechanically, her eyes distant.

A group of armed boys ran past, too young to know what they were doing. One glanced at me.

I barked something in Pashto, fast, confident: "There are infidels at the main gate! Go!"

They hesitated, then ran. I didn't look back.

We were halfway to the cistern when we hit a small courtyard. Two fighters turned from looting a body. One raised a weapon.

Baz moved without hesitation, knife out. He silenced the first with a slash across the throat. I dropped the second with a suppressed round to the chest.

Victoria didn't flinch. That worried me more than anything.

Then came the shot. A sharp crack behind us.

Riley dropped.

He fell mid-step, a bullet tearing through his neck. He hit the dirt hard, eyes wide.

"No!" Baz dropped next to him, grabbing at his vest.

I spun and, shrouded in the darkness of the entrance to a little cinderblock hut, was an old man with a rusted AK pointed at us. Without hesitation, I put three rounds in him and turned to check Riley.

I slid in beside him, hands already pressing into the wound, but it was no use. Blood fountained out, thick and arterial. Riley tried to speak, but only a gurgle came.

"Captain," Baz whispered, frozen. "He's..."

I grabbed Baz's vest and yanked him in close. "You move, or he dies for nothing. Do you understand me?"

Baz stayed frozen; his eyes were wide, fixated on Riley. I yanked him up. Hard. "Fucking *move* Baz! That's an order!"

He hesitated. Then nodded.

We moved again, leaving Riley behind.

The area around the cistern was half-buried in rubble from the tower, the very same access point we'd used for infiltration just hours earlier. I found the hatch where we'd left it—now covered in stone and soot.

Two fighters were nearby, scavenging gear from the dead.

I stepped forward, shouting in Pashto. "You two! Report to the main gate! Command needs you now!"

They turned, confused. One frowned. The other started to raise his weapon.

Baz slipped in from the side. His blade found its way between one's ribs. I fired at the second—one in the chest, then another in the head.

Victoria crouched beside the cistern. I opened the hatch. It groaned like an animal.

Baz dropped in first, then Victoria.

I lingered, just for a second.

From this spot, I could see the tower, where Kate and Fire Team Two had made their last stand. Smoke curled from shattered stone. Their graves now.

I dropped into the dark and closed the hatch behind me.

CHAPTER 23

March 2002
Qala-ye Khun, Northern Afghanistan, 0430 hours

We emerged from the tunnel into chaos.

Smoke hung low across the ravine, a choking fog of burnt flesh and diesel. Flames licked the sky from half-destroyed outbuildings. The stench of death was everywhere. The thunder of shouting men and the clatter of rifles surrounded us.

I pulled my scarf tighter across my face and glanced at Victoria. Her shoulders were hunched beneath her robes, her head low, keffiyeh wrapped tight to conceal her face and hair. In the low light and confusion, she passed as a scrawny teenage boy. Barely.

Baz stepped ahead, leading us into the current of fighters streaming toward the compound. Some were bloodied, some shouting in triumph. Many had no idea what had just happened—only that the Americans were retreating and that the sky had burned with the fire of the Prophet's vengeance.

We blended in, keeping pace, saying nothing.

A dead fighter lay sprawled in the dust, half his face missing. Another leaned against a burned-out truck, clutching his stomach and whimpering. The ground was slick with blood. I tried not to look too long at any one face, didn't want to invite conversation. Or suspicion. We got swept up into a crowd of laughing men who were gathered around a mule cart. We carefully made our way through the celebrating men, and as we got close to the center of the crowd, we saw what the fuss was all about.

Two naked bodies, filthy and limp, slung over the cart like sacks of meat. Red and Specs.

Someone had stripped them and painted slogans in black ink across their torsos. One of the bodies had a jagged blade sticking from its chest. The crowd roared around them, some throwing fists in the air, others laughing, dancing, spitting on the corpses.

Baz mouthed a curse and looked away. Victoria made a small sound, a gasp caught in her throat. I grabbed her wrist and squeezed gently. Not now.

We followed the slope upward, pushing toward the next ridgeline—the planned escape route that would lead us to the tertiary exfil trail, a footpath that curved around the mountain's western shoulder. But something was wrong.

The way was blocked.

Dozens of fighters clustered at the top of the ridge, some sitting, some standing with rifles, many scanning the horizon or arguing about the night's events. There was no way past without walking directly into their line of sight. We were too exposed. Too still.

Baz looked at me, then at Victoria. I could already see the decision forming on his face.

"You get her out," he said.

I shook my head, “What are you talking about, Baz? We blend in and wait until dark, then slip through."

"They'll spot her. You know they will. She's not going to pass close-up, not with eyes on her. We're out of time."

"Baz—"

He turned and gave me that stupid crooked grin. "Look after her, yeah, Capitano?"

Then he walked down the slope.

No hesitation.

Bold as brass, he moved straight toward the fighters on the ridgeline, pulling off his headscarf as he went, revealing his pale, sweat-soaked face.

And then—in the middle of that goddamn mountain, surrounded by death and fire and Kalashnikovs—he started singing.

"I've been a wild rover for many a year..."

His voice was hoarse, off-key, defiant.

The fighters froze, confused. A few raised their weapons. Others shouted in alarm.

Baz didn't stop. He lifted his arms like a conductor, his voice louder now, wobbling but clear: *"And I spent all me money on whisky and beer!"*

They tackled him.

He vanished beneath a pile of bodies. Boots slammed into his ribs. A rifle butt cracked across his face. A man pulled a machete.

But the ridgeline cleared, Baz had given us our window.

The crowd poured downhill toward the disturbance, howling for blood.

I grabbed Victoria's hand, and we ran up the open path, unnoticed in the chaos.

CHAPTER 24

March 2002
Afghan Highlands, 0500

The ridge was steep, littered with scree and the broken skeletons of scrub trees. We lay belly-down just over the crest, the darkness broken only by the fire-glow of the burning compound behind us.

Through a spotting scope, I watched Baz.

He was stripped to the waist, bruised, his arms lashed behind a crumbling stone pillar. Fighters surrounded him, jeering, throwing rocks, and spitting. Someone smashed the butt of a rifle into his gut. Baz doubled over and stayed down, coughing. His mouth moved. He was singing again, softly, but I couldn't hear the words.

Victoria sat beside me, silent under her dusty keffiyeh. Her eyes were locked on the scene below, one hand clenched on the rock, knuckles white.

"Spooky-1, this is Blackbird," I said into the radio, voice low, shaking. "I need a fire mission on the following grid."

I rattled off the coordinates—the crosshairs of my scope centered on Baz's crumpled figure.

Static. Then a clipped voice replied, "Spooky-1 copies. Confirm target is danger-close. Confirm fire for effect."

My finger hovered over the transmit button.

I stared at Baz. One of the fighters drew a blade. Baz didn't flinch. He stared right at the crowd, head high. Like he knew.

I pressed the button.

"Confirm. Fire for effect."

A brief pause.

"Roger that. Guns hot."

The AC-130 announced itself with a dull, distant thunder. Then the sky cracked open.

The hillside below us lit up in a sweeping blaze of destruction. Tracer lines stitched through the mob. The roar of the 40mm and then the 105mm—concussive, final. Stone and bodies evaporated in the flame. The scream of the crowd was swallowed by impact.

When the guns fell silent, nothing moved.

Only smoke, drifting up into the pre-dawn sky.

Victoria turned away, trembling. I watched the blackened earth, the spot where Baz had been, the blood still ringing in my ears.

Inside the compound, the tower was just a smoking skeleton. The courtyard was littered with bodies. The wreckage of the three helicopters still smoldered. I felt the grief well in my chest. And something else. Rage. Cold and absolute.

I thought of Kate, her sharp tongue, the night we'd shared beneath desert stars... her lies. Gone. All of them gone. Riley. Donovan. Even Hooper. My men reduced to silence and ash. We'd trained so hard, done everything right. And still, they were taken. By arrogance. By war. By betrayal.

The intel had been garbage. The enemy was waiting. This wasn't just a bad op. It was something else. Something deeper. I didn't have answers, but I knew one thing: someone had lied to us, and I was going to find out who.

I wanted to scream. I wanted to burn the world down.

Instead, I stayed still, the weight of it all pressing into my ribs.

I felt Victoria squeeze my hand.

"I'm sorry," she said softly. Silence for a moment, then, "We *have* to go,"

I nodded. I wiped the tears and soot from my face and stood. One last glance at the valley below, and then I turned my back on the fire and death.

Together, we disappeared into the mountains.

The wind carried the stench of war behind us.

Creighton's face was grim. He leaned back in his chair, hands folded tightly. For once, he didn't challenge the story or try to spar.

"Bad business, I knew Major Hooper; he was a decent man. Good family, his uncle was in my regiment." His eyes flicked to Churchill, but the older man offered nothing—just a sad, almost ceremonial nod.

Tom sat in silence, letting the weight of the memory hang in the room. The bunker's hum filled the void, steady and inhuman.

When Creighton spoke again, his voice had lost its edge. "And that, Mr. Harrington, is how it began. But I suspect you're not done with your story."

PART II

CHAPTER 25

May 2004
Stresa, Italy

The air in the room was heavy and stale, thick with burnt coffee and electronics working overtime. The window was cracked open, but the breeze didn't help. It was just more lake air, tinged with diesel exhaust from the water taxis.

We were four floors up, across the street from the Grand Hotel, crammed into a small hotel room that had once been charming. Now it was wires, screens, and two folding chairs. The bed had been dismantled to make space. The minibar was empty, the carpet stained.

The surveillance kit was standard: telescopic optics, wide-spectrum audio, encrypted recorder, and two backup drives. The whole thing fit in three suitcases. We kept them packed, in case we had to run. Clean passports were stashed in the bathroom vent. I checked it every morning.

It was just after 0600. The light outside was pale and metallic, the kind you only get in northern Italy before the sun climbs past the ridge. Lake Maggiore was flat as glass.

Marcus was halfway through a bag of crisps, crunching as if it were a protest. He'd been talking for an hour. About the waitress, about the bar, about how this whole op was a joke.

"I'm telling you," he said, gesturing with a greasy finger, "they've got Henry fucking Kissinger on a Segway down there. It's like watching Jurassic Park but without the ethics."

I didn't look. I was focused on Camera 1—wide shot of the

main entrance. Nothing much. Some Italian cops were standing around trying not to look bored. A dark Mercedes pulling up. Another name on the guest list.

“This is so dumb,” Marcus said around a mouthful. “We’re spying on people who brief our side anyway. What are we going to catch? George Soros picking his nose?”

“Just log the tape,” I said.

He muttered something and scribbled on the pad. I checked the next feed. A U.S. defense official ducked into the main entrance with a blonde in sunglasses. Not his wife. I noted the timestamp. 06:11.

Marcus leaned back in his chair, stretched. He was twenty-five and had a crush on the hotel bar waitress. The one with the nose ring.

“You should talk to her,” he said. “She thinks we’re Dutch intel.”

“You told her that?”

“I implied it. Look, you said not to say we’re Brits. I improvised.”

“Don’t fraternize with civilians on an op.”

“Relax. It’s Bilderberg. They’re all talking.”

Marcus wasn’t a field agent. He was SIGINT—surveillance, signal capture, bugging hotel rooms, and conference suites. He thought I was too. I didn’t correct him.

Officially, I was here because of my language skills. Monitoring the wires. Tuning out static. Harry had told me to loiter around bars off-shift, to listen for anything that slipped through the cracks—loose talk from defense ministers, oil execs, technocrats who drank too much when they were off-camera.

Unofficially, I suspected Harry still didn’t think I was ready to be back in the thick of it—not after Afghanistan. He hadn’t said it outright, but the assignment spoke volumes. I was still off my game and we both knew it. Light duty. A quiet lakeside op. No real teeth. He knew was still obsessively watching the helmet cam feeds in my spare time.

I stared at the monitors. My eyes were dry. I'd been up since midnight. Eight-hour shifts, split between two rooms. Watch. Record. Don't engage. Don't get caught. Don't get bored enough to start asking why we were here. Our tech team had slipped the cameras in weeks before the conference. Clean job. No alarms tripped.

Camera 4: Hotel lobby, wide angle. Security rotation. Then something flickered—'
'?movement, far right side.

A woman entered. Bright silk scarf, white blouse, sunglasses. Mid-thirties. Her stride was fluid. Unhurried. Familiar.

I sat up. Clicked for the alternate angle. Camera 5 gave me a profile. My stomach clenched, and the hairs on the back of my neck stood up, but I couldn't explain why. All my internal, subconscious instincts were instantly on high alert. I was wide awake now.

Marcus glanced up. "Something?"

I shook my head.

She crossed the lobby. Took out her Blackberry and rapidly tapped a message into it. Spoke briefly to a staffer. She turned slightly. Just enough for the angle to catch her cheekbone, jawline, the way she adjusted her scarf.

Camera 7 picked her up as she entered the elevator. No suitcase.

Then she was gone.

I rewound. Played it again—slower this time.

Kate.

It had to be.

Kate Prescott, late of the CIA. Kate Prescott, Smith College Graduate. Kate Prescott, former Booz Allen analyst. Kate Prescott, who had spent several nights in my bed. Kate Prescott, whose body was buried under the rubble of a Bactrian fortress in Afghanistan, along with a couple of dozen brave men. I had gone back myself months later to rummage through the wreckage, searching for answers. All we found were charred corpses, limbs like charcoal, gear melted into flesh. None of the bodies belonged to her, according to the DNA analysis we had done. But we told ourselves it was to be expected, not every fallen soldier is found. We needed the closure.

I watched the feed again. Her walk, the way her hair curled at her shoulders. You can fake documents, change your voice. But you can't fake a walk.

I felt cold sweat break under my shirt. My hands itched.

Marcus was still talking—something about the waitress and sangria.

I copied the segment to a drive. Slipped it into my inside pocket.

"I'm heading out," I said.

He turned. "What? Shift's not—"

"You've got it."

I didn't wait for a reply. I needed air. I needed movement. I needed to prove to myself I hadn't lost my mind.

The hallway was sterile and silent. Carpet too thick, like someone's grandmother's house. I didn't feel my feet hit the floor. Just that thumping in my chest. The kind you get when a sniper's watching and you don't know where from.

I hit the elevator button.

My mind reeled. If it was her—if it really was her... I struggled to wrap my mind around the implications.

The elevator opened.

I stepped in.

I'd seen the fortress go up in a fireball with my own eyes.

But dead women don't attend Bilderberg.

CHAPTER 26

May 2004
Stresa, Italy

The Grand Hotel's private security office was tucked behind a fake bookshelf near the spa wing—a nod to both discretion and bad taste. The wood paneling was real enough, but the hinges squealed when the concierge slid it open.

Inside, a cramped warren of monitors glowed blue in the morning dim. Cheap grappa stood half-finished in the corner beside a rusting fan. A photograph of a little girl at a carousel was crookedly pinned above the monitors. The man who rose to greet me—balding, heavyset, mid-fifties—wore a brown blazer with suede elbows and the distinct air of someone used to being underestimated.

"Lei è?" he asked.

I smiled, reaching into my jacket and pulling out the forged ID folder. "Capitano Luca Bianchi, SISDE. Regional security bureau, Milan. I'm here under the directive of the Protezione delle Personalità Commissione. We're conducting a quiet review of VIP protocol compliance during Bilderberg."

He squinted at the badge, fingers curling hesitantly around it.

"There was no notice."

"There wouldn't be," I said. "Ministerial directive. You understand."

He paused, then gave a grunt that could have meant anything. I added just the right amount of disdain. "Would you prefer I file a complaint about obstruction?"

That did the trick. He handed the badge back with a deferential nod. "Of course not, Capitano. This way."

Capitano. I winced, then caught myself and shoved the memory aside.

He gestured to the bank of monitors and offered a battered office chair. I sat. My eyes scanned the layout: ten feeds, one main console, a worn desktop running outdated software. Old enough to be hackable. A pad of handwritten notes. The smell of body odor and tobacco lingered thickly under the grappa.

Just then, a plainclothes carabinieri officer stepped in—thinner, late forties, sharp-creased jacket. Mirrored sunglasses pushed up onto his head. He didn't smile.

"Capitano," the head of security said. "This is Inspector De Luca. Liaison from the provincial command."

De Luca extended a hand, eyes scanning me before we even touched palms.

"Piacere," I said. Then, out of habit—God knows from where—I added, "Uè guagliò."

It slipped out too easily. The kind of local greeting you'd pick up while drinking cheap wine with old men in Naples. Not something someone from Milan—or Livigno, for that matter—should say.

De Luca's eyes narrowed, just slightly.

"You're from Naples?"

I paused half a second too long, cursing my carelessness. "No—Livigno. Up north. Near the Swiss border."

He nodded and gave me a flat, humorless smile. "But your greeting...that's Neapolitan."

I gave a sheepish grin, trying to roll with it. "Ah—yeah. My mother's side is from Vomero. She used to say it all the time when she was annoyed. Guess it stuck."

"Vomero," he echoed, folding his arms. "And you grew up in Livigno?"

"Born and raised. Ski patrol, small-town life. Got out as soon as I could." I made it sound tired and real. "Moved to Milan after conscription."

"Which office did you say sent you?"

"Milan HQ," I said, waving the forged ID again. "I'm with Internal Services, Regional Oversight Division. Handling a quiet sweep of security protocols while the conference is underway. Standard risk auditing. You know how it is—big egos, private security teams, no coordination."

De Luca didn't blink. "They sent you alone?"

I gave him a resigned look. "Welcome to the efficiency of the Italian state."

The head of security let out a small chuckle. "He's not wrong."

De Luca's gaze stayed locked on mine. "I'll be making a few calls."

"Of course," I said, all polite confidence. "But while you do, I'd appreciate it if we could continue the review. We're on a tight clock."

The head of security nodded, half-turning toward the monitors. De Luca gave a noncommittal grunt, then left, already thumbing numbers into his phone. He wasn't convinced. Which meant I had fifteen minutes, tops, before he found someone in Milan who'd never heard of Capitano Bianchi.

The door closed. I let out a slow breath.

"Don't mind him," the security chief said. "He's local. Doesn't like anything he didn't authorize."

I nodded, already shifting focus to the CCTV console. "Let's pull up this morning. Elevators and lobby cams. I'm looking for irregular patterns."

I pulled up the date-stamped feeds from the previous morning. Camera angles cycled: the lobby, the main entrance, a cluster of elevators. The place had been a fortress for the past two days, with names that would never appear in the press slipping in and out—ministers, bankers, deep-state nobility.

And then she appeared.

06:43 am.

Bright Hermes silk scarf. Sunglasses. White blouse. No bag.

I leaned closer, slowed the feed, adjusted the zoom.

There. Just for a second, the scarf shifted.

Cheekbone. Jawline.

My chest tightened. The back of my neck went cold.

It was her, alright. Kate Prescott.

I rewound. Slower. She moved with that same calculated fluidity, as if her hips and shoulders had learned diplomacy before language.

She tapped out a message on her BlackBerry, said something to the concierge, then entered the elevator.

I toggled to the elevator feed. She rode to the top floor. The penthouse.

Four hours later, she came down.

Same clothes. Same scarf. Same face.

No hallway footage from the penthouse level. I flagged the security supervisor.

He shrugged apologetically. "The client's personal security insisted the penthouse hallway feed be cut. Their own internal system."

"And who's the client?"

He hesitated, then tapped a few keys on his computer. "Helix

Meridian, S.A.; Registered in Luxembourg."

I gestured to the computer. "May I?"

I pulled up a browser. Traced the company through three levels of obfuscation—one holding company in the Caymans, another in Cyprus, until I hit a name I'd seen before:

Konstantin Varga.

The philanthropist oligarch. The man, some said, could crash markets with a phone call. The man who had heads of state on speed dial but was rarely seen in public. He operated a network of philanthropic NGOs, focusing on providing services and food to the developing world and encouraging the development of civil society. His most famous charity was NovaTerra, which was regularly featured in disaster areas on the news alongside the Red Cross.

"No one's seen him. His aides handle everything. One of them ordered ten crates of Austrian sparkling water yesterday. They carry it up themselves."

I copied the security footage to a thumb drive.

Twenty minutes later, I was back in my own hotel room, field report open on my laptop.

I filled in the usual boilerplate—event perimeter static, police posture tight, minor anomalies logged.

I left Kate's name out.

If she was alive, then someone lied. If she was here, then someone powerful sent her. The CIA? Varga? Both?

I closed the laptop and put the flash drive in my pocket.

Then I picked up the secure satphone.

"Harry," I said. "Listen—I'd like to take a few days. Follow up on something... unrelated. Just need a quiet window. That twerp Marcus can manage the surveillance for the last couple of days."

He asked questions. I answered vaguely.

He relented.

"I trust you," he said.

I thought about meeting Harry in his office two years earlier as he was on his way to a NovaTerra fundraiser. Could I trust Harry, I wondered?

CHAPTER 27

May 2004
Stresa, Italy

The next day, I began watching Varga's people. I told Marcus I picked up a stomach bug, and he agreed to cover for me.

A logistics man with Balkan scars handled deliveries. One woman with clerical credentials emerged from back rooms to shake hands with Russian oligarchs and oil executives.

A NovaTerra aide with perfect posture vanished between meetings. I tailed her to a café, then blinked and lost her. She knew she was being followed. Whoever she was, she wasn't a charity worker. She was trained.

As the sun set, on my way back from trailing the clerical woman, I spotted the suspicious detective from the hotel, this time carrying a tray of skewers from a street vendor. He looked up, saw me, narrowed his eyes, and quickly began moving my way.

I slipped into traffic, then a pharmacy, then disappeared down an alley. It took me twenty minutes to double back and clean.

I'd gotten sloppy; it wouldn't happen again.

That night, I found a dingy internet café just outside the old town. The smell of sweat and printer ink permeated the place. A pudgy, unshaven man with long, greasy, unwashed hair typed furiously on a keyboard and stared intently at his monitor while breathing hard. I didn't want to know what he was looking up. I plugged in the flash drive. Something I couldn't explain told me not to use OGI computers for this.

Kate, again. Frame by frame. Her walk. Her hair. The angle of her jaw. I zoomed in on the picture to an extreme close-up.

She was alive.

"How the hell did you get out?" I whispered.

Leaving the internet café, I drifted around the city, finally finding myself in the corner of a lakeside bar tucked away on a narrow side street a few blocks from the Grand Hotel—the kind of place with nicotine-stained walls, too many mirrors, and a bartender who didn't care if you drank in silence. I liked it for that reason. No tourists. No name tags. Just quiet. I was on my second whisky when I spotted them: two of Varga's aides—the ones I'd tailed that morning. They slid into a booth near the rear, half-obscured by a wooden column. I kept my back to them, watching in the mirror behind the bar.

They spoke in Hungarian, a language I don't know, but a few words pierced through the ambient noise: *Libya. Benghazi. Sirte.*

My blood ran cold. Those names were enough to raise every alarm in my body. OGI had been tracking black-market sophisticated weapons in North Africa for at least 18 months. Much of it appeared to originate from Libya.

I didn't move. Just listened. One of them gestured sharply, like he was sketching a map in the air. The other leaned in, nodded, lit a cigarette with a flick of his thumb. I caught the glint of a ring on his finger—the same one I'd seen earlier, when he passed through the NovaTerra security cordon.

I gripped the glass of whisky so hard I thought it would break.

And then, a voice behind the bar. Light. Cocky. Confident. A young waiter with a dish rag over his shoulder was grinning as he called to someone in the back, "Si, *Capitano!*"

It hit me like a punch to the gut.

For a moment, I wasn't in a lakeside bar in Italy. I was back in FOB Sphinx, back in the makeshift chow tent. Baz laughing, calling me that same stupid nickname. *"Hey, Capitano! Any more fit CIA birds around here, or you keepin' 'em all stashed in your tent?"* I could hear it perfectly. His voice. The grin. The way he threw his arms wide like he was playing to an invisible audience. Riley telling him to mind his paygrade.

And then: the hill over Qala-ye-Khun. The march. The song. His voice cracking as he sang *Wild Rover* with defiant, almost drunken pride, drawing every gun on the mountain to him. His body crumpled beneath boots and fists. The machete. My orders to the Specter Gunship. The smoking crater where Baz used to be.

I dug out my wallet and pulled out a battered, creased laminated card—Riley's prayer.

"If it be my lot to die, let me do so with courage and honor..."

I blinked. My throat was tight. My drink was still full.

I left a twenty on the bar and got the hell out of there.

I don't remember walking back to the hotel, only that I stopped at a corner shop and bought a bottle of scotch I couldn't afford. By the time I reached the hotel, it was half gone. I felt loose and reckless and full of something I didn't want to name.

The hotel bar was still open. Marcus was there, across the room, laughing at something the waitress said—the one he liked—the one with the dark eyes and a silver ring in her nose.

I made straight for the counter. Ordered a whisky. Then another.

Marcus's waitress approached and asked if I needed anything. I don't remember what I said to her. Something bold. Something crass. Something stupid. Whatever it was, it worked. She laughed. Caressed my hand. Whispered something in my ear. Marcus saw it, his face falling flat, wounded and silent.

I knew it was cruel. I didn't care.

The next morning, I woke with my skull cracking open and the taste of smoke and regret in my mouth. The waitress was asleep beside me, naked under the sheets.

I lay there, staring at the ceiling, head throbbing, the weight of it all pressing in. Kate, Varga, Baz, lies inside lies. Everything unraveling.

The waitress stirred and sat up, rubbing her eyes. She retrieved a cigarette from her purse and lit it. "You were so tender... not like the others. You are staying long?"

I gave her a noncommittal smile and lit a cigarette off the glowing ember of hers. I'd broken every rule of protocol. Compromised the op. Crossed lines I wasn't supposed to even approach. I knew this was the point at which I should walk away. Walk away, call Harry, confess everything.

I didn't care.

Whatever this was, whoever was pulling the strings, I was going to find out, even if it upended my world.

CHAPTER 28

May 2004
Provence, France

The road narrowed into crushed gravel and dust, lined with plane trees whose bark peeled in wide, clean flakes. The sun was low but still hot, and the air smelled of lavender and the sweet, sticky rot of overripe fruit. I parked beneath a crooked cypress and walked the rest of the way, boots crunching over the dry earth.

The vines ran in gentle, precise rows, their shoots trained on wires, heavy with green fruit still weeks from harvest. Somewhere, cicadas screeched. A breeze stirred the leaves but didn't reach the sweat on my back.

She was crouched between the vines, sleeves rolled, dirt on her knees. For a moment, I didn't speak. Just watched. Her posture was different now, lower to the earth, more grounded. But the line of her shoulders, the tilt of her jaw, was unmistakable.

She plucked a pale cluster of Viognier from the vine and crushed a grape between her fingers, inspecting the juice. A moment later, a black lab loped toward her, tail wagging. "Ne mange pas les raisins," she warned gently, nudging the dog aside. Then she spun.

The pistol came up fast, one-handed, a small black automatic steady in her grip.

"Easy," I said, hands raised. "It's just me."

Victoria Ashworth stared at me a beat longer, then exhaled

sharply. The gun lowered.

"Jesus, Tom," she said, tucking the pistol back into the waistband of her jeans. "You can't just walk up on people like that."

"I rang the bell. No one answered."

"We don't get many visitors." She dusted her hands on her thighs, studying me. "You look like shit."

"You always say that."

"Because it's usually true."

After Afghanistan, I had checked in on her about once a week, then once a month, but it had been 6 months since our last visit.

She turned and started walking back toward the house without another word. I followed. The vineyard sloped gently up toward a stone cottage ringed with oleander and rosemary. It wasn't large, but it was proud—its tiled roof sun-bleached, its shutters faded blue, the stucco cracked from a hundred summers.

We settled on the back terrace. A bottle of white wine was already sweating in an ice bucket. She poured without asking. The sun cast long, gold fingers across the hills.

"I didn't think I'd see you again," she said.

"You said that last time."

"That was different."

I took a sip. Crisp, acidic. Homegrown, probably.

"You've done well for yourself," I said.

She gave a small smile. "Inherited. From my mother's side."

I let the silence hang. Eventually, I pulled the photo from my pocket and slid it across the table.

Victoria stared at it. Didn't touch it. Her jaw went tight.

"That's Kate, part of the CIA team," I said.

"I know who it is."

"She's alive."

Victoria took a breath through her nose. The wind played with her hair.

"When was this taken?"

"Three days ago. Northern Italy. She came out of a penthouse rented by Konstantin Varga."

That got her attention. Her gaze snapped back to mine.

"You're sure?"

"I saw her."

She leaned back in her chair, wine forgotten. "Then this is bigger than the CIA—much bigger."

"I need help, Vic."

Her mouth twitched. I wasn't sure if it was sadness or amusement.

"It would seem so."

"I can't go through London. I don't trust my people right now. I don't know who's in Varga's pocket. I need someone who can dig through NGO records, UN filings, back-channel embassy cables, and pick journalists' brains. Someone who knows how the humanitarian shell game really works."

She stared at me for a long time, then reached for the wine and refilled her glass.

"All right," she said. "But you'd better be sure. Because if Kate's working with Varga, that means whatever you're chasing goes deeper than Langley. Varga is friends with my President *and* your Prime Minister. If you're doing this off the books, you're playing with fire—we *both* are."

I held her gaze steadily. "I need to know who's behind this and why. A lot of good men died that day. I figured you'd want to know too."

Her eyes narrowed, "I want them to *burn*—all of them."

CHAPTER 29

May 2004
Chamonix, France

The morning alpine air was cold, sharp, and clean. Fog crawled down the granite faces above like something alive. The village streets were quiet this time of year. No skiers, no tour buses. Just a few locals sipping coffee outside shuttered hotels, and the muffled clang of gondola cables echoing from the station at the base of the massif.

I didn't take the main road. Cut through a park, crossed an empty roundabout, and approached the gondola terminal from the rear access. There were a few hikers around, most of them British retirees with poles and overly bright jackets. I kept my pace casual, my eyes up.

She was waiting by the boarding gate, hood up, hands in her coat pockets. From a distance, she could have passed for anyone—an art history professor, a UN consultant, someone on sabbatical. But when she moved, I could see it. The tension. The coiled weight she carried now. She'd never quite shaken it off since Afghanistan.

We didn't speak. Just stepped into the next empty gondola and let the doors shut behind us.

The cable jolted, then pulled us skyward, the ground dropping away below. The cabin swayed gently, cables creaking. Fog pressed in on all sides, sealing us into silence.

Victoria sat stiffly, her back too straight, eyes fixed on nothing. She rubbed her fingers against her coat seam as if trying to scrub something off.

"This is bigger than we thought," she said finally, her voice tight and low. "Much bigger."

I waited.

"They're building something in Misrata," she went on, each word deliberate. "Not just logistics or cover ops—something structural, a sophisticated distribution network."

She exhaled hard, turned briefly to look at me. "You ever read a document that rewrites everything you thought you knew about history?"

I turned to her.

"Varga's name doesn't appear directly, of course. But there's a maritime logistics firm based in Valletta that has just secured exclusive rights to develop a deepwater port there. The money trail loops through Cyprus, then a series of Dutch trusts... and back to Helix Meridian."

"Same shell company that rented the penthouse?"

She nodded. "NovaTerra's footprint in Libya has tripled. Warehouses in Sirte. Community redevelopment contracts. And they've somehow obtained State Department clearance to move sealed shipments into the region. Diplomatic pouch. Uninspected."

"Pouch clearances are reserved for embassies."

"Unless you're Varga. Then Foggy Bottom rolls over."

The gondola swayed as it passed a support tower. We drifted into a low cloud. The world outside turned white.

"He also just acquired hangar space outside Benghazi," she continued. "At a decommissioned military field. The previous tenant? Some American security firm with old Blackwater ties. Now defunct. Conveniently."

I exhaled, watching the mist slide past the glass. "You found all this in a week?"

"I called in a lot of favors."

She reached into her coat and pulled out a slim manila envelope. It was soft at the edges, worn, sealed with a single length of red string.

"I also found this."

"What is it?"

"His father. Arpad Vargha. Not the official biography—the real one. Born in Hungary. Abwehr colonel. Embedded with Nazi intelligence during the war."

I took the envelope from her. It felt heavy, even if it wasn't.

"After the war, he cut a deal with the Americans. Sold out German networks in exchange for safe haven. The CIA smuggled him into Trieste in '47. He helped us run stay-behind operations across the Balkans. Recruited former Nazis. Hid them from Nuremberg."

"And the CIA let him?"

"They paid him. Called it containment. Arpad turned remnants of the Reich into Cold War assets. Built sabotage cells. Smuggled arms into Albania and Yugoslavia. By the time they realized what he was really doing, he was too valuable to stop."

I didn't say anything. Just turned the envelope slowly in my hands.

"He wasn't American. He wasn't Soviet. He wasn't even a Nazi anymore. He was something else. Something older. And Konstantin's not just his son. He's his legacy."

She leaned closer.

"You asked me to find out what Kate was doing with Varga. I don't have a clean answer. But she's not just meeting him for tea. Whatever's happening in Libya—it's big. Maybe a weapons depot. Maybe worse."

We said nothing for a while.

Then she added, more softly, "You should read the file in private. It's not something you forget."

The gondola began to descend. The cable groaned. The ground reemerged, trees and rooftops resolving in the fog.

I reached into my pocket and handed her a burner phone.

"Encrypted. Two numbers preloaded. Change SIM cards every 48 hours."

She took it without comment.

"If someone starts asking questions, go dark, be ready for multiple contingencies."

"I've already moved my laptop off-site. The documents, too. I've got safehouses lined up—my own ratlines, one benefit of being a trust fund baby."

The gondola touched down with a soft mechanical sigh.

The doors opened.

She stepped off without a glance back, melting into the crowd of hikers and tourists at the base station.

I stayed. A group of hikers moved to board my car, but I gave them a look that made them decide to take the next one.

The doors hissed shut again, and I began the slow return to the clouds, dossier in hand.

CHAPTER 30

The gondola hummed as it climbed back toward the summit. I sat alone in the swaying cabin, the envelope in my lap. I broke the seal. It contained a packet of official-looking typewritten documents on old, yellowing paper. I took a deep breath and began to read.

TOP SECRET // EYES ONLY
EXECUTIVE OFFICE OF THE PRESIDENT
Washington, D.C.
June 12, 1963

PRESIDENTIAL DIRECTIVE NO. 322-A

TO: The Director, Central Intelligence Agency
The Attorney General
The Secretary of Defense
The Director, Federal Bureau of Investigation

FROM: The President of the United States

RE: Formation of Presidential Commission on Axis Infiltration into U.S. Intelligence Services

In light of newly surfaced documentation and testimony relating to the postwar resettlement and employment of former Axis-aligned intelligence personnel by U.S. government agencies, and in response to grave concerns regarding the long-term consequences of such affiliations, I hereby direct the formation of a Presidential Commission to conduct a comprehensive investigation into:

1. The scope and scale of former Nazi and Axis intel-

ligence operatives integrated into American intelligence and defense services from 1945 onward.

2. The existence of any residual networks, corporate entities, or financial instruments controlled by said individuals or their descendants.
3. The potential compromise of U.S. national security policy as a result of these associations.

The Commission shall be chaired by a designated representative of the Attorney General's office and will have full authority to compel testimony, subpoena records, and coordinate with allied foreign governments.

This directive is to be executed with utmost discretion. Preliminary findings are to be submitted to my office no later than October 31st, 1963.

/s/ John F. Kennedy

TOP SECRET

TOP SECRET // EYES ONLY
CENTRAL INTELLIGENCE AGENCY
Directorate of Plans
Special Activities Staff
Washington, D.C.

August 18, 1963

TO: The President of the United States
FROM: Deputy Director Lawrence L. Cantwell, OSA
RE: SUBJECT DOSSIER: COLONEL ARPAD VARGHA

[BEGIN MEMORANDUM]

Mr. President,

As requested in your July memorandum regarding the disposition of former Nazi assets within the U.S. intelligence framework, I present herein a consolidated profile of Colonel Arpad Vargha, Hungarian-born intelligence officer and postwar CIA asset. Portions of this material have been suppressed from prior briefing records, including those made available to Congress. I advise against broader circulation.

SUMMARY:

NAME: COLONEL ARPAD VARGHA
BORN: 1899, Budapest, Austro-Hungarian Empire
DECEASED: 1958, Munich (car bomb)

Pre-War Ideological Orientation:
Colonel Vargha emerged from the collapse of the Austro-Hungarian Empire embittered and violently anti-Slavic. His hatred of Bolshevism bordered on religious. He was a military careerist by training and an ideologue by necessity, one who believed that the survival of the Western order depended on the subjugation or extermination of Communist structures. While not a doctrinaire Nazi, Vargha allied himself with the Abwehr in 1938 and remained their key Balkan liaison throughout the war.

WWII Activities:
In his capacity as Abwehr Section II field coordinator, Vargha oversaw operations in Yugoslavia and Ukraine. Reports attribute at least four partisan massacres in the Vojvodina region to fascist units under his indirect control. In one instance, following the sabotage of a German fuel convoy, Vargha ordered the public hanging of 43 villagers, including children. He is alleged to have personally executed a Jewish informant in Subotica with a pistol shot to the mouth.

In 1943, after a rival SS informant compromised one of Vargha's supply chains in Serbia, Vargha reportedly had the man's wife and daughters seized. The women were later found naked, strangled, and dumped in a cistern near Kragujevac. CIA archival testimony from a postwar double agent confirms Vargha had personally authorized the retaliation.

Postwar Exploitation by U.S. Intelligence:

Following Germany's surrender, the United States initiated Operation Paperclip to extract and employ German scientific and technical specialists. In parallel, select elements of Nazi military intelligence (Abwehr, SS) were quietly absorbed via the "Gehlen Organization" track, named for General Reinhard Gehlen, Hitler's former intelligence chief for the Eastern Front.

In May 1945, Vargha crossed over to American lines in Carinthia, Austria. He surrendered the complete organogram of Abwehr networks across the Balkans in exchange for exfiltration.

After being relocated to Trieste, Vargha served for over a decade as an unofficial CIA advisor. His residence doubled as a training site for anti-Communist émigré saboteurs, many of whom were themselves implicated in wartime atrocities. Vargha maintained close ties to ex-SS logisticians, Ustaše remnants, and elements of the Vatican's ratline network. He was instrumental in the extraction and reinsertion of assets into Hungary, Romania, and Yugoslavia.

Vargha formed several front companies during this period, allegedly to facilitate logistics and cover travel expenses. Internal audits suggest these firms were used to channel CIA funds and arms, but they also appear to have been used for personal gain. It is believed that by the time of his death, Vargha had accumulated a substantial personal fortune, shielded through these shell entities.

While still formally enrolled at university, his only son, KONSTANTIN VARGA, currently holds indirect control of several of these structures.

Vargha's Philosophical Outlook:

Transcripts from 1951–1957 reveal Vargha's worldview was explicitly post-ideological. He dismissed fascism, communism, and democracy alike as "populist theater." What he believed in was order: a world governed by those capable of wielding systems of power without moral restriction.

Notable quote from a 1953 debrief:
"A true order does not need to be loved. It needs only to be necessary."

Vargha advocated for the creation of a transnational, post-political elite, an intelligence class that would operate independently of national governments. He referred to this concept as the "*Silent Directorate*." While Agency leadership never formally endorsed these views, elements within the European Division reportedly found his thinking compelling.

Death and Legacy:
On June 14, 1958, Colonel Vargha was killed in a car bombing outside a CIA-run safehouse in Munich. The Agency attributed the attack to a Soviet wet team, though some internal reports suggest possible intra-service motives. Vargha had begun expressing frustration with Washington's "lack of vision" and was preparing to publish a pseudonymous white paper in West German policy circles.

He is survived by one son, Konstantin, who was present during the bombing. Aged 16 at the time, the boy was said to be covered in his father's blood. He was later placed under protection in Italy.

RECOMMENDATION:

It is my strong belief that any continued cooperation with known associates of Colonel Vargha must be subject to Presidential review. While the Colonel's operational utility during the Cold War is undeniable, the long-term consequences of enabling such men are still unfolding.

Respectfully,

LAWRENCE L. CANTWELL
Deputy Director
Special Activities Staff
Central Intelligence Agency

[END MEMO]

TOP SECRET

TOP SECRET // EYES ONLY
EXECUTIVE OFFICE OF THE PRESIDENT
Washington, D.C.
September 3, 1963

MEMORANDUM FOR THE ATTORNEY GENERAL

SUBJECT: Directive for Asset Tracing and Financial Audit of Arpad Vargha Network

Pursuant to Presidential Directive 322-A and the accompanying materials prepared by the Central Intelligence Agency, you are hereby authorized and directed to initiate a confidential investigation into the surviving shell companies, trust networks, and financial instruments previously associated with Colonel Arpad Vargha (deceased).

This audit shall determine:

1. The scope of assets still operational under Vargha's former holdings;
2. Any ongoing financial activities linked to his son, Konstantin Varga;
3. The existence of U.S.-based or allied facilitators knowingly engaged in concealing or utilizing these funds.

You are further authorized to coordinate with Treasury Department Financial Crimes units and appropriate legal attachés stationed at U.S. missions abroad. This operation is to be handled under Presidential Seal and is not to be disclosed outside cleared personnel.

/s/ John F. Kennedy

TOP SECRET

TOP SECRET // EYES ONLY
EXECUTIVE OFFICE OF THE PRESIDENT
Washington, D.C.
December 2, 1963

MEMORANDUM FOR THE DIRECTOR, CENTRAL INTELLIGENCE AGENCY

SUBJECT: Termination of Directive 322-A and Related Materials

Effective immediately, all activities pursuant to Directive 322-A are hereby suspended. The Presidential Commission on Axis Infiltration is to be disbanded. All copies of attached documentation, analysis memos, and asset tracing reports originating from the CIA Office of Special Activities are to be destroyed under the supervision of the Office of Security.

This memorandum constitutes final executive authority on this matter. Any future inquiries regarding Colonel Arpad Vargha or related materials are to be referred directly to the Director's Office.

/s/ Lyndon B. Johnson

TOP SECRET

When the gondola reached the summit, I tucked the dossier into my jacket and got off. The sky was clearing, but my mind was reeling. No wonder Victoria had been so spooked. The Johnson memo was dated one week after Kennedy's assassination.

Why shut the commission down? To protect the Agency from its own buried sins? To protect Varga?

A corner of my mind whispered the obvious: the Vargha file had the power to unravel things—old alliances, false narratives, careers. Could it have played some part in Dallas?

I shoved the thought aside. Too convenient. Too dangerous. Too Hollywood.

I made my way to the trail and hiked down into the valley to clear my head and plan my next move.

Kew Gardens, London
One week later

Harry Fletcher looked like a man at peace, which meant he was up to something. He was perched on a bench, sipping from a paper coffee cup, and fed crumbs to an irritable-looking robin.

I sat beside him.

"You look like hell," he said without turning.

"Vacation in the Alps. Didn't agree with me."

He waited.

I told him what I could: suspected weapons trafficking through North Africa, possibly connected to the network we had been trying to track for the last 2 years. NovaTerra fronts. A logistics pipeline moving through Misrata and Benghazi. Enough to spark interest, not enough to trigger oversight. I left out Victoria. I left out Kate. I left out old Nazi spy rings and Presidential assassinations.

Harry nodded slowly.

"What do you want?"

"A green light. Quiet. Just me."

He ran a hand over his jaw. "Observation only. You trip any wires, you're on your own. I'll let our man in Libya know you're coming. He's a useless tosser; he won't ask many questions."

"Understood."

He turned finally, met my eyes. "I'm serious. Varga's proper looked after, mate. I don't know 'ow far up it goes. You stir that hornet's nest, I ain't got the clout to fish you out."

"Would you even try?"

Harry gave a crooked smile. "I'm not yer fuckin' dad, Tommy. You wanna play Icarus, don't cry when your wings melt."

For a moment, he looked as if he was going to say something else, like something was weighing on his mind, but instead, he just looked away.

The robin flitted off into the trees.

So did I.

CHAPTER 31

June 2004
Libya

Benina Airport was a terminal in name only. Half the glass was cracked, and the other half was streaked with dust so thick it could have passed for paint. Checkpoints lined the tarmac like missing teeth, manned by boys in sweat-stained uniforms with too many rifles and not enough discipline.

I moved through the concourse in slow steps, breathing the heat, the diesel, the sunburnt silence of a place that hadn't quite decided if it was still a state.

NGO banners clung to the arrival gate like last year's party streamers. World Food Programme. Médecins Sans Frontières. NovaTerra—front and center, draped across the customs kiosk like a VIP pass to nowhere.

Passport control took longer than it should have. The guard wore mirrored sunglasses and an expression that suggested he'd shot someone for less than a typo. He flipped through my fake Maltese credentials, muttered to his colleague in Arabic, something about foreigners and forged paperwork, and looked up just long enough to meet my eye. I replied quietly, in Arabic, "Just here for the contracts, brother. No trouble." His eyebrows twitched in surprise, then he stamped the page with a sigh like he was signing a death warrant.

I thanked him and moved on.

The drive from Benina into Benghazi took just under twenty minutes, the radio played static, and the air conditioning didn't work. I passed a once-busy souk that now stood quiet, its awnings sagging like broken sails. A few vendors lingered like ghosts, sipping bitter coffee under collapsing awnings, selling nothing to no one. A billboard on the coastal road had been repurposed. Half of it advertising a mobile clinic funded by NovaTerra, the other still clinging to a sun-bleached image of Gaddafi mid-smile.

Teenage boys squatted outside what used to be a police station, playing cards with AKs resting in their laps. An old man watered the dust in front of a closed café with a cracked plastic kettle. It didn't help. Nothing here looked like it had been clean in years.

The OGI field office downtown was hidden behind a rusted gate and an old UNICEF logo. Inside: a concrete box with the charm of a bunker. Radios were silent. Cabinets half-open. The logbook on the desk hadn't seen a fresh entry since March. A ceiling fan spun lazily, like it too had given up. Whoever had been running things here was long gone in everything but name.

I didn't stay.

The OGI villa lay to the east of the city, past olive groves and shuttered petrol stations. It must have been grand once. Colonial-style, two stories, whitewashed walls faded to bone under the sun. A perimeter wall surrounded the compound, its iron gate rusted but intact. Cracked ceramic tiles led up to the main door. A generator chugged somewhere around back. I noticed empty beer bottles discarded beneath a hedge. The place had the look of a safehouse gone soft.

A young Libyan girl answered the gate. Barefoot, headscarf loose. Eyes sharp but hollow. She didn't speak English. Just stared.

I made a quick sweep as I walked the property. The wall gave good cover, the sightlines were decent. No CCTV. No obvious motion sensors. The roof had a view of the coast and inland. I logged the fallback options in my head.

The steward, Yousef, met me near the kitchen entrance. Late sixties, maybe. Grey stubble, sun-worn face. Ex-military, no question. The kind of man who could gut a goat or a diplomat with equal calm.

"Welcome, sir," he said quietly, and held out a glass of water.

I asked about the security package.

"No problems," he said. "Not yet. Standard field loadout is in the basement. Same as Lebanon. Same as everywhere."

"Good," I said. "I'll need a sidearm and some spare magazines."

"Yes, sir."

He led me out to the pool.

Sebastian Cartwright was tanning in a lounger, shirtless, perfectly bronze, sipping a gin and tonic. Twenty-eight, maybe older. Blond, handsome, Eton sculpted—the British version of a Greek statue with better teeth.

The girl returned with another cocktail. Still barefoot. She brushed her fingers against Seb's shoulder. He didn't notice. Or pretended not to.

Seb looked up. "Ah, you must be our man from Malta. Christ, you're a bit younger than I expected."

I just smiled and nodded faintly.

"Seb Cartwright. Head of Station. Well, technically. I'm being rotated out. Office in London. More clubs, less sunstroke."

He waved toward the villa. "Apologies for the state of the place. Haven't exactly been operating at full capacity."

He paused, waiting for me to say something. When I didn't, he launched into a ramble about his upcoming posting, dropping names with lazy familiarity. Old Rory from Balliol. So-and-so from Cheltenham. A woman from the Cabinet Office who apparently had a thing for champagne and junior officers.

I kept smiling and nodding.

He took a long sip. "This place could survive a bloody siege with that wall, eh? Shame I'd sleep through it." He giggled lightly.

"Come on, I'll show you the town tomorrow. Get you properly briefed, mate. I'll drive."

I tilted my head and dropped into a thick Mancurian drawl.

“Appreciate it, mate, but I'll probably poke around on me own. Used to do a bit of bouncing in Manchester, back before the Army. I'm used to bein' tossed into the thick of it—prefer to get the lay of the land meself.”

Seb blinked. Smile faltered. Recalibrated.

“Oh. Right. Of course.”

Yousef was still nearby, lingering at the edge of the veranda. He raised an eyebrow at the accent switch, the faintest flicker of amusement behind the stoicism. I gave him a quick wink.

Seb excused himself quickly after that, no longer keen on playing tour guide, claiming something about emails and the Seychelles. Perfect.

The dinner that night was served on the veranda. Grilled bream, sticky dates, fresh pita. The heat hung like a wet towel. A tinny radio played distorted folk music somewhere in the hills. Gunfire echoed now and then—celebratory, probably. For now.

Seb complimented the fish, then joked about catching dysentery. He talked without invitation or filter. Boarding school tales. Jokes about Harrow. Names dropped like confetti—Toby, Freddy in MI5, Arabella Devonshire with her endless legs and Oxford oar.

When he mentioned a butler's pantry at some country house dinner, I raised a brow.

“So, what's a butler's pantry then? That where you keep the silver caviar spoons? Or is that where the butler shags the maids?”

He laughed, paused, squinted.

I told him about bouncing in a Manchester nightclub. "Cambridge lads wandered in one night. Loud, drunk, clearly slumming it. One of 'em got mouthy about the music. Didn't go well. Had to drag his mate out by the collar before he bled on the cloakroom tiles. Amazing how fast they forget their Latin when there's a Manc boot in their ribs."

Seb stared. Tried to reclassify me again. Gave up halfway through the thought.

He got philosophical.

"You know, I used to think this job would mean something. Whispering to defectors in a backroom. Instead, it's spreadsheets and fundraisers and hoping the interns don't cry when the power cuts out." He waved his glass. "You ever been to a fundraiser for a warlord-sponsored food pantry? No? Had the most amazing veal at one of those."

I asked about NovaTerra. Casually.

He scoffed. "They throw parties. Hand out brochures. Fly in interns with teeth like toothpaste ads. PR with cocktails. Last one I went to, they flew in Perrier-Jouët. Gala for a 'rehabilitated' orphanage—Lady Cornwall's charity. All very moving. There was a slideshow. Do you know her daughter? No, of course *you* wouldn't. She was at Oxford with me—a bloody harlot that one."

He didn't wait for a reply.

"They even had a chamber quartet. One of 'em—Argentine, violinist, stunning—claimed she was here for 'civil society integration.' Think that meant shagging me between violin sets."

He chuckled. "I stay outta their way, and they stay friendly. Rhythm, you know? They pour the champagne, I shut up. Works rather well."

The lights cut out for a second. The fan died.

We sat in darkness until the generator coughed back to life.

Seb didn't react.

"I stopped asking questions. It's all theater. Donors get photos. Locals get a paint job. We get promoted. Just play your part, old boy. Smile. Sip the champagne. Or a can of Skol, if that's more your speed."

He stood. "I've got to call the Seychelles. Try not to steal the silver."

He vanished.

Yousef emerged from the shadows.

"There is a depot," he said. "Near the docks. NovaTerra owns it. It's always full—trucks arrive, supplies vanish inside. Nothing ever comes out. Not aid, not paperwork. Just silence."

He studied me.

"I don't think I need to tell you to be careful. You are a man who knows his business. Not like him." He gestured with disgust to the door through which Seb had disappeared.

He handed me a canvas bag.

Inside: a Glock 19, three mags, and a loose box of 9mm.

"Step lightly, my friend."

On the way to my room, I passed the kitchen. The girl, Layla, stood hunched over the sink, shoulders shaking, her sobs muffled by running water and the clink of cutlery.

I stepped in quietly and placed a folded wad of American bills on the counter beside her. She didn't turn, didn't pause. Just wiped her face with the back of her hand, took the money, and tucked it into a dented tea tin. She locked it in a drawer with a smooth, practiced motion. No gratitude, no hesitation. Just quiet, practiced survival.

That night, the fan in my room didn't work. The sheets stuck to my back. Gunfire cracked somewhere far off.

I lay in the dark, plotting.

Start at the docks. Go in quiet, local clothes. Ask the right questions. Watch the routes. Trace the corruption.

NovaTerra was a front. And OGI? It was rotting from the inside. Lately, I'd come to realize that men like Seb weren't outliers, they were becoming the norm. The type who coasted on connections, drifted through postings, and mistook inertia for competence. Harry's little empire was cracking at the seams, and not even he seemed to notice—or care.

CHAPTER 32

June 2004
Benghazi, Libya

The flat I rented was above an abandoned phone repair shop. Rust streaked the outer wall like dried blood. The tap ran red for five seconds before it cleared. No air conditioning, just a floor fan wired straight into a cracked fusebox, and a mat that passed for a bed. The shutters didn't close properly. Good. I needed to hear who was coming.

I rigged a cache behind the water tank in the bathroom: change of clothes, burner phones, three SIM cards, cash in dollars, dinars, and euros, and a fake passport. Enough to get me out or under, depending.

Nights were for movement. I darkened my hair with temporary dye, wrapped my head in a keffiyeh, and pulled on a worn djellaba. Henna on the hands. Ash in the nails. I walked like a man with somewhere to be and nowhere to go. I changed my route home each night. Circled the block twice. Left a hair on the latch. No one had been inside—yet.

My Arabic got me by. I traded gossip with a cigarette vendor near the port; he talked too much, but that was the point. I befriended a boy who slept under fish crates at the port. His older brother offloaded trucks for NovaTerra. I slipped the kid some dinar, and the next morning he handed me a folded scrap of paper with the week's delivery times.

I climbed rooftops and squatted behind air vents, listening to encrypted radio chatter, short bursts on UHF frequencies. Whoever these people were, they weren't distributing aid.

The so-called resettlement sites were theater. Tents in dusty lots, a couple of barrels painted with UN logos, and sometimes a dog chained up to bark when inspectors came. I slipped into one at night. The tents were empty. Some still had the price tags hanging off the poles.

One employee at the NovaTerra central office stood out from the parade of polished interns and swaggering field men. Slim. Early thirties. Always alone. No makeup. She left just after six each day, locking the door herself, the click audible even from my vantage point down the block. Long skirts, a gray blouse, hair wrapped in a plain scarf. She walked like someone braced for an impact that never came—shoulders tight, head turning more often than it should.

I didn't know her name. Not yet. But she was different. She was missing the easy, careless rhythm the others carried.

A few blocks away, a small warehouse near the docks drew similar attention from me. It seemed to be the main artery feeding the NovaTerra trucks. Three nights, I watched it from the roof of a crumbling customs office across the quay. Guard rotations noted. Generator hiccups timed. The 43-minute gap between the last truck leaving and the next patrol shift. On the fourth night, once I knew every pattern, every nuance of their schedule, I moved.

Dressed like a dockhand, I slipped behind a departing aid truck, ducking low, sliding behind a wall of crates, and crept toward the side door.

The lock was magnetic—old, dumb. I popped the panel with a rubber-wrapped hand drill, shorted it with foil and a probe. It clicked. Inside, it was cold. The warehouse was dank and filthy, rodents skittered in the shadows, and birds fluttered in the rafters. It was half full of wooden crates loaded onto pallets bearing markings such as "Portable Water Filtration Units" or "Shelter Tents". I cracked a box of filtration units; inside was a mix of sawdust and straw packing material. Buried in the middle were high-end water filters, wrapped in cellophane. No contraband, no smoking guns. Disappointment settled over me, and doubt began to worm its way into my mind. Was I barking up the wrong tree? Was NovaTerra really on the up and up?

I resecured the lid and let my eyes sweep the warehouse, weighing whether to press on or cut my losses. Then something out of place caught my eye—a shadowed corner where the dust lay heavier, undisturbed. I moved closer. Three hard-shell, molded-plastic cases sat forgotten behind a collapsed pallet. Not aid crates. Military transit cases. Four feet by three, with high-density foam interiors and a locking bar across the center. The foam was cut perfectly to house 10 M4 rifles, now long gone. Not a smoking gun, but it was a start. I slid the red filter over my headlamp and began taking photos.

At the far end of the warehouse, a narrow doorway led into a small, unlit office. An old metal desk squatted in the corner, its surface ringed with decades of coffee stains. I sifted through drawers—mostly pay slips, shift rosters, and stale paperwork. Then, buried in the back of the middle drawer, I found a wrinkled slip of paper. It was a shipping manifest, yellowed and creased from use. The cover sheet bore the NovaTerra letterhead, stamped with Benghazi's central office seal, dated August of the previous year.

The details leapt off the page. "Shipment ID: NT-2003-0518-A: Emergency water kits" routed through Station Alpha with customs pre-approval already arranged. Cold-chain vaccines were shipped to a place called Harvest Site under a network I'd never heard of. Solar lighting kits, maternal health modules, cholera barrels—all dressed up in the language of aid, every entry married to a different shell program or NGO. Air freight here, a truck convoy there, even a coastal skiff listed as if it were part of some standard supply chain.

To anyone else, it might have looked like bureaucratic trivia.

But I could see the potential pattern in the clutter: duplicate consignments under multiple covers, cargo split between modes, shipments hidden under UNICEF stickers. I folded the manifest and shoved it into my pocket. Not a smoking gun, just the first piece of the puzzle.

Outside, I heard the distant sound of footsteps and voices.

I killed the light, tidied up the desk, and peered out the door. The guards weren't visible yet, but their voices were growing louder. Arabic. I darted out of the door and made my way to some pallets near the side entrance. I pressed myself into the shadows as the guards passed, complaining about someone named Osip and arguing over cigarettes.

I moved fast—out the side door, panel snapped back into place. Slid into a dry canal choked with trash and stagnant water, knees bent low. I stepped on an aluminum can with a crunch. I froze.

Somewhere ahead in the dark, a faint scrape. My hand went to the Glock. I didn't move. Breathe shallow. A second scrape, closer. My mind started calculating exit routes, trigger weight, wind direction.

A cat padded out of the shadows, hugging the canal wall, eyes catching the dim spill of light. Just a cat. I exhaled slowly, but my heart was pounding. I kept moving, slower now, every step measured. By the time I hit the back streets, my pulse had settled enough to notice the sting in my side. Blood from a bent nail had soaked into my shirt, a dull, tacky warmth against my ribs.. Adrenaline kept me focused.

Back at the flat, I studied the shipping manifest repeatedly. What was really in those shipments? Where were they going? I called Victoria and gave her the names of the destinations and the recipient programs listed. Were they legitimate? Were they code?

The next few days passed in a rhythm of sweat, silence, and surveillance. By day, I watched the NovaTerra facilities, the camps, the offices, the warehouse, from alleyways and rooftops. By night, I mapped their patterns—when the lights stayed on, who came and went, which rooms stayed dark. Most nights, I ended up back in the flat with grainy photos sprawled across the tile.

My attention turned back to the girl in grey. She still locked up the office herself. No ride. Just a canvas bag and quiet steps through side streets near the university. She stopped frequently and looked behind her, as if expecting a tail.

I followed from the rooftops. Watched her apartment. Third floor. One broken window pane, covered with cardboard. I watched a little longer, then disappeared back into the dark.

It wasn't anything she did, exactly. Just the way she moved—too careful, too quiet, like someone who knew how fast things could go wrong. She didn't belong here, not with the others. And something told me she was my way in.

CHAPTER 33

June 2004
Libya

I had found out her name—the woman in grey was Amira al-Soudani. I kept my distance and learned the rhythm of her days. She left at the same time each morning, came back at the same time each night. No friends, no visitors. A stop at a café that allowed women, sometimes a bookstall or corner shop, but always alone. She lived like someone who had narrowed her world to the bare essentials. One hot evening, she stepped out of the office, locked the padlock with a practiced snap, and hesitated. Then her gaze climbed, searching the rooftops. It found me.

We made eye contact.

Just a flicker. I was crouched behind a rooftop vent across the street, keffiyeh drawn high, clothes local. But her gaze lingered half a second too long.

The next day, I staged an encounter.

She was managing supply distribution at a small satellite clinic east of the port—mostly cholera kits and expired antibiotics from some Swedish foundation. I dressed in Western casual: an untucked collared shirt, dusty desert boots, and an NGO badge from a Malta-based partner I knew no one would check.

"Excuse me," I said in Arabic. Halting, but polite. "I am looking for... logistic cooperation forms. Maybe someone can explain?"

She looked up from a shipping manifest, taking me in. Headscarf pale grey, blouse buttoned to the neck despite the heat. Her voice was even. "Your grammar's not bad, but you just asked to marry the supply tent."

I smiled. "That explains the silence."

A flicker of dry humor passed behind her eyes. "Who are you with?"

"Khyber Aid. UK-based, but my offices are in Malta. We're evaluating port partnerships. Supply transparency. Customs are being real bastards, they keep demanding paperwork no one's ever heard of."

She studied me. Not a hint of trust. But not hostility, either. "Talk to the Ministry of Planning. They write the rules. We just pretend to follow them."

I thanked her. She went back to work.

Two days later, we ran into each other again, this time near the old quarter, at a makeshift book stall beneath a leaning awning. She held a stack of documents. I picked up a battered volume of Ghassan Kanafani's *Return to Haifa*.

"Everyone reads Kanafani when they want to feel moral about war," she said without looking at me.

I nodded. "Or when they don't know how to talk about it."

This earned a glance.

We spoke for a few minutes about books, war zones, and how best to approach local humanitarian problems. I mentioned a story, half true, about a boy in Helmand whose entire family was displaced because of an airstrike meant for someone else.

She watched me carefully.

"What is it you think you're doing here?" she asked.

"Trying to help."

"There are too many people trying to help," she said.

A pause.

"There's a café, out near the edge of town. They serve women. No tourists. If you want tea, meet me there after eight."

That night, I sat across from her under buzzing lights and a rusted fan. The café was quiet—just the clink of glass and the faint whistle of wind against the tin awning.

She sipped mint tea. Didn't smile.

"Who do you really work for?"

I tilted my head. "No one interesting."

"That's not an answer."

I said nothing. Let the silence stretch.

"You speak Arabic well enough to lie in it. That narrows the list."

"I'm not here to hurt anyone."

"Everyone says that."

She reached into her bag and pulled out a folded envelope. Placed it in the ashtray. "Read it. Or don't. Just understand this —"

She met my eyes.

"If you're lying, lie carefully. The people you're lying to are worse than the people you're lying about."

And with that, she stood. Walked into the dark without looking back.

CHAPTER 34

I didn't touch the envelope until I was back in the flat. Under the red light, I opened it and unfolded the contents. The first was a memo. NovaTerra Foundation letterhead. Field Operations Directorate. Dated the third of June.

I scanned down the page, the language clipped and bloodless, the way bureaucrats like to bury rot under acronyms and logistics jargon. A "field operations review" signed off by someone called Rasmussen, Regional Logistics Coordinator for MENA.

The inspection notes were laid out like any audit trail—shipment dates, destination codes, and commodities. Water filters bound for Station Alpha. Desalination units through Iron Well. Bulk salts for Depot Echo. Maternal health kits to Cold Spring. Solar lamps, seed packets, surgical trauma kits. All of it dressed in the vocabulary of aid.

But the notes in the margins told the real story. Customs delays solved with pre-approvals, read: bribes. Pilot clearance issues "resolved in Geneva." Instructions to avoid coinciding with UN flights, to dodge inspection. Duplicate manifests for the same shipment filed at separate embarkation points—even a recommendation to rotate crews so the same names wouldn't keep surfacing.

To anyone else, it would read as operational housekeeping. To me, it was a blueprint for laundering: supplies disguised, rerouted, padded with ghost consignments. It wasn't sloppy paperwork. It was design.

The last page was different, no header, no logo. Handwritten. Amira's work. A list of airport codes, tarmac log entries, and arrival/departure stamps. The names matched the order in the memo's itinerary:

Station Alpha → BIAP (Baghdad, Iraq)
Iron Well → BND (Bandar Abbas, Iran)
Depot Echo → KDH (Kandahar, Afghanistan)
Cold Spring → ISB (Islamabad, Pakistan)
Sunrise Station → MGQ (Mogadishu, Somalia)
Field Post Zephyr → HGA (Hargeisa, Somaliland)
Blue Orchard Station → TIP (Tripoli, Libya)

I had part of the cipher—locations in warzones and terrorist hot spots. Enough to know they weren't distributing water filters or seed kits. Enough to know this wasn't a one-off.

NovaTerra wasn't moving aid along relief corridors; they were threading their way through war zones. Who was waiting at the other end? Militias? Warlords? I pictured soldiers grinding through the hellish maelstroms of Iraq and Afghanistan. Both had sunk into quagmires, the insurgencies too well-armed, too well-supplied. Was NovaTerra supplying these networks?

If so, I wasn't chasing phantoms anymore. I was chasing the same people who'd made Afghanistan a meat grinder, who'd sent us into unwinnable fights and called it progress. Sitting there in my flat, the fan rattling against the heat, I could still smell the burnt flesh from Qala-ye Khun, still see Baz's last stand in the smoke, Riley bleeding out. Maybe it had all been part of the same chain. The thought made my hands shake.

Amira knew.

And now I did too.

I called Victoria and gave her the news of my breakthrough. Then, I sat still for a long time, breathing in the musty silence and weighing the next move.

I needed to see her. The next afternoon, I slipped a cryptic note under her apartment door.

The garden café was almost empty when I arrived. Fading tiles curled around the courtyard, dust settled on old ironwork, and lanterns swayed slightly in the still heat. A waiter nodded without speaking. I took the back table, facing the wall.

I didn't know if she'd come.

She did.

Soft footfalls. A flash of grey. She sat across from me as if she'd always belonged there, drew her tea close, and said quietly, "So. Not Khyber Aid, then."

I smiled. "Not Khyber Aid."

She exhaled deeply. Not angry. Just tired. "I used to believe the paperwork. That's how it starts, you know. You tell yourself you're helping. That the crates mean something. That the fuel we track is going to clinics, not... wherever it goes."

"Wherever it goes," I echoed. "You stayed longer than most."

"Because I thought I could do some good. Maybe that makes me naïve."

"Or brave."

She shook her head. "No one's brave here. Just trapped."

She set her tea down and folded her hands in her lap. "You know, I studied in Tripoli—public health. I wanted to join WHO, maybe. Do something that mattered. Then the sanctions came, and the ministries changed overnight. Foreign programs pulled out. Budgets vanished. And..." She trailed off, but her eyes stayed fixed on mine.

"I took the job with NovaTerra 6 years ago. They flew me to Geneva for training. Gave me a laptop, a stipend, and a stack of idealism. I thought, finally, here's a chance to rebuild something. To help."

She gave a dry laugh.

"But all I did was shuffle manifests and sign for boxes no one ever opened. They'd send press teams with cameras when the supplies arrived. Then they'd vanish. And the aid? It went somewhere else."

I kept silent. She wasn't finished.

"I tried to quit. Two years ago. They flew in a security officer from Tunis. Sat me down. He smiled the whole time. Said it would be 'unfortunate' if someone misunderstood my resignation. That people might think I was making accusations."

Her voice had gone low, almost flat.

"My brother lives in Tobruk. We don't talk much, but they mentioned him by name. Just... casually. Like they knew where he bought his bread."

She looked away. "So, I stayed."

Her hand trembled slightly as she lifted her cup. She caught my gaze and tugged her sleeve down a little more.

"This city eats people," she murmured. "Slowly. Like rust."

A series of cracks echoed in the distance—gunfire, maybe a Kalashnikov. It rang across the rooftops and then faded. Neither of us moved.

"You don't flinch when you hear gunfire," she said.

"Neither do you."

"Then maybe we're both too far gone."

I slid the sugar bowl toward her without looking up. She smiled, the smallest, saddest smile.

"What's your real name?"

"Tom."

"No Arabic alias?"

"Not one worth remembering. Is Amira an alias?"

She laughed. It was the first time I had seen a genuine smile on her face.

"It suits you."

"Does it?"

"It means 'princess.' But also 'leader.'"

"I don't feel like either."

The lanterns began to go dark, one by one. The waiter yawned and disappeared into the kitchen.

"It's too dangerous," she said. "This."

"Then tell me to walk away."

She didn't.

Instead, she reached across the table and took my hand. Tentative. Searching. I turned my palm up and laced my fingers through hers.

No words.

We left together.

The flat smelled like sweat and old plaster. She removed her scarf slowly. I turned away.

We didn't speak as we undressed. Not passion. Not escape. Just... the need to feel something unguarded. Something human.

Afterward, we lay tangled on the thin mattress. Her fingers rested lightly on my chest.

"If I close my eyes long enough," she whispered, "I can almost believe we're in Malta... anywhere clean. Somewhere free. A place where I'm not followed to work, where crates don't arrive in the dark, and I don't sleep with a bag packed by the door. Somewhere I could read in the morning sun and not listen for boots in the stairwell."

She paused.

"Would you take me there?"

I didn't answer. I kissed her forehead.

She saw it. Said nothing more.

The next morning, I brainstormed how to get Amira out of the country. I seized upon the idea of a UK student visa—fabricated enrollment, host family, bank account balances. I had half the story sketched before I began to think clearly.

If OGI was compromised, this wasn't a rescue. It was a death sentence.

Instead, I called Victoria. I threw half-baked ideas at her—journalistic visas, refugee routes.

"You want me to run an asylum channel," she said flatly.

"Yes."

A long pause.

"You'd better be sure. Once we enter her into the system, there's no pulling her out. You know that, right?"

I did.

That week, pressure mounted. NovaTerra staff were being pulled aside for questioning. Amira's desk mate—a shy accountant with a pink plastic calculator—disappeared overnight. No one would say where she went.

I found a chalk mark on my doorframe one night. A signal? A warning?

The next day, I found a small folded scrap tucked into the crumbling mortar beside the courtyard fountain at the old café, where we had set up a dead drop to limit public meetings.

"We need to stop," it read, in her careful, slanted hand.

I slipped my reply behind the third stone from the base, where the grout had split wide enough to hold a secret.

"Disappear. For your own safety."

But she came anyway.

That night, she knocked once and let herself in. Her shoulders were tight, eyes raw. She placed a small stack of documents on the floor—contracts, manifests, encrypted communication schedules.

“I told myself I wouldn’t,” she said, voice cracking. “But you think I don’t know how this ends?”

I kissed her gently, then quickly flipped through the documents. The top page was a shipping invoice in French, the consignee listed only as *Société Maritime du Levant*, a company I’d never heard of. Tucked inside was a photocopied customs clearance sheet bearing an address on the outskirts of Misrata—industrial park, Lot 17—marked in pencil with a small ‘2.’ Beneath that, a partial floor plan with bays numbered, one circled twice. I didn’t have the whole picture yet, but something in my gut told me I was looking at the other end of NovaTerra’s pipeline.

She shook her head. “I just didn’t want to go quietly. That’s all.”

I pulled her into my arms. We didn’t speak. She fell asleep against me, breathing shallowly. The fan buzzed, useless against the heat.

I stared at the ceiling. She wasn’t just a source anymore. Not an asset. Not an angle.

She was something else.

And I knew—I had signed her death warrant.

CHAPTER 35

The second NovaTerra warehouse sat just outside the city limits, beyond the cracked tarmac and rusted petrol drums that marked Benghazi's industrial edge. It had once been a refrigerated food depot, according to the faded signage near the gate. Now, it flew a new vinyl banner: "COLD CHAIN STORAGE - EMERGENCY VACCINE LOGISTICS."

The security was polished and professional-looking. Motion lights. Biometric locks on the admin office. Fluorescent fixtures that cast everything in an antiseptic glow. Humanitarian theater, staged with precision.

I arrived in a borrowed van just after sundown, posing as a Geneva-based logistics auditor with forged paperwork Amira had helped me fabricate. A clipboard, a vest, a perfect Swiss accent, and enough bureaucracy to appear legitimate got me inside the front-loading bay.

Inside, the warehouse was cold, clinically lit, and spotless. Steel racks rose twenty feet, stacked with neat blue crates stenciled in three languages: *Emergency Nutrition Kits. Maternal Hemorrhage Response. Cold Storage – Authorized Personnel Only.*

It was almost convincing.

Almost.

It might have fooled anyone who hadn't seen the codes before. But I had. KUF-MED-17. ZEL-NSL-42. The same cryptic tags from the manifests Amira had smuggled to me. One shipment supposedly bound for a rural clinic that had burned down years ago; another for a psychiatric ward that existed only on paper.

I walked the aisles at a casual pace, jotting notes. The air smelled wrong—less like disinfectant, more like fuel. Somewhere in the mix was the faint metallic tang of gun oil.

Near the rear wall, a half-sealed crate labeled *Refrigerated Medical Supply Modules* caught my eye. I flipped the lid. Inside were custom-cut foam slots—each the exact dimensions for a shoulder-fired surface-to-air missile tube. Empty now, but no mistaking the shape. The lid's tamper seal was counterfeit, a crude heat-gun job.

I checked another crate: stenciled for *Emergency Water Purification*. Beneath a top layer of cheap Chinese filters lay rows of ammunition tins marked in Cyrillic, the lacquered green of Russian 7.62×39mm rounds.

And then the clincher—a pallet still wrapped in clear film. The label read *NSL-42 / Cold Spring / Maternal Health Modules*. I slit the wrap, peeled back the cardboard, and found an HK-branded weapons case. Inside: a disassembled MG4 light machine gun, spotless and freshly oiled.

The code broke itself in my head as I moved from pallet to pallet. Location code. Cover commodity code. Content code. Every false aid label mapped to a weapons category—SAL for small arms, NSL for NATO-standard light machine guns, MED for narcotics precursors, AGR for explosives packed as "agricultural equipment." The destinations were all in Amira's list. Iraq. Afghanistan. Somalia. Chechnya.

This wasn't mismanagement or "grey routing." This was sophisticated, an industrial-scale distribution network to insurgents across every conflict zone on the board.

Voices echoed from the admin wing—two men, one speaking Russian-inflected Arabic, arguing about "the Tripoli mix-up" and a shipment to "the Hargeisa buyers." Boots thumped closer. I slid behind a stack of shrink-wrapped "mosquito netting" and stayed low, hand on my sidearm.

They passed without looking my way.

Three minutes later, I walked out through the main entrance, calm, nodding at the guard. Paperwork and confidence—the best camouflage in the world.

Back at my flat, I updated my wall. The cheap plaster was already pitted from too many pushpins, curling tape, and the heat. Dead center went a fresh printout of the second warehouse's floor plan, to the left, Amira's annotated airport logs formed a tight column, each destination code now marked with its true counterpart: Kandahar, Baghdad, Tripoli, Mogadishu, Bandar Abbas, Hargeisa, Islamabad. Cross-referencing with internal memos had cracked the content cipher—MED-17 was never "Maternal Hemorrhage Response Kits." It was M4 rifles. AGR-22 wasn't "Agricultural Seed Kits" but crates of anti-tank munitions.

On the right, personnel rosters sat beside passport scans—drivers, loaders, and guards tied to Russian Private Military Contractors and defunct Balkan freight outfits. Some still had dormant Interpol red notices for trafficking; others had been erased entirely from public record, existing now only in my photos and cross-referenced manifests.

Above, I pinned Victoria's latest drop. Dossiers on names absent from NovaTerra's books but pulling its strings from the shadows: a Gulf defense minister who chaired NATO procurement; a retired U.S. general fronting a think tank that funneled contracts to Varga's shell firms; a Brussels commissioner with voting power over sanctions lists; a Russian oligarch sanctioned in name only, still moving steel and fuel through EU ports; a British peer whose family trust financed "development" in every war zone NovaTerra touched; and—most chilling—a former UN humanitarian envoy who had brokered ceasefires in exchange for smuggling lanes. Each face was tagged with a red paperclip, strung along the top like a gallery of kings and kingmakers—people who could pick up a phone and start a war, or make one vanish.

I stepped back, the paper edges lifting in the damp night air. From a distance, it no longer looked like an investigation—it looked like a coup, the kind history never admits to. Not smuggling, not corruption. A shadow state with its own generals, treasurers, and diplomats. I lit another cigarette and watched the smoke drift toward the cracked ceiling. Part of me wanted to call Harry, dump the whole thing in his lap, let him make it someone else's problem. The other part knew the second I did, this would disappear into a locked archive, and I'd be next on someone's list.

I couldn't sit still. I left the flat and drifted through the city's narrow streets, following no route, just the pull of my thoughts. Every shadow felt heavier now, every motorbike tailpipe an exhaust plume from some unmarked convoy. Should I tell Harry? Even if OGI was clean, did Harry have the power to do anything? Either way, handing this over could be suicide for both of us. By the time I looped back toward the old quarter, my lungs ached from smoke and the salt air. I found myself in the courtyard of the Amira's cafe, the fountain gurgling in the dark. I checked our dead drop, and tucked in the hollow beneath the third tile by the fountain's edge was a small note.

"A delegation is arriving. One is an important woman. I saw her before—at the docks. She doesn't wear a badge. Everyone moves aside when she enters. There was a man following me today. Second time this week. We talked about Malta once. Would you take me there?"

My hand tightened on the paper. I reread her letter on the walk home, folding and refolding it until the creases formed a map of worry. Should I take her to the villa, I wondered? But what then?

CHAPTER 36

The shed smelled like hydraulic oil and sun-baked metal, and felt like the inside of a furnace. My joints ached, and I was drenched with sweat from twenty-six hours in the same cramped square of corrugated tin, living off warm bottled water and flatbread so dry it turned to paste in my mouth.

Light came through the warped shutters in narrow, fixed bands. Every fifteen minutes, I'd lift the scope and check the runway. Same bored guard at the fence post, cigarette hanging like he'd been born with it. Same gull hopping onto the blue fuel drum, pretending to discover it all over again.

Twice, a maintenance worker wandered too close, close enough that my hand found the Glock without thinking. Once, a stray dog nosed the door. We looked at each other through the gap for a second before he lost interest and padded away, nails ticking on the concrete.

Time stretched and warped in here. Long elastic minutes that snapped tight without warning.

Late afternoon, the heat rising off the tarmac turned the far hangars into something unreal—paper cut-outs in a mirage. Then a mid-sized private jet came in low and smooth.

The stairs were wheeled up before the engines had even spun down.

She came out first.

Kate. Laughing at something over her shoulder, hair catching the light. Last time I'd seen her in person, she'd been dust-streaked and sunburned at the FOB in Afghanistan. Now she looked untouchable, like she'd walked out of a magazine spread.

And then Voss.

For a second, I thought my eyes were playing tricks on me. Gone were the gym shorts, the scuffed ballcap, the sweat-dark tank top. He was in a pale linen suit, cut so sharp it could've drawn blood. Expensive dark lenses hid his eyes, but the cocky arrogance was still in his gait.

Two men I didn't recognize followed them down the stairs. They crossed the tarmac together toward a waiting black Mercedes convoy.

Through the parabolic mic, I caught fragments—commentary on the heat, a burst of laughter. It didn't matter. Seeing them alive, together, was enough to hit me low in the gut.

The ghosts weren't just back. They were thriving.

I packed my gear fast and darted to the sad little car I had procured. The battered Peugeot started after sulking for a moment, and I eased out of the airfield service road, two cars back, one lane over.

The city was in its evening rhythm. Flat light on the harbor. Street lights flickering to life one at a time. Motorbikes darting between taxis. The kind of slow bustle you can hide inside.

The convoy pulled under the awning of a waterfront hotel, dusty palm trees swaying in front.

The valet line swallowed the convoy; I let a taxi slide between us and parked a street over in the shadow of a shuttered travel agency. I took the bag with my kit and walked like I had a reservation somewhere. I found a service stairwell in the building across the street, four flights, push-bar door, rooftop gravel still blisteringly hot from the afternoon sun.

From there, the sea was a pane of black glass scored with silver where the streetlights hit it. The hotel restaurant's top-floor windows glowed the color of warm brass. I hoped this was where they were headed. I crouched behind a wheezing air-conditioning unit and put the kit together the way I've done it a hundred times: parabolic on the short tripod, gaffer-taped low to cut the wind; laser mic on a foam block, the beam skittering until I calmed it with a thumb and a breath. Every rumble in the street made the glass vibrate; I dialed out the jitter, adjusted for thickness, and waited for the hiss in my ear to turn into voices.

The private room was just inside the glass. Four seats, linen, polished silver, a waiter doing the quiet dance of someone who knows his tips will be good.

Through the scope, I found Kate first. She leaned back with her hair tucked behind one ear, at home in her skin. Voss sat to her right—heavier across the shoulders than I remembered. Opposite was a pale Englishman in a linen jacket, fifty-something, academic tan that never quite takes, and a darker man with gold cufflinks and careful posture, the look of old money raised on discretion.

Cutlery chimed, the waiter poured wine. The mic steadied. Then Kate's voice, clean through the hiss, as if she'd leaned toward me.

"I thought you were a Budweiser man, Voss."

He laughed, low. "I'm branching out. Spent a week in Provence last year—figured I should at least learn what the fuss is about."

The Englishman: "And?"

"Turns out French wine doesn't taste like it's been filtered through a gym sock. Still can't pronounce half the names, but I'm making progress."

Kate smiled. "Next thing you know, he'll be reading poetry."

"Don't push it."

The tanned man tipped his glass toward Voss. "Ever try Douro reds? Portuguese. Stronger than they look."

"I'll put it on my list."

I shifted my elbow, felt hot tar grit bite through fabric. A slight breeze coming from the sea occasionally gave a welcome respite to the heat and the smell of roofing tar. Inside, the talk wandered to holiday houses. The Englishman—Harcourt, I learned three minutes later—had closed on a place in the Azores. His wife was "bossing builders around." Kate liked Amalfi—"if you know the right Italians"—and Voss said he preferred any place where you couldn't see your neighbor's windows.

It would have been easy to forget why I was there. People, wine, a view. Then Harcourt swirled his glass and made things interesting.

"Did you ever close that thing in the Congo?"

The darker man, Duarte, sighed. "Closed, yes. But twenty-seven warlords claiming the same diamond pits make for a headache. They'll shake you down twice before breakfast if they think you've got an extra truck in the yard."

Voss leaned back, half-grin in place. "We should consolidate them somehow."

Kate speared an olive, didn't look up. "We did that in Sierra Leone in '99. Played the Revolutionary United Front remnants off each other until one swallowed the rest. Only had to bribe one man after that."

Harcourt chuckled. "And that one man owed his throne to you."

"Not owed." She set the fork down. "Rented. We stopped paying, he stopped being useful."

Laughter. Light, unforced.

"Remember Chad?" Voss said. "Three million to unseat a president, and they still thanked us in the press release."

"Mali was cleaner," Kate said. "Less budget, better ROI. Sometimes chaos is the sustainable choice."

Duarte chuckled.

"To a healthy return on investment..." Harcourt lifted his glass.

The recorder's red light ticked steadily in the corner of my eye, logging every word. Through the scope, I watched the waiter's hands—steady, respectful, practiced. Four people eating dinner with the kind of composure you get from being protected by money and men like Voss.

More shop talk about past operations ensued: A militia commander who inflated his headcount by counting village boys with rusted hunting rifles, then swore the "faulty British maps" had made him overestimate his own army. A "training mishap" at an airstrip in Kivu that destroyed the only functional transport plane for the opposing side, forcing their retreat without a single shot. A food aid "partnership" in Monrovia, where half the rice shipment went missing in port, only to reappear weeks later in the militia's own supply tents.

Then Duarte leaned in.

"And tomorrow's client?"

Kate: "Met him once in Aleppo. Runs a disciplined crew for his size. Keeps the splinter factions in line—for now."

Voss: "Manpower's solid. Funding depends on Gulf backers staying interested."

Harcourt: "Distribution's stable. Tripoli to Mersin is fine as long as Turkish customs keep looking the other way. Beirut's still tricky."

"Once tomorrow's meeting is sealed," Kate said, "we're ready to execute inside six weeks."

Voss's grin sharpened. "He calls it a franchise model. Says an al-

Qaeda branch is more profitable than a McDonald's franchise—better brand recognition where he's from."

"Just make sure the press don't run with that line," Harcourt said.

Duarte set his glass, "Corniche Club, yes? The embassy crowd likes to see us 'networking.'"

"Private terrace," Voss said. "Seven sharp."

They were back to wine after that—vintages, vineyards, the Azores again. Through the scope, Kate's face softened into a smile I'd seen once before in a dusty Afghan FOB, when the world was simpler because I didn't know what it really was.

I let the mics run until the conversation thinned into comfortable silence and the check appeared in the waiter's hand like a conjuring trick.

I packed in reverse order, quickly disassembling all my equipment, then made for the stairwell door. At the bottom of the stairs, a kitchen boy smoked by the exit and didn't look at me.

I threaded through some stinking back alleys until I came to the Peugeot. I jumped in the car and headed to the waterfront. I parked three blocks off and walked the rest, staying under the shade of the trees that lined the street. From the landward side, the Corniche Club looked like every other piece of Gulf vanity architecture: white façade, too much glass, a revolving door where the valets smoked until a guest appeared. Security drifted in pairs, not enough to rattle the clientele, just enough to give them stories to tell. Cameras sat where you'd expect. Sightlines were clean. All of it ordinary, until you thought about why people chose to eat here.

I circled the block and came down to the waterfront. The club's terrace clung to the seaward side, perched over the Corniche like a glass jaw daring you to swing. From the sidewalk by the seawall, I could see the neat rows of tables, all turned toward the bay where fishing dhows and cargo haulers slid past on different schedules. White railings caught the light; the sheet of glass behind them bounced the sun back into my eyes. It was perfect theater—every diner framed against the horizon, pretending to watch the water while watching each other.

From the sidewalk, I felt like a man standing under a floodlight; anyone on the terrace could have looked down and picked me out. I fretted about how I would listen in on tomorrow's conversation. The sea and the wind created enormous noise pollution, and the glass on the terrace was angled just enough to redirect the laser on my parabolic mic. My surveillance kit would be useless. If I wanted to eavesdrop on this meeting, I'd have to be inside, close enough to smell the tobacco on their breath.

I bought a newspaper from a boy running his route and stood at the seawall staring at the terrace, over the open paper. Seven o'clock tomorrow evening, they'd be out there, selling terror like a pyramid scheme. Kate would sell the illusion of control. Harcourt would sell banking services. Duarte would sell him shipping routes. Voss would sell him the idea that he mattered.

I folded the paper, dropped it in the bin, and checked my watch. I'd be spending my evening working on a convincing disguise.

CHAPTER 37

They had already finished their first bottle of champagne when I took my seat. Voss motioned to the waiter and ordered a bottle of Châteauneuf-du-Pape. Kate leaned in, smiling at something only meant for him. They looked comfortable, like this was their natural habitat, not the shadows where I'd last known them.

Being in close proximity to them together hit me harder than I expected. Every bone in my body screamed to cross the terrace, drag Voss out of his chair, and put a bullet in his brain. Kate wasn't any better; she was supposed to be dead, and yet here she was, laughing like the grave had been just another cover story.

I forced my hand to stay still on the table, keeping the napkin draped across my lap. A little directional mic rested under it, angled at their end of the terrace. A discreet earpiece fed their conversation to me.

I'd spent the morning dyeing my skin a shade darker, my hair a matte black, beard trimmed into the style you saw on men back from Dubai. Cheap cologne dulled the last trace of dye and ammonia. The clothes were just right for the part—pressed shirt open at the collar, gold-plated watch, shoes polished but cheap if you looked closely. Not perfect, but good enough for a man eating alone in a room full of merchants and contractors who'd come home with pockets full of Gulf money.

My burner phone buzzed on the table as I studied the Nova-Terra group using my peripherals. A message from Victoria. Short, clipped, like everything she wrote these days: "Rome contact secured. Visa in motion. Clearance in days."

For the first time in weeks, I almost believed there was a way out. Maybe there was still a way to end this without another body in the ground. I typed back that I'd call her after the meeting at the Corniche Club, that I would move Amira to the villa.

I slid the phone into my pocket and told myself I believed it. Then I lifted the glass and glanced across the terrace. Harcourt quaffed his bubbly, the casual academic. Duarte grinning at some joke, too perfect teeth flashing white. Kate sat poised, at home, eyes flicking between them like she was running a chessboard. And Voss, cocky as ever, the center of gravity.

Their buyer entered without ceremony, flanked by two aides. I recognized him instantly, Abu Khalid, an up-and-coming player among the Syrian resistance movements organizing to overthrow the Assad regime. The man I'd seen in classified reports, cables, and grainy photos wearing tribal robes, a uniform cap, the long beard of a warlord who wanted his enemies to tremble. Now he wore an Italian suit, charcoal with a faint pinstripe, cut to fit. His beard trimmed short, hair slicked. Not a desert chieftain. A client who had learned the language of boardrooms.

The waiters moved fast, pulling a chair, pouring wine he didn't touch. Voss greeted him like an old friend, laughter loud enough to draw a glance from another table. Kate stayed quiet, sliding documents across, her voice low, professional.

I adjusted the tiny mic under my napkin, the feed crackled, then cleared.

Voss's voice, smooth: "Delivery in two weeks. Three if you want the full complement of launchers. Transit under aid convoys, paperwork airtight."

"Not surplus stock. New issue, latest generation. Trainers will embed just long enough to make your men proficient, then disappear," Kate added.

Abu Khalid leaned back, letting silence work for him. When he spoke, it was deliberate, measured. "The price is high. Too high. Risk is higher still. For that number, I expect more than promises and two dozen launchers."

Voss smiled. "You'll have enough to blind a squadron. That's worth the ticket."

Abu Khalid shook his head, a small, contemptuous flick. "I want drones. Not toys, not castoffs. Eyes in the sky, Western tech. And body armor. Plates that don't crack like tin."

For a moment, the table was quiet but for the clink of glass. Kate leaned in, voice even but edged. "That can be arranged. The package will expand to two UAVs with encrypted control and ceramic plates. But the window stays the same. Two weeks."

Abu Khalid let the corner of his mouth curl, a predator's grin. "Better. Still not enough. You want my signature tonight, you cut the price by a fifth. Otherwise, I walk, and you sell your toys to children."

Harcourt leaned forward with a patient smile, "A fifth is blood from a stone." He held Abu Khalid's gaze, then gave a small shrug. "But perhaps we can bleed together. You'll have your discount this time. Consider it a gesture of goodwill to seal a new friendship."

The glasses touched at last. The deal, and the danger, sealed.

I kept my head down, fork halfway to my mouth, body tight. It should have been just another meeting to record and report. But listening to Kate pitch missiles and Voss grinning like it was business as usual, I saw the fallout in my head: smoking wreckage on desert runways, dead Americans and British boys like Baz and Riley zipped into bags, civilians shredded because someone wanted leverage. Another war fed, another million graves dug. Every nerve in my body wanted to flip the table and end it right there. Instead, I chewed, swallowed, and stayed still.

Voss poured more wine, laughing at a line I didn't catch. Then he leaned back and let his eyes wander lazily over the terrace.

When they reached me, they paused. His gaze lingered a beat too long, then a devious grin slid onto his face, slow and certain. A hunter spotting a footprint.

I kept my head down, looking at my plate, cut into the lamb, chewed like I hadn't noticed. But I knew. He'd seen through the dye, the beard, the posture. Not the surface, but my habits. How I checked exits. How I smoked. The things you can't paint over.

The little mic felt like an anvil on my thigh. I drained the last of my glass, dropped bills on the table, and rose. Walked out calm. Every step wired with the urge to run.

The fountain was as it had always been: dry, broken, and ignored. The café beside it was shuttered now, but I remembered the first time I'd seen her there. She'd looked up from a chipped porcelain cup, those hunted, dark eyes boring into me.

I crouched, fingers finding the loose tile by muscle memory, and slid the note underneath: *Compromised. Get to villa immediately. Bring nothing.*

Tile back in place, I scanned the street corners. No tails. Not yet.

I straightened, kept moving, blending with the late workers trudging home. The Peugeot was three streets over, sulking where I'd left it. I didn't go for it. Not yet. First, the flat. I needed the tranche of evidence that I had stashed.

My key slid into the lock. Quiet. Wrong quiet. I paused. The hair on the door jamb was gone.

I pulled out the Glock, threw open the door, and dove into the dark room headfirst just as several shots rang out from a dark corner by the window. The muzzle flashes illuminated a large, bearded man. I put two rounds in his belly and one in his throat before I hit the ground.

Before I could regain my feet, the second one was on me, kicking the gun out of my hand and slashing wildly with a knife. The back of my left shoulder exploded in pain as the scything edge of the blade caught it. I backpedaled, hands up in a defensive posture, eyes trying to adjust to the darkness. I heard the scuff of sneaker against floorboard to my left and sidestepped just as another onslaught began. I redirected my attacker using his own momentum to drive his skull into the wall with a sickening thud. I brought a heel down hard on his jaw to make sure.

Silence. I stood shaking, wiped my face with the back of my sleeve. I went for the rucksack—photos, recordings, everything that mattered. I dug out my field medical kit and found a medical stapler. I doused the seeping wound with betadine, closed it up, slapped on a dressing, and bolted out to the Peugeot.

They'd be swarming the city soon.

The old car turned over with a cough, then roared as I jammed it into gear.

Flickering streetlamps illuminated shuttered shopfronts. I cut across alleys, through market stalls closing for the night, tires screeching at every turn. My eyes flicked from rearview to windshield to side mirrors, half-expecting headlights locking on.

In the glass I saw my own face, streaked with sweat and blood. Saw ghosts of Baz, the Major, Sergeant Rai, of every dead man I thought I'd buried back in Qala-ye Khun.

CHAPTER 38

The drive back to the villa was blind panic. I killed the lights a hundred meters out, let the car roll the last stretch with only the tick of the cooling engine for company. I sprinted to the gates, pounding on the metal with my fist.

The bolts drew back, and Yousef's narrow face appeared through the crack, pistol in hand. He looked me up and down, saw the blood on my shirt, the wildness in my eyes.

"Open the safe," I said. My voice was raw. "Now. We're out of time."

He hesitated, trying to get a question out, but I shoved past him. Whatever explanation I owed would have to wait.

Seb was in the living room. Half-drunk, shirt half-open, sprawled across the sofa like he was a permanent feature. Layla, the young servant girl, was kneading his shoulders, a glass of Scotch balanced in his hand. The television played to itself in the corner, some old British comedy on satellite.

"Get up, they're coming—we need to get ready."

Seb squinted up at me, bleary-eyed, annoyed. "Stop barking. You'll frighten the girl."

I hauled him upright by the collar and slapped him hard across the face. The glass shattered on the tiles.

"Men are coming here to kill us," I said. "Get off your ass."

He staggered, blinking, slack with disbelief. "Don't be absurd. They wouldn't dare. This is British property."

"Tell it to them." I dragged him toward the basement.

The safe was already open when we got there. Yousef had pulled the steel door wide and was laying out weapons across the concrete floor in neat rows.

I took quick stock.

- Two M240 machine guns.
- Six L119A1 carbines.
- Ten Glock 19s.
- Claymores, grenades.
- Plate carriers.
- NVGs.
- Suppressors.
- Crates of ammunition

Yousef was already working methodically, checking bolts, ejecting a faulty magazine, setting it aside. His hands were steady. "I told them this day would come," he said. "They laughed."

He slid a pistol into his belt and picked up a rifle, weighing it in his hands. "My brother died with nothing in his hands," he said. "I won't."

Seb swayed against the doorframe, staring at the kit with thin disdain. "Jesus Christ. What is all this? Some bloody commando fantasy?"

No one answered.

We worked fast. The villa groaned with the noise of preparation: sandbags thumping on the tiles, rifles clattering, grenades rolling into corners. The place turned inside out.

Yousef hauled the machine guns to the roof. We found a forgotten pile of sandbags behind the shed, rotted and hard, but usable. We stacked them in the night wind and built crude nests facing the street and the terrace. He lined the belt through the receiver, tested the arc of fire.

I wired claymores to the outer approaches—the front gate and the entrance to the terrace. Firing cables trailed back through broken windows, taped down against the tiles.

Spare rifles went into stairwells, behind courtyard walls, under overturned tables. Ammunition was redistributed into small stashes, tucked into window alcoves, and under rugs.

In the courtyard, we dragged discarded cinder blocks into breastworks. My hands were raw, my clothes heavy with sweat, my fresh knife wound screaming against the staples.

Yousef watched me with quiet respect. "You've done this before," he said.

"Not like this," I told him. "Never like this."

Seb came down again while we were working. He waved his phone like a weapon.

"London isn't answering. I've called half a dozen numbers. Nothing. Not even the Duty Officer number at the Main Office. They can't just leave us here."

"They're not coming," I said.

He stared at me, white-faced. "Christ. *Jesus Christ—*" His voice cracked, then his shoulders went limp. He looked at the armor piled against the wall. Slowly, as though it weighed a hundred kilos, he picked up a vest and strapped it across his chest. Fumbled with the straps.

"Do tell me if I've put this on backwards," he said. "Would be just my luck to die in the wrong kit." He checked the fit with shaking hands, then reached for a rifle, tested its balance, checked the sights, and chambered a round, his mouth set. "We'll see. I did well enough during my field training. Maybe it will all come back to me."

There was something steadier in his voice now. Dry, fatalistic.

A flicker of the old Eton polish.

"I'll go barricade some windows."

The girl was still in the living room, pressed small against the wall. I pulled her aside, found a vest that was almost her size, and slipped it onto her narrow frame.

"It's too heavy," she whispered.

"Better than nothing." I pressed a pistol into her hand, showed her how to line the sights, and squeeze the trigger. "Stay low. Stay hidden. Only if you have to."

She nodded, eyes shining with fear and something else. Pride, maybe. "I will."

We did final checks in silence. Body armor cinched tight, NVGs clipped to helmets, magazines filled and slotted into pouches. Radio checks. Red-lensed torches kept the house in shadow. Every window was black. The villa seemed to be holding its breath.

In the courtyard, Seb leaned against a cinder block wall, armor loose on his thin frame, rifle heavy in his hand. For once, he wasn't shaking. His voice had that old half-drunk dryness again, but steadier now.

"Suppose I fetch us a whisky while we wait?"

I shot him a look.

Seb shrugged. "Shame. Got a bottle in there worth a small fortune. Hate to leave it for the bloody heathens."

He continued, "The Colonel, my father, used to bore me senseless with stories of Arnhem, you know, Operation Market Garden? Every bloody Sunday at the club fire. All the colonels and brigadiers rattling their glasses, going on about how the Empire was held together by chaps who stayed cheerful while the whole world fell on their heads. The Colonel said I'd never be half a man unless I learned how to die properly."

He gave a small, bitter smile. "I thought it was nonsense. Sandhurst myths meant to scare us into becoming little tin soldiers. But here we are, eh? No cavalry, no evacuation boats. Just us, holding the fort like it's 1944 and the Huns are closing in."

He checked the rifle, pulling the bolt back just enough to verify a round was chambered, and looked at me. "Suppose the old bastard would say this is character-building." His mouth twitched. "*How can man die better than facing fearful odds, for the ashes of his fathers,*
And the temples of his Gods?"

I had no answer.

From the roof, Yousef's voice cut the silence. "Vehicle! Fast! Coming straight for the gate!"

Seb straightened and raised the rifle to his shoulder. I slid to the gate, weapon up, pulse loud in my ears. The engine noise filled the night.

Headlights flared, then a battered car slewed to a halt against the sandbags. The door flew open.

Amira stumbled out, eyes wide, terrified, scanning behind her.

"Thank God you made it," I breathed, swinging the gate open, rushing to pull her inside. Relief flooded me. Now I could protect her; now she was safe.

She slipped through the gate, clutching at my arm. Seb called from behind the wall, half a laugh in his voice. "Well. Reinforcements, after all—"

The night cracked.

One rifle shot.

Amira jerked hard against me, breath leaving in a gasp, crimson blooming across her back. She sagged in my arms, eyes wide with shock.

The echo of the rifle rolled across the street, flat and endless.

And then there was only the sound of her breathing, shallow and failing, and the weight of her in my arms.

CHAPTER 39

Amira's breaths were shallow, ragged whispers rattling through her chest. I held her hand as if I could will her to stay, fingers cold against mine. The courtyard around us was lit only by the glow of a lantern on its last fumes. Somewhere beyond the walls, engines growled in the dark.

Her eyes found me one last time. The fear was gone. What was left was something harder, something almost like defiance. Her lips moved, but the sound was no louder than a sigh.

I bent closer. "I'm here."

Her hand twitched once, then stilled. Her head lolled to the side, the breath leaving her. For a moment, I stayed there, fore-head pressed against hers, the world held at arm's length.

A shout from the roof broke it. Yousef, urgent, already moving to the gun. And the engines I'd heard were closer now, roaring, headlights bouncing across the dirt road toward the gate.

I swallowed, lifted Amira into my arms. She weighed nothing. I carried her inside, past the threshold, into the cool dark of the villa. I lay her down on a couch and brushed the hair from her face.

Then the villa shook with the first hammer of Yousef's gun, the roar rattling through plaster and stone. The battle had come, and there was no time for grief.

I shouldered my rifle, stepped back into the furnace night.

Tracers ripped across the gate and found the trucks. One windshield exploded inward; the Toyota veered sideways and ploughed into the stone wall. The other skidded to a halt, its bed already half-empty — men tumbled off it like burning leaves, their bodies shredded mid-jump.

Some of them made it. Three, maybe four, crouched low behind the twisted gate, spraying wild bursts through the bars. Rounds pinged off the stone, whining past my ear. Seb was next to me at the cinder-block barricade, tight grin under his sweat. We popped up in short bursts, answering with sharp cracks, stone dust spraying the wall where their rounds hit.

I saw the flashes through smoke, two men crouched low, pressing forward behind the wreckage. I thumbed the clacker. The world went white. The concussion slammed me back behind cover, the gate blown outward in a fan of blood and smoke. When the ringing cleared, nothing moved. Only the sound of a dying engine ticking itself out.

No time to breathe.

The machine gun opened up again. "East wall! They're over!" Yousef's voice cracked through the radio, sharp with strain.

"Hold the courtyard!" I shouted to Seb, already moving. Rifle up, I sprinted along the villa's flank, keeping tight to the wall, its shadow wrapping me close. I sliced the corner, careful not to expose my body.

Halfway down, I saw them. Three shapes in the gloom. One barely a teenager, another old enough to be his grandfather. Both held their rifles wrong, eyes wide, faces frozen in fear. Terrified.

The third man was braver—or more desperate. He was at a shuttered window, smashing the butt of his rifle into the wood, each blow sending cracks splintering across the frame.

The boy and the old man went down in pairs of shots, center mass. Quick. The window-man got a burst that blew him sideways into the shutters.

The silence felt strange and uneasy. My shirt was soaked with sweat under my plate carrier, sweat stinging in my eyes. I swapped mags, then started back toward the courtyard.

Then the world shook again.

A dull, heavy thump from the terrace on the north side of the villa, followed by the sound of debris raining down. Plastic explosives. I knew the sound, the sharpness of it. Local militias for hire didn't use plastics. This wasn't the work of amateurs. My stomach knotted. Someone else was out there, pulling strings. I pushed towards the terrace.

I rounded the corner in time to see five figures charging through the breach. Yousef's heavy gun tore into two of them, their shredded bodies falling into the pool, threads of red streaked the blue water. I opened up on the three survivors, who were out of Yousef's line of fire. I dropped one, and the other two peppered my position with 7.62.

There was a flash like a sun switched on in the middle of the night. Both men vanished in fire and dirt. Yousef had lit off the claymore. The shockwave knocked me back, and grit sprayed into my mouth. I gagged on the taste, eyes watering. I forced myself back toward the courtyard.

Smoke drifted in lazy sheets, the air burnt and sharp. Our cinder-block cover looked like something out of Stalingrad: chipped to hell, pocked with holes. The body armor we'd draped across it was torn open, Kevlar spilling out like tufts of cotton.

Seb slid down against it, wiped sweat across his forehead, and uncapped a leather flask with that permanent half-smirk.

"Might as well drink up before the Empire falls." He took a swig and offered it to me.

I hesitated, then drank deep. Expensive scotch. The burn felt good going down, but not enough to drown the thought of Amira lying on the couch just inside. I lit a cigarette.

"Got any more of those?"

I looked up. Yousef's head edged over the roofline. I tossed the pack. He caught it one-handed, lit up, and the smoke drifted down toward us.

"You think this is bad? Beirut, '86. Half the city was burning, shells dropping every night. At least here we know who's shooting."

Seb let out a bark of laughter and took another swallow. "Christ, the Colonel would've loved this. Shame we don't have scarlet tunics, bugles, and regimental colors."

The unmistakable whine of an incoming RPG sent us diving behind our wall. The impact slammed the twisted gate clean off its hinges and blew it inward in a storm of iron and fire. Smoke and dust filled the courtyard, thick enough to choke.

Then the Molotovs came. Bottles shattered, flames spreading across stone and tile. The heat clawed at us as we ducked low behind what cover was left. Seb batted fire off his sleeve, cursing, while rounds hammered our position, sparks strobing the air.

We returned fire in bursts, timing shots between ricochets. I pitched a grenade through the smoke. The blast doused some of the fire and scattered shadows at the gate. Seb followed it up with one of his own. "That'll keep them honest," he said through gritted teeth.

Yousef's voice crackled through the radio. "Moving to MG1." Seconds later, his gun tore back into life, hammering over the shattered gate, keeping us from being buried alive.

Thank God for Yousef and his 240s. We might ride it out yet.

Then came his voice again, grim now: "More men, north wall breach. Moving back to MG2."

The heavy gun on the north side of the villa opened up, fast, sharp. Then it stopped. Mid-burst.

Silence.

I called his name over the radio. Nothing. Seb didn't look at me when he said, "That'll be the end of Yousef then."

Gunfire raked both sides of the villa. More Molotovs sailed in, flames licking high against the courtyard walls. Seb shouted that the cinder blocks wouldn't hold another minute.

I grabbed his arm and dragged him toward the villa. The courtyard had become a furnace. Fire, smoke, and muzzle flashes blended into a single nightmare strobe.

I glanced up at the roofline before ducking inside. Where I'd tossed the cigarettes moments earlier, only a limp foot hung over the roofline. We slammed the doors closed, gunfire chewing the walls outside.

CHAPTER 40

The formal reception room stretched wide, with marble floors, arches, and a chandelier swaying faintly from the shock of the last blast. It should have felt grand. All I could see was the couch.

She looked small there. Amira's body lay where I'd placed her, the linen of her dress dark with a thick bloom of dried blood. One arm dangled limply over the cushion, her head was turned toward me as if she were only sleeping. For half a second, I thought she might stir, open her eyes.

Seb was already moving, rifle up, eyes cutting across the corners.
"Stay sharp," he yelled. "They'll be inside any second."

Movement. Shadows flickered through the glass doors that opened onto the terrace. I snapped three rounds. One figure crumpled and stayed down.

"Dining room!" Seb barked.

Something metal clattered across the tiles: a flash, a crack like the world splitting open. Everything went white, sound sucked out, vision scorched to nothing.

Instinct drove me. I hurled myself toward where I'd last seen Seb, colliding with him and dragging him down. My ears rang painfully, and the smell of hot magnesium burned my nostrils. Shapes moved in the arched doorway. Black figures flowed in low, weapons up, sweeping corners with practiced precision.

Not boys. Not farmers. Four professionals, stacked tight, splitting left and right.

We were in a tangle behind the bulk of a couch out of their line of sight. For now. I drew my Glock and leaned around one corner of the sofa, releasing rounds low, rapid fire. The first man on the right went down screaming, several rounds slamming into his legs and groin. The second whipped his gun towards me, but praying Seb would handle the other two, I surged up before he could level, working the trigger as fast as I could, rounds tearing into his plates and his arms. He staggered. I crashed into him, grabbed him by the collar, wrenched him upright into a choke, and dragged him back. His body was jerking, the ceramic plates pinging, as incoming fire from his friends slammed into him. A warm fountain of blood sprayed me as one round ripped through my human shield's neck.

Seb was still down, blinking the stun out of his eyes. He finally popped up, like he had been awoken from a deep sleep, and sent several controlled bursts into the two remaining attackers. One spun into the dining room doorway, a round had caught him in his side, where there were no ceramic plates to protect him. Seb cut him down with a follow-up to the head. The last man dove for cover behind a toppled chair, firing wildly.

I let my shield drop, hauled my rifle up from the sling, and laid down suppressing fire. Seb army crawled to the other side of the room, leaned into the sight line, and put the last man flat with two more rounds.

"Christ almighty. Got him," Seb said, a hint of surprise in his voice.

For a moment, the only sounds were my breathing and the wet rattles of the men dying on the tiles. Seb crouched against the wall, sleeve black with blood, rifle still steady. His eyes met mine, sharp but rattled.

"What do you reckon? What are our odds of getting out of here?"

I didn't answer.

"That good, eh?"

I heard footsteps in the dining room. Careful, deliberate.

We gave each other a look and brought up our rifles.

A shadow broke, a face caught in a sliver of light: thick beard, eyes like pits. Voss. We fired as one. Plaster stung my cheek. Seb opened up, too late—Voss had already slipped back into the east wing.

At the same time, a crash echoed from the west wing: glass breaking, furniture going over, voices in Arabic, a door hinge tearing loose.

Seb started after Voss, grinning like a man headed to the gallows. "Let's have him."

"No." I grabbed his sleeve. "He's serious business. You'll get yourself killed. Clear out the west wing."

He bristled, eyes bright with the idea of Voss, then swallowed it down and gave me a thin, aristocratic smile. "Do try to not embarrass me." He swapped magazines and went west, boots skidding on broken glass.

I reloaded, let one breath settle my hands, and pushed alone into the east wing.

The east wing turned the villa into a claustrophobic kill zone: tiled corridors, archways that framed a man like a target, rooms half-dark behind broken shutters. Broken glass signaled my location with every crunch under my boot.

His voice traveled ahead of me.

"Sorry about the girl, *Harrington*," Voss called, light and conversational, somewhere down the hall. "Was she yours? That bullet was meant for you. But one less whore in the world makes for a nice concession, don't you think?"

I ground my teeth until my jaw hurt. *How the hell does he know my real name?* I kept moving, rifle tight in my shoulder, breath coming ragged.

I came to a room and checked the angles before making entry. A sitting room. Overturned chairs and a rug skewed like it had been dragged. A shadow at the edge of my vision disappeared through a side arch. I bolted after it and carefully rounded the corner, finding only a long, empty passage and my pulse hammering in my ears.

He let his voice drift closer. Amused. "Did you really think anyone bought that SAS act?"

I swept a study: scattered papers, a desk knocked sideways, a smear of blood on the jamb. Clear. Empty.

"We had your name before you set foot in Whitehall," he went on, and then two suppressed shots cracked from the dark. I dropped behind a pillar and sent a burst back at the muzzle flash. Nothing.

My throat went dry. "They knew the whole time," I said, barely hearing my own voice.

He laughed, nearer now, as if he were circling me without moving his feet. "OGI thought they were clever. Sending Fletcher's little American burglar boy to play soldier. You weren't undercover, Harrington. You were useful."

Boots pounded somewhere behind the walls. Seb's side? A deeper thump shook dust from a beam. Grenade? I pressed on.

"Why do you think you and the girl survived Afghanistan?" Voss asked, almost bored. "You think it's because you're good? We *let* you live. Somebody had to tell the story. You played your part beautifully."

The temperature in my skull went up ten degrees. Rage is a sharpener if you let it be a tool. It's a blindfold if you let it lead. I kept my muzzle where it needed to be and pushed through the last arch into a larger room.

A library. Or had been. Shelves along two walls, books tumbled like bricks, a table on its side. I cleared left, right, center—

He hit me from the blind side.

We went through the table, and the floor came up hard. My rifle clattered and yanked against my sling, banging my ribs. Voss's forearm slid under my jaw and cinched tight. Not a clean blood choke. He was crushing the windpipe because panic is faster than technique. It still did the job. The edges of the room went black. I clawed at his arm and found rock. He had the angle, his weight, and the confidence of a man who had done this before.

A voice at the doorway, thin with fear: "Stop—"

Layla. She was shaking so hard the pistol trembled in both hands. Tears stood in her eyes, but the barrel didn't waver from Voss.

Voss didn't loosen. He turned his head just enough to see her. "What's this?" he said, almost gently. "A little Joan of Arc?"

He pulled his own sidearm in a blur and fired once.

The shot slapped Layla into the wall. She crumpled, gasping. The round had smacked center mass, but the vest I'd strapped over her dress caught it. She was alive. Maybe.

The shot gave me the inch I needed. I sank my weight, trapped his choking arm with both hands, curled my chin, and twisted hard into him. Space opened for half a second. I drove an elbow back into his ribs and kicked my hips out. Voss and his pistol went flying, and air tore into me like knives.

He didn't give me time to be grateful. Before I had time to bring my rifle up, he came in again heavy, trying to tie up my legs, hands going for eyes, for anything he could tear.

Voss's hand shot down and caught the gun, jerking hard. The sling yanked me sideways like a leash, my shoulder slamming into a wall of books hard enough to rattle my teeth. Books avalanched. Snarling, I clawed at the buckle, popped it free, and let the rifle fall. In this kind of fight, the gun was dead weight.

I hooked my instep behind his calf and swept, going down with him as he fell, and came up knee-on-belly. He bucked like a bull, grabbed for my groin, headbutted my face, bit at my forearm. Dirty and effective. I drove my knee harder, tried to isolate an arm for a submission. He ripped free and rolled. We crashed into the scrollwork of a half-broken chair and broke it the rest of the way.

He backed off two steps and grinned, blood on his teeth. "Is this what they trained you for? Rolling on the floor like a street thug?"

I didn't answer. He wanted to talk; I wanted his airway.

He lunged low, and I sprawled, captured his head and arm, and spun for a triangle. He stacked me, slammed me into the tile, and I let the setup go before he could spike me into unconsciousness. We scrambled to our feet at the same time, both slick with sweat and blood, both breathing like runners.

"Whatever happened to that incompetent little shit in Afghanistan?" he asked between heaving breaths, circling. "*Baz*, was it?"

I feinted high, then yanked his wrist and hauled him over my hip with a throw. He slammed onto his back, and his breath burst out in a grunt, yet he was still fighting, boots kicking at the tiles. I dropped across his chest, pinning him sideways, and wrenched his right arm up against the bend of his shoulder.

His free arm clawed at me, fingers raking across my face, shoving at my ribs, trying to buck me off. I felt his nails catch skin, but I kept cranking the trapped arm higher. His left hand hammered uselessly against my vest, smacking, pushing, anything to break the hold.

"Motherfucker," he hissed, teeth bared.

I cinched down harder, using my weight and both hands to twist his shoulder back. The joint began to creak under the pressure. He thrashed, arching his hips, but my knee dug into his ribs, keeping him pinned. It was all leverage now, his strength against the angle of his own body, and he knew it.

We slid in the dust and splinters, each of us fighting for an inch, the whole world boiled down to bone, pressure, and pain.

He drove an elbow into the stapled wound at my shoulder. White flare. I loosened for half a breath. He heaved and got free and came up again with the same nasty little smile.

Somewhere to the west, a burst of automatic fire rattled the walls. A man screamed and kept screaming until his air ran out. "Come on, you bastards!" I heard Seb's aristocratic voice yell in the distance. I had seconds to finish this before the next wave found me.

We closed again, fists and elbows glancing off shoulders and arms. I faked left, then cut right and yanked his head forward while I kicked his leg out from under him. His balance went, and he crashed hard onto the tiles.

He rolled to his stomach, trying to push up, but I was already on him. I drove my legs around his hips, locking myself to his back, and hooked my heels inside to keep him trapped. My arm slid across his throat, tight and low.

He clawed at my hands, trying to tear them free, but this time I didn't crush his windpipe. I slid the crook of my arm under his jaw, locked my other hand around my bicep, and squeezed with everything I had.

He went wild. Fingers clawed at my eyes and nose and bit at the meat of my hand. I tightened. His thrashing lost rhythm. His heels drummed. The world narrowed to the sound of our breathing and the thud of his heels and the slight, satisfying sleep of the muscles under my arm.

He went limp.

I held a second longer to be sure, then let him sag. My own lungs tore air like it was new. Layla lay where she'd fallen, groaning, trying to breathe through the shock. I crawled to her, pulled her vest straight, checked for penetration. The kevlar had done its job. Her eyes fluttered and found mine, and she made a choked sound, half-sob, half-laugh. I squeezed her hand. "Stay down. Don't move. It's all right."

I went back to Voss, rolled him onto his back, and stripped his gear. Then I grabbed his collar and dragged him. He was heavy, and I was more tired than I wanted to admit. The hall seemed longer than it had been on the way in. We left a smear behind us that didn't belong to just one of us.

Gunfire crackled from the west wing, and something heavy fell. "Seb!" I shouted. No answer. I kept moving.

The basement stairs were narrow and warm, the day's heat trapped in the stone. The exhaustion was hitting me; my knees almost gave out as I half-lifted, half-dropped him onto the landing and let him bounce down the last three steps. He didn't wake up. A bare bulb buzzed overhead, casting everything in a sickly hue.

There was a dusty metal chair in the corner. I hauled Voss into it. He groaned back into consciousness as I got a cuff around his wrist. He jerked once, hard, testing, and I broke his rhythm with a punch to the sternum that knocked the air out of him and maybe a little of the arrogance. Then I cuffed the other wrist. Ankles next, locked tight. I added flex-cuffs around the chair back and his forearms for good measure. He wasn't going anywhere unless I wanted him to.

He slumped, then raised his head. There it was again, his infuriating trademark look, like he wasn't the one handcuffed to a chair. "You think this is over, *boy*?"

I crouched until we were eye to eye. The basement hummed. Somewhere above us, the house moaned under the weight of boots. "No," I said. "I'm just getting started with you, Voss."

CHAPTER 41

The first floor was wrecked. Sprawled bodies, splintered furniture, slick pools of half-congealed blood, and spent shell casings were scattered everywhere.

Bursts of automatic fire thundered from the second floor, hard and fast, rattling through the villa's bones. Someone was laying it on thick, hopefully Seb. I moved for the staircase. More bodies lay slumped at its base, weapons kicked from their hands.

The stairs themselves were a mess of brass and plaster. Every step sent casings tinkling down the stairs. The banister was slick with a handprint of blood, the trail smearing halfway up before vanishing.

At the top, I froze. Three more fighters were crouched just a few meters ahead, their backs to me, firing down the corridor at a barricade. Return bursts snapped back, ricocheting off plaster.

The hallway was a slaughterhouse. Eight lifeless bodies, discarded rifles, empty magazines spilled like loose change. They'd tried to charge the barricade and paid for it in blood.

I moved fast, low. The first man never saw me. Two rounds through the back of his head, and he folded forward like a dropped marionette. The second spun, gun rising. I beat him to it, a center-mass burst slammed him back against the wall, a wet smear trailing as he slid down. The third got half a shout-out before I put him down the same way.

The gunfire stopped. The sudden silence was somehow more jarring than the noise had been.

"Friendly!" I called out down the hall.

"Thank Christ for that!" was the reply.

I shouldered past the barricade of overturned furniture, a desk, a wardrobe, splintered from the impacts of rounds, and into the bedroom beyond. Seb was inside, slumped against the wall, rifle still in his lap. Blood soaked his sleeve, and another dark stain spread across his thigh. His face was pale, but his eyes locked on me, sharp even through the pain.

"About bloody time," he rasped with a forced smile. He nodded at the hallway carnage. "You've missed the party."

I dropped beside him and yanked my med kit open. The smile he gave me was all bluff; he was bleeding out. His skin was chalky, lips edged blue. The wound in his thigh was a mess. Through and through, blood pumping slow but steady. I cinched a tourniquet high and tight. He hissed through his teeth, then flashed me his crooked smile.

"You know," he said, "it's almost a shame I survived. The family would've *adored* a martyr. My portrait in oils, hung in a place of honor in the old pile, all stern jaw and noble sacrifice. 'Here lies Sebastian Cartwright, who died bravely while others did the hard work.'" He barked a short, bitter laugh that ended in a cough. "Now I'll just be the cripple they wheel out at Christmas."

He fished out his flask, and we both took a long pull. He groaned, then whimpered as I shoved QuickClot packets deep into the wound. Once the bleeding slowed, I slapped dressings over both holes.

"Better a cripple than a corpse."

He grimaced, then let out a ragged laugh. "Spoken like a man who's never met my family."

I handed him back his rifle. His grip trembled, but he still worked the bolt and checked the chamber with mechanical care.

"Still in the fight?" I asked.

He smirked faintly, breath ragged. "For now. Go finish your business. I'll make sure no one redecorates the hallway."

I gave him a nod, then stood.

The rest of the house was quiet. I swept room to room: guest suites with broken doors, bedsheets blackened from muzzle flashes. I found Layla, still cowering in the east wing, and sent her up to the second floor to look after Seb.

Amira's body was still on the couch, in the reception room, untouched amid the wreckage. I paused only long enough to cover her with a curtain torn from the wall.

I cleared the courtyard last. The fire had burned itself low, embers hissing on the stone. Our makeshift defensive cinder block walls shattered. Spent brass covered the ground like autumn leaves. Bodies slumped where they'd fallen. No movement.

The silence broke in fragments. First the hiss of wind through broken shutters, then the groan of the villa's beams, then the sound of my own ragged breath.

It was finished, for now.

I turned back inside. There was work left to do in the basement.

CHAPTER 42

I sat across from Voss, smoking and studying him. The bushy beard, the black eyes, the weathered lines on his face. On the table between us: pliers, a hammer, a kitchen carving knife, a hacksaw, a roll of tape, a tourniquet, and a bottle of Seb's expensive scotch.

He tried a smile that didn't belong to his face anymore. "What's this then? You going to sit there and brood me to death?"

I poured myself a large measure of the whisky and drank.

"I've never had someone stare at me this lovingly," he went on. "You gonna interrogate me or fuck me, Harrington? Sorry, but I'm taken."

Silence. Smoke.

"You're not man enough for this. You don't have the stones."

I picked up the pliers and rolled them in my hand.

"I've been through worse," he said, leaning forward as far as the cuffs allowed. "You'll quit before I do."

He pitched his voice high like a child. "Pleeeease, pleeease, don't hurt me." He laughed at his own joke.

I stood. Walked around behind him. Took his right hand in mine and set it on the chair arm. He tried to jerk it free. The cuff stopped him. I gripped the nail on his index finger, snugged the pliers, and pulled.

He snarled.

"That all you've got?" He was panting now. "I've had hangnails hurt worse."

I took the middle finger next. Then the ring. Metal, pressure, tear. The sound of it was small and precise, like staples pulled from wood. Sweat ran off him in sheets. I could tell it was getting harder for him to hold the screams in.

A memory wormed its way to the forefront of my mind: for a moment, I wasn't in that basement. I was twenty-one again, Paris, wrists bound, Lucien Moreau leaning in with the same tool in his hand, my own screams filling the dark. The taste of blood in my mouth. The certainty that I wouldn't live to see morning.

I shoved the memory back down where it belonged. Another finger. Another scream.

I set the pliers down, picked up the hammer, and laid his hand flat again.

He panted, sucking air. "You don't even know what you're asking me for," he said. "Break every bone in my body, and I'll still die with more secrets than you'll ever hold."

I brought the hammer down once. A crack. He jerked and howled. I reset his hand. Brought it down again, a different finger, a different pitch of break. Then another, and another.

"Jesus Christ," he spat, voice shaking. "You think this makes you a man? This makes you pathetic."

I didn't answer. I set the hammer down, took the knife, and cut open his trouser leg. I put the tourniquet on his right leg, up high, and cinched it as tight as I could. I put the hacksaw on the table where he could see it.

He tried to square his shoulders, but fear had already climbed into his eyes. "You're stalling," he said, forcing arrogance he couldn't carry anymore. "I see it. You haven't got the stomach. Go on then, cut. Or are you waiting for Fletcher to hold your hand?"

He pivoted to bargaining. "Listen—listen. I'll tell you what I know about NovaTerra. I'm low-level, but I can give you names. You've seen the warehouses in Benghazi, haven't you? That's one hub. Just one."

I didn't reply. I slid the blade under his skin and went to work.

Color drained from him. "You can't," he moaned.

I kept working.

Desperate now, panic in his voice: "You can't do this. We're both professionals. You need me alive if you want answers."

I picked up the saw.

He broke. Screams tore at the ceiling and died there. He thrashed until the chair rattled, begged until the words fell apart, promised anything, everyone, the whole world, if it would stop.

I finished what I'd started. When it was done, the room rang in the sudden quiet like a bell.

He sagged, chin to chest, drenched in sweat. The tourniquet held. The stump wept anyway.

"...enough," he whispered, voice raw and small. "Enough. Please. I'll talk. Christ, I'll give you everything. Just...stop."

I took the cigarette from my mouth and ground it out on the concrete. My first words since it began were simple. "Then talk."

He talked.

The Afghanistan raid was theater. Karim wasn't some wild dog running a fortress in the hills; he was on their leash. Varga's creature. The CIA's too. For years, he was the perfect cutout: opium moved out under protection, rifles and missiles funneled back the other way. The profits kept their black programs humming and bought half the politicians in Kabul.

But Karim saw opportunity in the smoke of 9/11. The Americans were about to flood the country with troops, cash, contractors. He figured he could use the war to build his own empire—unite all the tribes under his banner, maybe rule all of Afghanistan.

"When he took that journalist, Ashworth, it forced Varga's hand. Forced Langley's too. Karim wasn't just a partner anymore. He was a liability, a man who knew too much and thought he could write his own script," Voss said.

"So they staged a raid. Turned it into theater. You think it was about hostages, about destroying a fortress? Bullshit. It was about clipping wings. Karim had to be shut down, discredited, buried under rubble, so no one would ever trace the heroin or the weapons back to Langley. Or to Varga."

Voss described how Varga ran logistics. Not the face in the compound, the hand behind the curtain. Money in, guns out, cutouts layered through shell companies, charities, and "development" fronts. The CIA took its share for projects you don't brief the Hill on. Politicians got theirs, greased palms wrapped in patriotic speeches. Varga's empire grew, quiet and clean.

He kept talking because my silence gave him no place to stop. "You think that was it?" he said, a half-laugh breaking on his teeth. "A castle in the Afghan hills? That was nothing. A link in the chain. This runs globally. Africa, South America, the Balkans. Drugs, guns, cash. Aid crates one way, medicine stamped on the side, rifles the other. Private security firms, NGOs, and foundations with marble lobbies. Half the men giving speeches at the UN owe their careers to it."

He lifted his head. Blood stained his teeth when he smiled. "What do you think you're going to do, Harrington? Take on the whole power structure of the world? Prime ministers, senators, heads of state? You're not at war with one man. You're at war with the system that owns everything you touch."

He coughed until it bent him. When he could breathe again, he forced the old smirk. "Varga's the only one bold enough to stop hiding," he said. "He's building something permanent. He says his father dreamed of something called a *'Silent Directorate'*—

a new aristocracy of the best and brightest, chosen to run the world cleanly, without the chaos of the old order. Varga's the son who listened."

I let him ramble until the edge left his voice and all that was left was the kind of honesty men find at the bottom of pain. I didn't chase footnotes. I took the pieces I needed and laid them where they belonged in my head.

He slumped back, eyes unfocused. When he spoke again, it was almost gentle. "They tortured you once, didn't they? In Paris? I saw it in your file." His lips lifted. "Now look at you. You think you win by breaking me? You've already lost. This work, this world Harry dragged you into, it eats men like you alive. The more you fight it, the more you become it. One day you'll look in the mirror and—"

I reached into the small of my back, pulled out the Glock, and put a single round through his head. The sound slapped the walls and was gone. His smile left with it.

I sat, poured scotch. Seb was right, it was expensive. I lit an equally expensive cigar I'd found in Seb's humidor while I was gathering the tools. Smoke rose and held in the bulb's cone of light.

Paris came back the way bad dreams do—sound before picture. Water in my lungs; Lucien Moreau's voice, patient, almost kind, asking the same question over and over. The horror of the pliers. Electrodes next. Begging him to stop. Twenty-one, stupid, and convinced the world was a fair fight if you shook hands before you started.

The scotch burned on the way down. For a second, the basement felt like that same room, only I'd changed chairs: the smoke, the smell of sweat and mildew.

Upstairs, the house settled into its wounds: beams creaking, wind finding gaps in broken shutters. I sat with him in the quiet until the cigar burned to a nub and the bottle was nearly gone.

Before the sun rose, I buried Amira and Yousef on the bluff behind the villa. A patch of ground with a view of the sea, with nothing but the wind and the salt air for company. Then I loaded Seb and Layla in a car and burned the villa and the bodies. I left Voss's body dangling from the roof by his remaining foot, clothes cut away. I dropped Layla at the bus station, pressed a roll of American bills into her hand, told her to leave Benghazi and not look back. And Seb, I hauled half-drunk and half-broken, onto the first flight out of Benina with a letter to Harry tucked in his coat.

CHAPTER 43

The Benina Airport looked like every airport in the world at seven in the morning—sickly fluorescents, dull echoes, a smell of old coffee and floor polish. I moved through the terminal half on instinct, half on fumes. Everything hurt. My ribs throbbed with every breath, and my left arm barely worked.

I just wanted out of Libya. Out of the heat, out of the blood, out of the memory of Amira bleeding out in my arms.

I spotted her before I heard her.

Kate. Standing alone beside a column, hands tucked into the sleeves of her jacket. Too still. Too composed. But her eyes were tired. Rimmed red, dark circles.

"Tom," she said softly.

I stopped so fast the people behind me veered around.

"Don't."

Her lips parted like she'd been slapped. She took half a step forward.

"I came to—"

"I know what you came to do." My voice carried farther than I intended. Two men by the window glanced over. I lowered it. "Save the performance. I heard you. You and Voss talking about your 'business' like you were discussing the weather."

I thought I had quenched my rage at the villa, but one look at her and it was back, hot and sharp.

Kate blinked, and for the first time since I'd known her, she looked unsure.

“You’re no innocent,” I said, struggling to keep my voice low and calm. “Not after what you did at the villa. Not after what happened to *her*.”

The last word almost cracked. I forced it steady and stepped toward her, fists clenched, then caught myself. Passengers breezed past us. Wrong place, wrong time to settle scores.

Kate swallowed hard. Her hands tightened in her sleeves, and she seemed to almost disappear into her jacket.

“You’re right,” she said. She stared at the ground, her voice shaking slightly.

“I was part of it. I didn’t want to see what it really was. I told myself I could steer things. Influence decisions. Make it less ugly from the inside.” She let out a hollow breath. “I lied to myself.”

I said nothing. I didn’t trust my voice.

“When they decided you were expendable,” she said, “that was the moment it stopped being theoretical. That was when I realized how far I’d let myself drift. That was when it became personal. I tried to talk them out of going to the villa.” She looked up at me, eyes soft, pleading. “I went to your flat in Benghazi to warn you. You were already gone. I found the two men they sent for you.”

A boarding announcement crackled overhead.

“Varga’s people are suspicious of me now,” she said. “They think I hesitated. They think I warned you.” She shook her head slightly. “They’re watching me. I’m on borrowed time.”

I wanted to tell her I didn’t care. I wanted to turn and walk. But something in the way she shifted her weight, leaning lightly against the column as if her legs were tired, made me hear her out.

“And now you want sympathy?”

Her gaze drifted past me, toward the windows overlooking the tarmac and the dark beyond.

"Tom... haven't you ever wanted to just walk away? Disappear. Start fresh. Be anonymous?"

I stiffened.

She kept going, her voice soft, almost conversational—except she wasn't talking to me. She was talking to memories.

"I think about London sometimes," she said. "Your little apartment, eating take-out noodles. The pub around the corner. For a few weeks, I let myself imagine a normal life. One with a boyfriend and no handlers." A bitter smile flickered. "I held onto that longer than I should have."

She looked at me again, and for a moment, just a moment, and the mask dropped completely.

"I waited too long," she whispered. "Varga doesn't let people walk away."

I didn't believe most of her act. But some part of me wanted to.

"He won't get away with what happened," I said. It came out low and raw. "Not after this."

She studied me, eyes watery, makeup a mess, this wasn't the carefully composed Kate I was used to.

Then she said, almost idly, "He'll be in Paris for the next month."

My pulse ticked.

"Private dinners every night at nineteen hundred," she said. "Same room. Same seat. He likes routine."

She waited to see if I'd stop her. I didn't.

"There's a wine cellar directly beneath the dining room. A delivery entrance that's barely monitored. Minimal guards posted inside. It's... a vulnerability. If someone wanted justice," she said, "that's where it could happen."

I knew she was steering me. I wasn't blind to it. I needed a target. I needed an outlet for my rage. Paris and Varga worked.

Kate stepped closer, not too close, just enough that her voice didn't need to rise.

"Be careful," she said. "Please. You're the only one in this mess I didn't want to lose."

A lie? A confession? Maybe both.

My boarding group was called. People rose, collected bags, shuffled toward the gate.

Kate stepped back, "Goodbye, Tom."

She turned and walked into the crowd without waiting for an answer.

PART III

CHAPTER 44

Creighton leaned back, pen tapping against the metal table.

"So that's Libya."

"That's Libya," Tom said.

"Why is it that everywhere you go, there's a trail of bodies and wreckage?"

Tom folded his arms across his chest. He said nothing.

Churchill broke the silence first, leaning in over the table.

"Let's talk about Paris."

"I studied his routine, every security measure. I learned the background of every employee, every vendor. I built the picture piece by piece."

Churchill cocked his head. "You created a case file, didn't you? Like you were working a sanctioned mission."

A flicker of something, wryness, or weariness, passed across Tom's face. "Old habits die hard."

Churchill reached for a leather briefcase at his feet, drew out a thick folder, and slid it across the steel table.

"This one?"

Tom stared at it for a while, then finally nodded. He opened it and began leafing through his own handwriting, his finger pausing here and there on a line.

"Why don't you walk us through it, the surveillance, the planning?" Churchill said.

Creighton's mouth twisted. "Was the girl, Victoria, involved?"

Tom's hand stilled on the page. He didn't look up.

"No. I cut her off after Libya. There was no need for both of us to go down. She's been through enough."

Tom turned another page, and when he spoke again, his voice had changed; colder, more distant, as though it were coming from a different place. The case file pulled him back to Paris.

I took a fifth-floor flat across from the gates. Curtains drawn, camera lens pressed against the glass. A parabolic mic dressed as a satellite dish on the balcony.

From there, I watched. Timed guard patrols with a stopwatch. Logged how long it took them to move from the gate to the garden hedge. Forty-five seconds, every time. I catalogued faces, printed photos, numbered them, built my own roster of who belonged. Drivers, guards, household staff.

The pattern emerged. SUVs rotated at the corners every four hours. Cameras swept on a twelve-second cycle. Catering vans arrived in the late afternoon.

One day, I dropped a shopping bag near the gate with a recorder inside, just to see. Nobody touched it. Civilians were ignored unless aggressive. It went into the notes. Every detail mattered.

Watching gave me rhythm. But rhythm isn't context. For that, I followed staff.

A bakery driver, a guard off duty, a caterer who liked cheap bars. I bought drinks, said little, let them talk.

One of the drivers rubbed his back, cursed about lugging wine crates down a narrow stairwell while the guards smoked above. He didn't know it mattered, but it confirmed what Kate had told me. A cellar. A blind spot.

I ran vendor plates through a contact in city records. Every service company checked out. No false fronts. Which meant the chaos was real, not manufactured. And real chaos leaves seams.

Varga had the house renovated three years earlier. French law required the architects to file their plans with the Hôtel de Ville.

I broke in one night, forced a filing cabinet, and photographed the drawings under a desk lamp.

The blueprints showed what the chatter and timing already suggested: a service stair leading to a cellar directly beneath the dining room. Heavy timbers above. Reinforced concrete underfoot. The diagrams were sterile, but I filled the margins with notes. Camera angles, silhouettes in the windows, lights switched on and off. Piece by piece, the picture sharpened.

Observation and hearsay weren't enough. To be sure, I had to test the seam.

I tailed a Maison Comtois employee home and noted where the uniforms were laundered. A stolen badge, a borrowed jacket. I shaved, pressed trousers, and clipped the badge to my chest. At dawn, I joined the catering crew at the depot.

At the gate, two guards flipped badges more than scanned them. I was waved through.

Inside, the service corridor stretched long and tiled, harshly lit. Cameras swept every junction—twelve seconds between passes. Two posted guards blocked the junction leading to the main house. They didn't search trays or crates. Catering was assumed clear.

Two Malinois paced the hall with handlers. One pulled at the leash, staring at us. The other whined at the cellar stairs, refusing to go down. The guards laughed, stayed upstairs, and left us to haul the crates below.

I mimicked the staff's body language. Eyes down, quick steps. I carried a crate into the stairwell, narrow, one person at a time. A bottleneck. Vulnerable.

In the cellar, I counted half-empty racks; the floor was concrete, and heavy beams supported the dining room above. Six minutes unsupervised. Then I walked back out, heartbeat steady, teeth clenched. The test was complete. Barely.

I went back a week later. Same cover. Same risk.

Churchill broke in, "Twice inside, without backup. One slip and you'd have been burned before you began."

Tom shifted uncomfortably. "I needed to be sure. I couldn't carry out an assassination based on one single data point."

Churchill nodded skeptically.

This time I lingered. Pretended to straighten bottles after dropping the crate. I saw electrical conduits, cameras above the stairwell, but none in the cellar itself. A blind spot.

I traced the room against the blueprints. The ceiling beams aligned exactly with the position of the dining table above.

I tested the acoustics, clinking bottles. The sound barely carried. Noise wouldn't betray anything down here.

The dogs again. Same pattern. One handler forced the nervous Malinois down two steps, then gave up. The animal wouldn't patrol the cellar.

As I left, a guard stepped into the stairwell. His eyes lingered on my face too long. I thought he'd stop me. I held his gaze, then dropped it like a real caterer trying not to get yelled at. He muttered "temp" under his breath and let me go.

I was convinced now: the seam was real. The bomb plan would work.

"So, your answer wasn't a bullet or a knife, but a bomb. In the middle of Paris," Creighton cut in. "The girl told you to jump, and you asked, 'How high?'"

"Catering gave me cover. She was right. The cellar was the heart. A shaped charge hidden in a wine crate, triggered remotely, would end him without touching the perimeter."

"You'd have blown up half his staff," Creighton said.

"Collateral is inevitable. But it would have been surgical."

Churchill said nothing, but he pursed his lips in disapproval.

On the fourth day, I watched his aide load three heavy cases into the Mercedes. The car drove south, toward Orly. It came back empty. That night in a café, I overheard catering staff gossip about a farewell dinner on Thursday. Varga was leaving Paris.

I only had four days.

My notes grew shorter. Numbers circled, underlined. The script turned jagged. No more patient logs of patrols and cigarettes. Just a deadline.

Creighton shook his head. "That's when you stopped building a plan and started unraveling."

"Focused, not unraveling. I stripped the noise away. Four days, that was the only clarity that mattered. It was my only opportunity. You don't get a second chance with men like him."

Then the Secretary of State arrived. Black SUVs, diplomatic plates, DSS sweeps, Paris police choking the corners. Catering through metal detectors, every crate opened.

My heart sank. Everything I'd built, the patterns, the risks, the hours, it collapsed the second her motorcade turned through the gates. Weeks reduced to ash in an instant.

I lit a cigarette and told myself I could adapt. But I knew, deep down, a bomb was now impossible. Killing her would have ignited an international incident. The new checks meant discovery. The only option was proximity. Collapse the distance. A badge, a uniform, the catering flow, leverage my knowledge of their routine. From there, it would be simple.

Churchill's tone was quiet, almost pitying. "So in your mind, the solution was proximity. Get close enough to shoot him."

"Yes."

Creighton snorted, "Simple? After all the notes and diagrams, you just decided to walk in and shoot him?"

Tom's jaw tightened. "It wasn't crude. Routes, timing, disguise —every skill still applied."

"Don't dress it up," Creighton snapped. "You threw away weeks of planning for a suicide run."

Tom closed the folder and pushed it back across the table. He shrugged, his gaze fixed on the ashtray, smoke curling upward between them. He couldn't meet Creighton's eyes. For once, there was nothing left to say.

CHAPTER 45

The mansion woke like a stage set. Lights on every cornice, engines low and expensive at the curb, police radios chattering in two languages. Diplomatic Security Service agents in dark suits hovered near the gate, earpieces tight, eyes scanning. I tucked in behind the Maison Comtois crew, forged badge and stolen jacket, a crate in my hands that felt heavier than it was.

The queue moved. Metal detectors. Bags on tables. The caterer in front of me cracked a joke about the Americans and got pulled over for a pat-down that went on too long. I kept my eyes on the trays, the floor, and the body language. Shoulders forward, head down, the soft impatience of men paid by the hour. My badge got a glance, and a hand waved me through. The field of cameras watched without blinking.

Inside, the service corridor ran bright and tiled, hot with steam and hurry. Staff and guards filled it the way water fills a narrowing pipe. I waited for the camera to pan off; it took twelve seconds, as always, and I walked when it turned its face the other way. The junction to the main house had two posted guards tonight, eyes more alert than before. I kept moving with the flow, tray up, spine loose. If they looked at you as passing traffic, you became passing traffic. I cleared them without changing pace.

This is what preparation buys: twelve seconds of borrowed invisibility.

At the next choke point, the catering line bunched and stalled. I slid out along a side corridor like a strand of thread slipping from the weave. The guard I'd clocked in my trial runs was there, exactly where he should be. He had the habit of taking a breather there, rolling his shoulders, rubbing the back of his neck, while the other thumbed a Blackberry, the screen glow lighting his face.

I came up behind him and looped my arm around his throat. No speech, no warning. He flailed; his elbow banged the plaster and scuffed my wrist. I hauled the choke tighter, felt the panic leave him in a small collapse as his windpipe collapsed. His aftershave was cheap and cloying. I dragged him into a service alcove that had been left for mops and forgotten things. The jacket came off, and the earpiece came free with a slight tug. I stripped us both and swapped clothes with him. The pants were a bit too loose and short, the jacket a little big, but the disguise should hold. Pistol to my waistband, radio wire down under the lapel. I waited for someone to round the corner, for a shout, for anything.

No one came. The corridor stayed empty.

In uniform, the building seemed to change its posture around me. The earpiece hissed with the flat comfort of routine: acknowledgements, door checks, a request for ice in the west salon that made two men laugh. I knew the routes and walked them as if I'd always walked them. A uniform is half a disguise; the rest is cadence. You don't play a role, you inhabit a rhythm. Heel, toe, head level, eyes bored.

The guards I met gave me the quick glance that said *seen you before, can't place you, don't care*. The Americans were a different ecosystem. Too much gym, the boxy coats, the hard eyes that flicked past staff to the perimeter. They were looking outward. Everyone was.

I cut through the service wing on the times I'd memorized weeks ago. Rotations rose and fell in me like tide tables. It all held perfectly. A DSS man swept a corridor just ahead, and I ducked into a stairwell on instinct, pressed flat against cold paint while his shadow went long and then vanished.

He didn't check the door. He didn't double back. The earpiece crackled: someone needed a cart; someone's battery was dying. I breathed once, slowly, and went on.

The door to the private apartments sat at the end of a short, tasteful hall, the wallpaper quiet and expensive, the carpet so thick it ate the sound of my steps. A trusted guard stood post. He had the weight of a man who'd been given a narrow task and intended to do it. I expected trouble. I palmed an empty silver tray from a sideboard and let it slide, gentle at first, then loud, clattering away down the marble like a coin in a basin. The guard's head snapped toward the noise. He muttered something about kitchen boys and stepped off to look.

Just like that, the path was clear.

I went through, adrenaline sharp and steady, and told myself I'd earned it. Read the seams, exploit the seams. That's the only game there is.

The corridor beyond was quieter, the air cooler. Paintings watched with old eyes. At the end, the double doors I knew by their proportions and the carpet napped outward in the center, as if feet chose that path when they were tired, was the study. I knew the room from the blueprints, the dimensions laid over in my head like a transparency. Desk on the far side. Window to the right. A sofa near the fire.

I checked the pistol I'd taken, mag seated, slide snug, and found my hands weren't doing what I told them. A small tremor. I tightened my grip until it stopped. Everything I'd built, every hour, every margin note, every lie I'd told myself to make it through led to this door.

I set my hand on the knob, forced the tremor still, and began to turn—

"You really thought this was *tradecraft*, Harrington? It wasn't skill, it was a red carpet." Creighton cut in. "The only thing missing was a band and side boys."

Across the table, Churchill looked down and shook his head.

CHAPTER 46

The doors gave way under my shoulder, and I came into the study with the pistol up, barrel sweeping corners, heart pounding. The room was warm with lamplight, first editions on mahogany shelves, and curtains drawn against the Paris night. And behind the desk, Konstantin Varga sat as though he'd been waiting, a hardback in his hand.

He didn't flinch. Didn't startle. He finished the last line of his paragraph, slid a bookmark between the pages, and closed the cover with deliberate care. Only then did he look up at me.

No fear. No anger. Only the faintest curve of amusement at the corner of his mouth.

He wore a tuxedo shirt, the bow tie undone, the jacket draped neatly across the back of a leather chair. He looked less like a man about to be assassinated and more like a host readying himself for dinner with the Secretary of State.

I held the pistol steady, but the quiet in the room pressed hard against me. My eyes flicked across the walls. Behind his desk, a gallery of power:

A faded military map of Hungary from the 1940s, framed like art, villages circled in German script.

A framed sepia photograph showed Varga, young and lean, standing half in shadow behind a knot of well-dressed, important-looking men. A brass plate beneath it said: *Bretton Woods, 1971*.

On a side table, easy to overlook, a leather-bound field notebook, initials pressed in Gothic script: A.V. Perhaps, a memento from his father, I wondered.

Gleaming amidst the mementos on the wall, a medal in a velvet case stood out proud, its silver cross catching the light.

“Do you like it?” Varga said at last, his voice low, unhurried. “A little token of appreciation from the Order of Charlemagne. The Archduke himself put my name forward.”

“Stand up,” I said. My voice came out harsher than I intended, my breath came heavy. I knew this was the end.

His eyes lingered on mine, curious, almost kind. “Men like you only know the hammer, and so you only see nails. But real power is the fox, not the hammer. It lives in treaties and boardrooms, not in stairwells and pistols. Kick down all the doors you like. You’re still just a tool someone else will throw away. And, here you are, a hammer in search of a nail.”

I fired before he could say another word. Once. Twice.

The cracks split the air like thunder, but the sound was wrong. Muffled. The bullets slapped flat against something invisible. Spiderweb fractures spread in front of his desk, glass glinting under the lamplight where there should have been only empty air.

Varga leaned back, still smiling, the way a teacher might at a child’s failed trick. He shook his head lightly, almost pitying.

The door behind me exploded inward. Boots thundered on parquet. Shouts in French and English overlapped as a dozen men poured in, armored vests and rifles, beams of light cutting across gilt frames. A gloved hand smashed the pistol from my grip, another drove my face into the carpet. My arms were wrenched behind me, cuffs ratcheting down so tight my hands went numb in seconds.

I spat blood and tried to look up.

Kate entered last. She strolled through the scrum of police like someone coming home late to a dinner party. Her eyes found mine. For a second, I thought I saw compassion. Then she spoke, and the softness curdled.

"You never did know when to stop."

I was roughly hauled upright. Varga raised a hand, and they froze. He came around the desk, shoes quiet on the Persian rug. Up close, he studied me the way a scientist studies a pinned insect. The lamplight glinted in his eyes.

"All this effort," he said. A pause. "And you could have simply asked for a chair at the table."

Then he turned his back, already bored.

Kate leaned close, whispered something I couldn't catch. Varga gave a small nod. She straightened and addressed the lead officer without hesitation.

"I'll ride with him to the airport."

The men nodded, and the hands on my arms tightened. They pulled me toward the door, the study shrinking behind me, Varga already lowering himself back into his chair, reaching for his book.

The spiderwebbed glass caught the lamplight one last time as the doors shut.

CHAPTER 47

The steel door slammed shut, and the world narrowed to a dim red bulb buzzing in its cage overhead. The air in the armored transport was hot and metallic, thick with the smell of oil and rubber. I sat shackled at wrists and ankles, chains biting into my skin every time the vehicle jolted. Across from me, alone in the bench seats, sat Kate.

For a while, she said nothing. Just watched me. A strand of hair had slipped loose from behind her ear, and with the same unconscious grace I remembered from London, she tucked it back. The gesture pulled me back for an instant. Captain Avery's apartment, sheets tangled, her hair falling across her eyes while she laughed at something I'd said. Funny how you can miss something that never existed. I hadn't realized how much I'd leaned on the lie. Then the moment was gone, and she was only Kate again, smiling faintly in the dark. The hum of the engine and the occasional crackle of a police radio filled the silence. Her legs were crossed, hands folded lightly in her lap, as though this were nothing more than a late-night train ride.

"You should have left well enough alone, Tom." Her voice was quiet, almost gentle, the kind of tone she'd used once when neither of us wanted to fight anymore. "You could've had a life. A small one, maybe, but a life."

I stared straight ahead, chains clattering when the van braked.

She tilted her head, a small smile breaking across her face. "I did like you, Tom. That part was real."

The light caught her eyes as she leaned forward, conspiratorial. "You remember that little Indian restaurant in London?

God, the samosas were amazing. It almost felt like a normal date. Almost." Her voice softened further, wistful. "I don't get to go on real dates anymore. Thank you for that."

The smile slipped. She leaned back, fingers drumming against her knee, voice sharper now, "But you had to keep pulling at the thread. And here we are."

I finally made eye contact with her. "How's Voss?" I allowed myself a small smile.

Her face hardened, her eyes flashed with rage, and her lip curled in a sneer. She slapped me, sharp and fast, the sound swallowed by the van's steel walls. The sting burned across my cheek, but she was already talking.

"There are rules in this business." Her voice was cold now, clipped. "You broke them. You were never going to win." She let the silence stretch, let me taste the truth of it.

Then, as if a switch had flipped, her tone warmed again, almost admiring. "Konstantin liked you, though. Admired you. Thought you had potential. On paper, you were the perfect recruit. The troubled youth turned spy. I told him you were too stubborn. Too short-sighted. That you lack vision."

The van swayed, the chains bit into my wrists. I stayed silent.

"When he offered me a place," she went on, her smile returning, "I didn't hesitate. Why would I? You saw the room, Tom. You saw the walls. That's where real power lives. Men like you blow things up, wave guns around, spill blood on the carpet. Men like him set the table."

The transport rolled to a stop, brakes hissing. The rear doors banged open, floodlights bleached the interior white. A strip of runway stretched out beyond, a military cargo plane idling with its tail ramp yawning like a steel mouth.

Hands were on me immediately, dragging me down the steps, boots scuffing against asphalt. Shackled, bent forward, I moved like freight. The wind howled, bringing the smell of jet fuel with it.

Kate's fashionable heels clicked beside us, in stark contrast to the tactical boots of my escort. She raised a hand. "Wait."

Rough hands jerked me to a halt.

She slid up next to me until I could smell her perfume: faint citrus, remembered too well from another life. Her lips brushed my cheek, and I felt the press of something small and hard into my palm.

Her voice dropped to a whisper, intimate, as though no one else in the world could hear.

"It's the least I can do. Better this than what they'll do to you... don't say I never gave you anything."

I glanced down: a capsule, smooth, faintly ridged. Cyanide.

PART IV

CHAPTER 47

Tom's story complete, he sat quietly, his face impassive. Across from him, Creighton leaned forward like a man waiting for a fight; Churchill sat slightly back, his hands folded, his expression flat but tight.

Finally, Creighton and Churchill exchanged the look men share at the end of a too-long dinner. Churchill gathered his papers into a neat stack, squared the edges with a precise tap, and slipped them into his briefcase. Creighton stretched, hiding a stagey yawn behind his fist.

"Well," Churchill said, rising with the briefcase in hand. "We do thank you, Mr. Harrington. You've been remarkably forthcoming. But surely you see—what's done cannot be undone."

"Quite," Creighton added, the false joviality back in his voice. "You've had your say, the record's complete. Best to leave things where they lie."

Chairs scraped. Latches clicked. Tom exhaled smoke, eyes half-lidded. Then he said, evenly:

"There's *more.*"

They froze mid-motion. Churchill paused with a pile of folders half-lifted; Creighton's irritation flared in a sharp stare.

"You think you have the whole picture," Tom said. "You don't. Not even close."

He let the words sit.

"During my time with OGI, I had unrestricted access to RIPA intercept databases. Call logs, faxes, encrypted emails, text messages—bulk collection dressed up as oversight. You both know the truth. Most of the queries were warrantless. Illegal. Everyone knew. Nobody cared. Before I left Libya and went underground, I took what I needed. Defence cables. Treasury traffic." He looked at them in turn. "The Prime Minister's private line."

Churchill set his notes back on the table without a sound and sat down heavily. Creighton leaned forward despite himself.

"You think Washington cornered the market on illegal surveillance?" Tom said. "Britain's no better. Do you know what your Defence Ministry did, Mr. Creighton? They opened the vault to contractors and turned a blind eye. Unlimited queries. No warrants. No oversight. I was inside the system."

He flicked ash into the tray. His voice stayed level, almost bored.

"The Prime Minister doesn't sign off policy until Varga's men red-line it first. I've seen the drafts, the tracked changes. Even Defence White Papers. Edited in Varga's office before Parliament ever touched it."

Creighton's scoff died in his throat.

"And your Defence Minister," Tom continued, "his brother's shipping firm in Limassol? Routing NovaTerra contracts through shell fronts. Guns, heroin, pick your poison. I've got the invoices." He didn't blink. "Then there's his daughter in Zurich. Her heroin habit isn't gossip in the corridors. I've got the clinic invoices, charged to an MOD black fund."

Churchill had a vacant stare and was absentmindedly scrubbing his glasses with his tie.

"As for Washington," Tom said, "your former CIA Deputy Director's already got his retirement packaged and ribboned: a board seat, seven figures a year, quid pro quo to keep Treasury off NovaTerra's back. I have his signature on a secure fax." He let the next words fall like stones. "And when he travels, it's not Geneva or London. It's Nairobi. Manila. Young boys from local orphanages 'valet' for him when he's in country. There are files. Hotel receipts, passenger manifests, internal investigations that were buried."

Creighton went white.

Then Tom twisted the knife.

"And let's close with your Prime Minister. He keeps a pied-à-terre in Madrid. You've both heard the rumors." He blew a cloud of smoke in Creighton's direction. "I've seen the phone records. Calls at all hours to one number. A young bartender. Spanish. He flew under diplomatic clearance once, on the PM's jet." Tom tilted his head. "Shall I continue, gentlemen?"

Churchill winced, then there was silence. Thick enough to touch.

Creighton broke first. "Fabrication. Treason. Delusion. You're a disgraced nobody telling bedtime stories, Harrington. You think this posturing—"

Tom lit a fresh cigarette in the middle of the tirade and watched the flame catch. He didn't bother to answer until Creighton ran out of breath.

"If I disappear," he said, "all of it goes public. Not rumor, not conjecture. Original signatures. Transcripts. Emails. Hotel receipts." His gaze didn't leave Creighton's. "Even the recent incident in Brussels… you know which one I mean."

Churchill's breathing had gone slower, heavier. He laid the glasses down, his hand betraying a slight tremor, and laced his fingers, saying nothing.

Tom leaned, "I've built a dead man's switch. *Multiple* dead man's switches. I get so much as a paper cut, it all gets released to every major newspaper, news network, and conspiracy blogger in the world."

Creighton swallowed whatever was left of his fury and growled between gritted teeth, "What do you want?"

Tom stubbed the cigarette half-finished, as if bored with it.

"My life... and Varga's. Then I forget this wretched little conspiracy ever existed, and I disappear."

Creighton smoldered, jaw tight, eyes hot with things he couldn't afford to say. Churchill studied Tom like a man measuring a detonator he'd rather not touch.

Tom reached for the bottle, found only a swallow left, and poured it. He raised the glass in a careless half-toast.

"To the hammer in search of a nail."

He paused, glass just short of his lips, then added, "And the Prime Minister's boyfriend."

Finally, he drained it, leaned back, the faintest suggestion of a smile at one corner of his mouth.

Across the table, Churchill and Creighton exchanged a look and slumped back in their chairs.

CHAPTER 48

Danny's boots scuffed the corridor, loud against the concrete, almost a shuffle. His head stayed down, hands twitching as he checked his gun belt for the third time. Beside him, Geoff walked briskly, clipboard tucked under his arm like a shield, jaw set in that professional mask he wore too tight.

"Christ, Geoff," Danny said, voice thin with nerves. "Why's it got to be us again? Couldn't they send someone else?"

"Because it's our shift," Geoff said. "And because no one else volunteered."

They stopped outside the reinforced cell door. Geoff pressed the intercom button, his voice clipped, parade-ground sharp:

"Prisoner. Face the wall. Interlace fingers behind your neck. Go to the deck, one knee at a time. Cross your feet and sit back on them."

Silence. Then the faint scrape of movement inside.

The bolts rolled back. The door opened.

Tom was already kneeling, hands laced neatly behind his neck, his face unreadable. If he'd heard their nerves through the wall, he gave no sign.

They moved in, the air thick with their unease. Geoff's motions were precise, mechanical, as though reciting a ritual: left wrist, right wrist, click, check, chain. Danny's hands shook enough to fumble the cuff before he got it latched.

Tom watched him. Eyes steady, unblinking, the faintest curl of amusement at the corner of his mouth.

"Release procedure, section four," Geoff droned, eyes on his clipboard, voice as flat as a catechism. "Manacles secured. Prisoner compliant. Transfer commencing." He never once looked Tom in the eye.

They hauled him to his feet and started down the corridor toward the elevator. The chains rattled softly, Danny's nerves louder still.

And then Danny's mouth ran away with him.

"Funny thing, this," he blurted, voice high and quick. "Sort of reminds me of the other weekend, bloke got kicked out of the club, yeah? Slapped the ass of one of the dancers—Crystal, she's got a tattoo of a, of a..." He faltered, color draining. "In any case, this bloke, he wouldn't go quiet, kept shouting at the bouncer, and then—ah, there was this other girl, one of the dancers, she—she had a cousin, I think—no, wait, maybe it was her boyfriend—bloody *Christ...*"

His voice collapsed into silence, the story unraveling into fragments.

Geoff groaned, pinching the bridge of his nose. "Bloody hell, Danny. *Shut it.*"

Danny snapped his mouth shut, lips pressed white. His hands trembled.

A few steps later, he risked a whisper. "Your eyes... they didn't blink. You didn't move. How...?"

Tom's gaze slid to him, calm, almost kind. "An old trick a Sergeant Major taught me during SAS selection. You put yourself in a sort of meditative state. Rest, but aware."

Danny swallowed hard. "How'd you know the Ministry blokes'd be comin'?

Tom gave a small laugh, "Standard procedure. They break you with sleep deprivation for three weeks before they start asking questions. It was day twenty-one."

The elevator doors opened with a groan.

They stepped out into the facility's main entrance. Beyond the blast doors, an unmarked white van rolled down the access road, headlights haloed in the damp.

Tom leaned a fraction closer, his smile slow, deliberate. He pitched his voice into Danny's accent, whispering:

"Maybe I'll see you out at your club, Danny? Yeah? You can finish telling me about Crystal's tattoo. Drinks are on me."

Danny flinched as if burned, fumbling the keys, nearly dropping them. Geoff cursed under his breath, set his jaw stoically, but the clipboard in his hand rattled before he steadied it.

A bag went over Tom's head, and he was roughly bundled into the back of the van.

"Till next time, boys," Tom called out lightly, voice muffled under the hood.

The doors slammed.

Unlike Danny, whoever was in the van kept their mouths shut. No chatter, no coughs, not even a shift in the seats. Just the low drone of the engine and the occasional jolt when the road gave out. Time dragged.

Finally, the van slowed. The cuffs were removed, but a pair of rough, burly hands held his arms twisted behind him. The side door of the van slid open, the bag was yanked free, and with a rough shove, Tom hurtled out of the van. He tumbled roughly into a wet ditch that ran next to the road. Cold air bit his face; it felt sharp and raw after spending weeks in the cell.

Tom pressed a hand to the grass, felt the damp earth under his palm. It was real. He looked up just in time to see the red taillights vanish into the gloom. Stark moors stretched in every direction, rolling and uneven, ridges fading into fog that clung low to the earth: no trees, no houses, no sound but the hiss of the wind through the grass.

CHAPTER 49

"Mary Queen of Scots was held at Bolton Castle in 1568, for six months..."

The guide droned on about Mary Stuart's retinue of thirty and her embroidery frame. Tom let the words wash past as he studied the soot-blackened hearth, the window slit, the iron latch that would've closed the chamber off from the rest of the castle. Tourists snapped pictures and leaned in, taking in every detail.

Tom slipped away from the tour. Through a passage where the plaster had fallen away to rough stone, down a tight turn of stairs, he came out into the open cut of the ruined range: walls broken to sky, wind shouldering through the gaps, nettles pushing up where floors had been. Families drifted past with guidebooks; a boy clacked a plastic sword against a parapet and got scolded.

Tom found Harry in the dungeon, staring intently at some rusty manacles bolted to the stone wall. Long coat, collar up, paper cup of coffee steaming. The castle's tourist brochure was tucked under his arm. Tom slid beside him without looking over. As he stared at the manacles, Tom instinctively rubbed his wrists.

"You're out," Harry said. "You'll never work in Whitehall again."

"Was I ever really in?" Tom said.

Harry huffed a single laugh, cut it short, eyes drifting to other artifacts of the dungeon, a pair of thumbscrews, an iron maiden (likely a Victorian tourist artifact). "Damned foolish thing you did. Brazen. Never bite the hand that feeds you, Tom. We taught you to nick secrets, not crown heads. Now you're walkin' about like a bloody king-slayer."

Wind in the weeds. Camera shutters somewhere above.

Harry reached into his coat and pressed a thick envelope into Tom's palm. It had the reassuring weight of cash, the hard edges of passports, and a cheap phone. "Lay low a bit after you finish this. They may come for you. Once things quiet down a bit, I'll sling what work I can your way, off the books. How you sorted, money-wise?"

Tom weighed the envelope once, then tucked it into his jacket. Said nothing.

Harry leaned closer, voice dropping though no one was near enough to hear. "You serious about goin' after him?"

Tom nodded.

"You'll be the death of both of us," Harry said, half to himself. "Either we trained you better than we thought... or you won't need that money after all."

They walked a little, ducking under a jagged arch into the colder shade of the lower range. Rusted bars covered a small opening that read "Cellars and Stores." Tourists gave it a glance and moved on.

"He's in Scotland," Harry said at last. "Hunting lodge. Old family pile. If you're fool enough to walk into it..." He let it hang.

Tom waited.

Harry looked at him then—hard, appraising, the old street in his eyes under the Savile Row exterior. "He's got the dirtiest bunch of killers in the business on the doors, sensors on the tracks, a whirlybird sat fat on the lawn for bad weather. You still goin'?"

"Yes."

"You reckon putting Varga in the ground'll fix you?

"It's a start."

"Men who say that never stop."

"I will."

"That's what they all say."

"I want to see what life looks like when no one's pulling the strings but me."

"I thought you didn't want to be a planner."

Tom fished a cigarette out of his pocket and lit it, not meeting his eyes.

Harry nodded once, like a judge passing sentence. He took a slow sip of coffee, shoved a cigar he hadn't bothered to light yet into his mouth, and leaned against an arch, next to a plaque that read, "Chapel."

Their eyes met.

"Right then," Harry said, walking towards the exit. "Off you go, King-slayer. Don't say I didn't warn you."

CHAPTER 50

The boathouse looked like a postcard as they approached down the path. A squat, stone Victorian cottage, gables pitched against the sky, smoke curling from a bent iron chimney. Its windows had a flawless view of the loch. For a fleeting second, Kate imagined it empty, quiet, a place to write or read.

Inside, the illusion collapsed. The neat little cottage had been colonized, turned into a barracks and bachelor pad in equal measure. Four guards sprawled around a scarred table, cards in hand, half-eaten sandwiches among empty tins of lager. Boots and rifles were dumped wherever they fell. A radio crackled faintly on the counter, ignored.

Kate's escort, a tall ex-paratrooper with a wrestler's neck, nodded at them. "We're taking a boat out," he said, already moving toward the back door that opened onto the moorings. One of the guards looked up long enough to grunt, then threw another chip into the pile.

The boat was small but expensive, eighteen feet with a clean white hull and teak trim, the kind of runabout built for weekenders on the Riviera but just as happy nosing across a Scottish loch. The stainless cleats gleamed; the nylon seat covers were still beaded with last night's rain.

Kate stepped aboard lightly, ducking into the cockpit. She flicked open the engine bay, checked the battery cut-off switch, and gave the bilge pump a quick test. "Don't just stand there," she said over her shoulder. "The battery switch is right there—red handle. See it?"

He bent, frowning, reaching toward the wrong panel. She

laughed, pushed his hand aside, and turned the switch herself. The gauges on the console ticked alive, needles quivering.

"Oh, never mind. I'll do it. Army guy, huh?" she said, with a sharp grin. "Can you at least take the covers off the seats?"

He muttered something under his breath and removed the covers, revealing the rich leather seats, while she slipped behind the wheel, pressing the ignition. The inboard turned over once, twice, then caught, a smooth purr vibrating through the deck. She eased the throttle, listening with the ear of someone who had grown up around engines.

Lines were cast off in quick, practiced motions, and she steered them clear of the moorings. The nose swung toward the center of the loch, mist curling low across the black water. She opened the throttle for a while and let the engine hum, reveling in the thrill of the wind whipping her hair.

They came to a rocky outcropping a few miles west of the estate. She cut the engine, let the boat drift, and baited a hook with neat, practiced fingers.

Her father's voice surfaced uninvited, as it often did near water: *Slow down, Kate. Be patient. Not everything is a fight.* She pushed the memory aside and watched the ripples spread as she cast the line. The Highlands rose around them, black-green ridges with slashes of purple heather, tops lost in weather. You could disappear here, she thought. Buy a cottage with a wood-burning stove and a view of nothing. No phones. No meetings. Just quiet.

The float ticked with the swell. She closed her eyes, envisioned the little cottage on a loch, nothing around for miles... she could almost feel it.

Then the rain came, fine and needling, dimpling the surface of the water. It slid down her cheekbones, clung to her lashes, pulled her back to the present. The Highlands blurred, grey on grey, the ridges half-swallowed by weather.

Kate blinked, sighed, and reeled in the line. "Back to the bloody house," she said. The engine coughed once, then caught, its hum breaking the silence. She swung the bow towards the estate, the loch's black water parting before her.

On the outer perimeter, a bulky man in a soaked field jacket walked his sector with the numb patience of a professional. The rain came thin and steady, beading on the brim of his cap and running down his collar. He was from the Balkans and carried the comfortable fatalism of a man who'd changed uniforms more than once. The command post had warned that the CCTV was down again; a technician was "en route," which meant hours. Fine. He had boots, a pattern, and a radio. Patterns kept men alive.

He checked the treeline, scanned the track, turned to sweep back, and saw a figure ahead on the estate road.

Tall, slender. Tweed baker boy cap, green Barbour jacket, corduroys, cashmere sweater, the kind of boots that looked hand-stitched. Striding along, as if the estate belonged to him.

The guard shifted his strong hand to the butt of his pistol and lifted his off hand. "Private property. You turn around now."

"Oh, thank God," the man said, the vowels light and educated, a Highland lilt overlaid on an old school. "I've been trying to find someone in authority. I've just purchased the neighboring estate, you see, and my ghillie—*idiot*—shot a buck that wandered over your line. I'll settle it, of course. Wouldn't want accusations of poaching. Dreadfully embarrassing."

"You go gate," the guard said. "Make appointment."

The man bristled, as if the rain itself offended him. "Good God, man, must we stand on ceremony in the bloody rain? I'd expect more initiative from your sort. Tell your superior, Sir Ian MacArthur, is here to see the gamekeeper."

"Against tree." The guard's tone didn't change. He pushed the man, patted him down, professional hands running over ribs, waist, ankles. Nothing obvious. He stepped back and lifted his radio, thumbed the transmit.

A breath of static.

The knife went in over the collarbone, quick and clean, a sliver of steel hugging bone and vein. The guard's free hand shot to his pistol on reflex, but the Barbour man had his wrist, turned and pinned, driving both of them into the ditch. The radio hissed against mud; the guard's breath sawed, then hiccuped, then slowed. The man in the tweed cap held his gaze and nodded with a half-smile, making shushing sounds. When the life left his eyes, he eased the guard down, cleaned the blade on the dead man's jacket, and took the pistol and the radio with a small, economical motion. He straightened his cap, stepped back onto the road, and kept walking purposefully toward the house.

The main office looked like every Highland fantasy a banker ever paid for: dark wood, a stag in oils over the fireplace, tartan heavy at the windows. Konstantin Varga sat behind a desk the size of a small boat, reading glasses low on his nose, a sheaf of reports turned to angles that made sense to him and no one else.

Varga adjusted his reading glasses and tapped a line on the report with a gold fountain pen. "Local militia, Kivu. Line four. Intelligence says they're shifting their smuggling from the road to the lake." He looked up at Maddox. "If that's true, what does it mean for us?"

Maddox sat sprawled in the opposite chair, jacket open, tie crooked. He looked more like a soldier awkwardly dressed for a boardroom than a partner in a baronial office. "How about we kill their chieftain and be done with it?"

Varga sighed, the patient irritation of a man obliged to say simple things twice.

"Because then another steps up," he said. "Kill a leader, you make a martyr. Buy a cousin, you make a dynasty." He set the glasses back on. "That's how the world is run."

Varga leaned back in his chair. He was about to launch into another lecture, then thought better of it. These ex-military types could be infuriatingly obtuse—he'd be wasting his breath.

Maddox shifted, restless. He wistfully eyed the crystal decanters of whisky that lay on an ornate table in the corner of the room.

A sharp knock at the door cut across the room.

"Enter," Varga said without raising his voice.

The head of security slipped in, rain still dripping from his jacket. He was a compact man gone loose in the middle, the kind of ex-military hire chosen less for his trigger finger than for his planning and paperwork, the steady hand who knew how to shuffle guard rosters and keep the estate's logistics neat.

"Sir," he began, his voice apologetic, "CCTV is still down, and now we've got multiple guards not responding to radio checks. I've recalled the off-duty detail, sent the maids and kitchen staff home, and we're issuing long guns."

Varga looked up from his papers, lips pursed.

Maddox gave a dry, disdainful laugh, shaking his head. "And this is the grand design, is it? All your clever little machinations, and the whole house of cards collapses because your cameras go out. You hired planners when you should've hired professionals."

Varga's gaze settled on Maddox, calm but cold.

"Well, Mr. Maddox," he said at last, "if you think the house is collapsing, then by all means, join them. Go earn that exorbitant salary I pay you."

CHAPTER 51

The runabout slid back into its moorings with barely a ripple. Kate stepped off first, taking the line while her escort awkwardly looped the stern rope and cinched it off. They made their way back up the short path to the little boathouse. The rain had thickened to a fine mist, clinging to her hair, softening the lines of the cottage until, for a heartbeat, it looked almost like her fantasy retreat again. She thought about how she would decorate it: old leather chesterfields and tartan.

"Something ain't right," her escort said. His voice cut the reverie in two.

Kate blinked. Up ahead, the door to the boathouse hung slightly ajar, rocking faintly in the wind. She remembered distinctly when they left, one of the guards had knocked it shut with a casual kick.

Her escort's hand went to his sidearm. He slowed, shoulders tensing, scanning the shadows under the eaves. The faint yellow light inside seemed wrong now, blurred and uncertain.

Kate's pulse quickened. She smelled oil and damp wood, the ordinary scents of the place, but beneath it—something metallic, something acrid.

They edged closer. He pushed the door with two fingers. It swung open on its hinges with a low groan.

Inside—

The illusion of the idyllic cottage collapsed.

The interior was unrecognizable now. Blood was everywhere, pooled across the flagstones, spattered on the whitewashed walls. The poker table had collapsed under the weight of two bodies, cards scattered across the floor like dead leaves. Sandwich bread was still laid out on the counter, crusts soaking red.

Kate froze.

Her escort's pistol was in his hand instantly, sweeping corners. "I'm going to the big house. You stay here." He didn't wait for her answer, just moved fast and low through the door, vanishing into the wet.

Kate's eyes flicked once more across the carnage—four men butchered with surgical efficiency. Something primal screamed at her: *Get out. Now.*

She moved with cold precision. What did she need? She grabbed a discarded rucksack and started shoving supplies into it. A sidearm from one of the bodies. Spare magazines. She rifled through dead men's pockets, stripping wallets, peeling out cash. Next, she moved to the kitchen, grabbing bread, tinned vegetables, chocolate bars, anything quick.

One of the guards' phones buzzed weakly with a low battery warning. Kate snatched it up and, moving back down to the docks, entered a number from memory.

"I need an exit route," she said. A pause, then, more urgently: "No. This is *bigger*. Broken Arrow. I need to go deep under."

Static, then a reply only she could hear. Her lips tightened. "Okay. I'll see you in Dublin."

She ended the call, hurled the phone, and watched it splash into the black loch.

Outside, Varga's thirty-five-foot cruiser bobbed against its cleats, paint gleaming, stainless steel glistening. She jumped aboard, working fast at the mooring lines. Her movements were precise—until her hands started to shake.

The knot was simple, but she fumbled with it, her fingers losing all dexterity. She yanked at it, cursed it under her breath, but the tremors grew worse, her chest tight, her breath coming in gasps. She slammed a fist against the rail and let out a raw, guttural scream that echoed across the water. Tears blurred her vision, hot and sudden. Her whole body trembled.

"*Get it together, Kate.*"

She ripped the last line free, stumbled back into the cockpit, and fired up the inboard. The engine purred awake, steady. She shoved the throttle forward gently, eased the boat out into the loch, hugging the dark shoreline.

Her face was smooth now, mask restored, but her eyes shimmered.

The estate's walled kitchen garden would have been idyllic and serene under different circumstances. Maddox almost expected Peter Rabbit to poke his head up, with an armload of lettuce. Rain tapped the greenhouse glass and ran in thin streams down the panes. The tranquil scene was shredded as Maddox and his men moved in silence, rifles sweeping. He had chosen three of the best operators in the security detail to accompany him. One, a former SAS man; another, a dishonorably discharged Delta operator; and finally, a former SEAL, like him.

They fanned into a staggered line, each man covering a different angle. The point man swept the hedgerow with his muzzle, the second checked the wall above, the third drifted back-to-back with Maddox to cover the blind side. No words passed; only hand signals, crisp and economical, guiding the advance row by row.

The silence broke in a series of rapid suppressed cracks.

His men dropped where they stood, bodies jerking once before stilling. Each shot placed perfectly in the unprotected gaps of plate and vest.

Maddox whirled, weapon sweeping, teeth bared. Silence answered him.

He shifted a step, boots crunching in the gravel, carbine pressed so tightly into his shoulder the stock creaked. His eyes desperately scanned for his opponent, but the walled garden gave him nothing back but dripping leaves and the slow sway of apple branches. Somewhere, a loose shutter tapped against stone.

He tried to steady his breathing, but every exhale seemed too loud. His men were sprawled at his feet in neat, unmoving heaps. Whoever had done it could see him now. Could have already taken the shot.

Maddox's skin crawled. He swept the muzzle across the hedgerows again, then up to the wall tops, expecting movement, a shadow, anything. Nothing. Just the hiss of rain in the soil.

"What the *fuck* do you want?" he finally roared, voice echoing against the stone walls. "Come out and show yourself!"

A voice, calm, familiar, cut through the rain.

"What do you say, Maddox? Let's finish this... no guns."

Maddox froze, trying to place it. Then he laughed low, a growl of recognition. "*Harrington*? Christ. I heard they buried you. Guess they didn't dig deep enough." His grin widened, sharp and cruel. "No guns? Sure. Let's dance."

Tom stepped out from a cluster of apple trees, rifle at the low ready. They circled each other, rifles slung off, tossed aside. Pistols followed, skidding across wet soil.

"You're a bit overdressed, aren't you?" Maddox sneered, eyes raking Tom's Barbour and tweed.

Tom said nothing, only shifted into a fighting stance, balanced, waiting.

Maddox grinned as he drew a small knife from his boot. Tom answered with a thin knowing smile as his hand disappeared into his coat, emerging with a small pistol.

Maddox blinked, confused for a half-second.

CRACK

The shot punched into Maddox's thigh. He screamed and collapsed into the mud, knife flying from his grip. His hands clawed at the wound, blood spilling between his fingers.

"You—you bastard," he gasped. "Fight me—you coward—fight —"

Tom slowly walked towards him.

"No."

Maddox tried to crawl backward, dragging his leg through the muck, leaving a dark smear behind him. His eyes darted for the knife, but it was too far away.

Tom stopped a foot from him.

Maddox looked up, teeth gritted, eyes wide.

Tom put the gun to his head. Maddox's mouth worked, but no sound came.

The gun barked again, and Maddox slumped into the mud, eyes open but empty.

The main house loomed above the loch, all turrets and stone, Highland baronial whimsy at its finest. Its windows glowed warmly through the rain, curtains drawn, promising safety and civility. Tom mounted the front steps, carbine up and ready, without slowing, boots hammering on wet flagstone. His blood was up. No flanking, no subtlety. Straight through the front.

The oak double doors gave way under his shove, swinging wide into the grand entry hall. Antlers and oil portraits loomed over tartan carpets and polished wood.

A shape lurched into view at the far end of the hall: the head of security. His face was grey, lips thin, rifle clutched white-knuckled. For a heartbeat, both men stared—one panicked, one implacable.

Then the guard broke, panic taking him. He yanked the trigger, and the lobby erupted in a full-auto scream. Bullets ripped chandeliers, shredded stags' heads, burst plaster from the walls. A spray of glass cascaded from the mezzanine windows. Almost everything in the room was hit except his target.

The bolt of the rifle locked to the rear; the magazine was empty. The security man's chest heaved as though he had run a marathon, eyes wide.

Tom put one round through his forehead and moved deliberately towards the stairs.

He climbed the stairs slowly, past faded banners, gilt-framed maps of old campaigns, oil paintings of famous battles. The office door waited at the end of the corridor, ajar, lamplight spilling across the carpet.

Tom dropped the carbine to the floor, drew his pistol, and pushed the door open. A fire guttered low in the grate. The desk was a mess of reports, one glass overturned, scotch bleeding across figures. A host of crystal decanters gleamed from a sideboard. On the desk next to a pile of envelopes lay an SS dagger, its Totenkopf grinning in silver, its edge dulled now, pressed into service as a letter-opener.

Tom's eyes moved across the room. More mementos littered the walls and shelves, like the study in Paris. An antique dueling pistol, a Montblanc fountain pen that was used to sign a treaty, a framed picture of President Kennedy, smiling from his limousine in Dallas. Tom's head whipped around towards a large antique wardrobe that dominated a wall. A slight scrape had come from within. He strode up to it and flung the doors open.

He found Varga crouched inside, a revolver trembling in both hands. His glasses were skewed, his tie crooked, but when he saw Tom, he composed himself, sat up straighter, lifted his chin. He carefully set the gun aside and stepped out of the wardrobe, smoothing his jacket and straightening his tie.

Without asking, he crossed the room to the decanter and poured two drinks. The crystal clinked faintly against the glass. His hand was shaking despite the practiced motion.

"There's no point, you know," he said. "Kill the King, and there are a hundred waiting to take his place. The only question is—who will sit on the throne?" He drained his glass and poured himself another.

Tom kept the gun trained on him and said nothing.

"We didn't give you a seat at the table—you took it at gunpoint." A thin, wry smile tugged at Varga's mouth. He picked up the other glass of whisky and offered it to Tom.

Tom didn't move.

"Bottled in '39, from Churchill's private collection." He extended the glass a little further. "This is what real power tastes like."

Tom let it hang.

"Go on, you've earned your place at the table."

The pistol bucked once. Varga's head snapped sideways, and he collapsed, blood spattering the desk.

Tom worked in silence. He dragged bodies, loaded them into the estate's Polaris, and dumped them in a heap in the lobby of the main hall. Guns went into the loch, vanishing into black water.

He ransacked the house for cash, found several thick bundles, and stuffed them into a satchel with the contents of Varga's humidor. He set aside two bottles of 50-year-old single malt found in the bar.

The smell of petrol filled the house as he splashed gasoline across the floorboards and curtains, twisted open the gas lines, let the air grow heavy and dangerous.

In the foyer, he struck a road flare, the hiss popping loudly in the silence. He tossed it into the dark and turned away.

The explosion rolled across the loch, fire blooming against the rain. The old pile burned bright, a pyre of stone and timber.

Tom walked briskly back down the road he had come in on, a bottle of whisky under each arm, whistling *Wild Rover.*

Epilogue

The cottage sat so close to the surf it seemed one hard wave might tear it free and carry it out to sea. From the sand, it looked idyllic: weathered shutters, sun-bleached clapboard, palm fronds rattling in the trade wind.

Kate—these days she answered to *Claire Jensen*—stepped barefoot onto the porch in a linen shirt and sunglasses, steaming coffee in hand. She lifted a hand to the old fisherman down the beach, who sat cross-legged over his net, needle flashing through twine. He waved back without pausing his work.

Farther out, her boyfriend's voice carried from the water. "Oi, coffee addict!" He splashed like an overgrown child, hair blond and sun-browned shoulders gleaming. He taught surfing at a resort up the coast, a happy drifter who'd washed into her life and stayed. He knew nothing of dead drops, dossiers, or soft power. She liked it that way.

She smiled and waved, but her eyes lingered on the horizon, scanning. Always scanning.

Inside the cottage, paradise wore a different face. The shutters were not wood but steel, painted to fool the eye. The locks on the doors were triple-barred. A pistol slept under her pillow, and hidden in the closet, a half-packed rucksack with cash and spare passports. The alarm system threaded silent currents through every frame and sill. And two local bruisers she paid in cash drank rum most nights on the far end of the beach, shooing away curious tourists and reporting if any foreigners asked the wrong questions.

Later that morning, she and Freddy walked the beach together, arm in arm, their bare feet sinking into damp sand where the tide had turned. He talked as he always did, easy, rolling stories that came out like songs. This one was about a tourist who had downed too many rum punches, staggered onto a surfboard, and toppled off in a spectacular splash before he even got his balance. He laughed as he told it, his hands sketching the wobble, the crash, the foaming wave.

Kate smiled in the right places, but her eyes never stopped moving. The treeline at the edge of the sand. The blind curve of the bay where the reef rose dark beneath the water. The fisherman's shack half-hidden in palms.

"You okay?" he asked after a while, catching her silence.

She nodded, but it was too quick, unconvincing.

"Your mind's always somewhere else," he said. His hand squeezed hers, gentle, almost pleading. "Can't you just... be here? Be present?"

She stopped walking, let the surf hiss around her ankles. For a moment she let herself look at him, really looked. The sun-browned shoulders, the crow's-feet lines carved by salt and laughter, a man who could belong to this place in a way she never would.

Her smile was faint, sad. "I wish I could," she said, and her voice nearly broke on it. "You've no idea how much I wish I could."

The waves whispered against the shore. He bent to kiss her temple, still thinking she was only distracted, only tired. But Kate knew the truth. The beach, the laughter, even the man beside her, none of it could ever belong to her.

At sunset, she dined in the old quarter, where tourists pressed into narrow streets lit by strings of bulbs and the smell of grilling fish. She chose her seat by instinct: back to the wall, facing the exits. Her spoon never clinked against the plate. She laughed, tipped generously, lingered over wine, but her eyes never stopped moving.

She left the restaurant just as the evening light began to thin, slipping toward that golden, honeyed hour when everything looked kinder than it was. Down the street, a pack of children was playing fútbol with a half-flat ball, chasing it through puddles, shrieking with delight. Kate slowed, drawn in despite herself.

The ball came skittering down the cobbled street, bouncing off a shutter before rolling to her feet. The children shrieked with laughter, their bare legs flashing as they chased after it.

Kate trapped it under her sandal with a smooth stop, the motion so familiar it startled her. For a heartbeat, she was twelve again, on a patch of Long Island grass, her father's voice sharp but amused: *Keep your knee over it, Katie, don't let it get away from you.* She nudged the ball back, and the kids erupted in cheers, one bowing theatrically before darting away with it.

She stayed there, smiling, letting the sound of their game wash over her. The late light caught in the puddles, turned the air gold, softened everything. She could almost believe she belonged in this place, just another woman walking home after dinner, no shadows to chase, no masks to wear.

The ball thudded against a wall. A boy's shout echoed down the narrow lane. She lingered too long, letting herself feel the warmth in her chest, a strange ache of wanting.

That was when the shadow detached itself from the mouth of an alley.

One of her hired watchers, wiry, pockmarked, a cigarette clinging to his lip, sidled close, so quietly he seemed part of the street until the last second. He didn't raise his voice. He bent as though sharing a joke, eyes never leaving the children.

"Señora," he said, soft and flat, "a tall white man. Seen here. Diving near the reef. Asking questions. Hanging around too much."

The warmth drained from her in an instant. Her smile stayed in place for the children's sake, but her body was rigid, the skin at the back of her neck prickling. She slid him a folded note, crisp, ready, into his palm.

"Gracias," she whispered.

He nodded once and melted back into the dusk.

Kate's gaze lingered on the children one last time, their voices rising in a chant as the ball smacked stone and feet. For a heartbeat, she envied them the simplicity of their joy. Then she turned on her heel, walking fast toward her moped, her stomach a knot of ice.

Moments later, she was tearing through the lanes on her scooter, wind in her face, heart pounding.

Back at the bungalow, Kate all but slammed the door behind her, breath ragged, heart thundering in her ears. She dropped the first bolt, then the second, then dragged the crossbar across with a grunt until the frame shuddered. The shutters came next—steel masquerading as weathered wood—crashing shut with hollow bangs that echoed through the cottage. Each one sounded final, like sealing a tomb.

She moved room to room in a frenzy that only looked methodical. Her fingers shook as she checked the seams. The hair she'd left across the back door was still in place. The kitchen blind hung at the same angle. The tripwire at the sand line unbroken. Relief came in jagged little gasps—but it didn't slow her. If anything, the confirmation made the fear worse. Whoever was out there hadn't come yet... but they would.

The Beretta slid into her grip from its hiding panel. She racked the slide, the metallic crack splitting the silence, and jammed spare magazines into her pockets with fumbling speed.

From behind a row of wine bottles in the kitchen, she pulled down a small steel box, the kind no thief would look twice at. Inside: passports under three different names, currency in five denominations, prepaid SIMs, two burner phones, and a rucksack already packed with the essentials—clothes, antibiotics, iodine tabs, a roll of dollars rubber-banded tight.

She powered one phone on, the cheap screen flaring bluish in the dark. Dialed from memory.

"Where are you?" The voice on the other end was low, untraceable.

"They found me," she whispered. "I need the boat. Now."

A pause. Then: "Understood." The line went dead.

She killed the phone, pulled the SIM, snapped it in two, tossed it in the sink.

Next came the power. She moved toward the breaker panel, intending to cut power. Standard procedure: deny any intruder the cover of appliances, of humming machinery, control the dark herself.

But as her hand reached for the switch, everything went black.

Total blackout.

The refrigerator gave one last sigh, the ceiling fan clicked once and stopped. Even the security light above the porch snuffed out.

Her breath caught.

Gun raised, flashlight in her off hand, she began clearing

rooms, slow and methodical. Her own heartbeat sounded too loud. The sea hissed steadily outside, but inside—nothing. No creak, no scuff, no sound of another human being.

She slipped into the bathroom last. Reinforced door, no windows, tiles she'd lined with a second skin of Kevlar. Her safe room. The place she'd hold out until extraction.

She swung the light, scanning.

Freddy was sprawled in the tub, dumped there like garbage. One arm dangled over the edge, fingers grazing the tiled floor. His throat was carved to the spine, the wound gaping, flies already twitching at the edges. One of his eyes was half-shut, the other staring. Dried blood crusted in the basin, dark smears dragged across the rim where he'd been hauled in.

Kate screamed, staggered, flashlight jerking wildly across tiles.

She spun, pistol up, back against the wall, heart slamming. The light steadied on the sink—and caught something that didn't belong.

A small dish. Inside it, carefully placed, perfectly centered: a ridged capsule. Cyanide.

The gun trembled in her hands.

Her silhouette shook in the moonlight spilling through the slats, her breath breaking into soft, strangled whimpers.

A CONVERSATION WITH THE AUTHOR

Q: Is *The Silent Directorate* based on real events?
A: Of course not.
Officially.

Q: That's not reassuring.
A: It shouldn't be.

Q: Does a "Silent Directorate" actually exist?
A: Not in any building you can Google. Not with a sign on the door.
But if you believe power structures dissolved when the Cold War ended, I have a bridge in Berlin to sell you.

Q: Konstantin Varga feels disturbingly plausible. Is he based on a real person?
A: He's based on a type.
Men who never appear on ballots but attend every summit.
Men who fund both sides of conflicts and call it "stability."

If you can't think of one, you're not paying attention.

Q: Is Tom Harrington a hero?
A: He wants to be.

That may be the problem.

Q: He tortures. He kills outside the rules. Some readers may struggle with that.
A: They should.

Tom begins the book as part of a system. Then he tries to pull at the threads.

What he discovers is that the threads are woven into everything — including himself.

Q: There seems to be a mirroring between Tom and Lucien Moreau from *The Phoenix Gambit*. Was that intentional?
A: Very.

Systems replicate themselves. Even through the men who fight them.

Q: So is he becoming what he hates?
A: He's terrified that he already has.

Q: Why doesn't he walk away?
A: Because walking away doesn't undo what you've learned.

And it doesn't undo what you've done.

Q: Are readers meant to approve of his choices?
A: No.

They're meant to feel the weight of them.

If you're comfortable when Tom crosses a line, something's wrong.
If you're uneasy but understand why he did it — that's where the story lives.

Q: There's a strong theme of betrayal—especially among allies. Why?
A: Because betrayal rarely comes from enemies.

It comes from the people sitting next to you at the briefing table.

Q: The book suggests humanitarian aid can be weaponized. Are you making a political statement?
A: I'm making a historical one.

Aid, trade, religion, democracy — every ideal can be repurposed by power.

That isn't cynicism. It's precedent.

Q: Is Kate Prescott alive?
A: That depends on who you ask.

And what version of events you believe.

Q: Will Tom ever get peace?
A: Define peace.

Q: What's the most dangerous idea in this book?
A: That systems don't drift toward corruption.

They are built to absorb it.

Q: Final question: Should readers be worried?
A: You already are.

That's why you finished the book.

A FINAL NOTE

If you enjoyed *The Silent Directorate*, consider leaving a review or sharing it with someone who enjoys morally complex thrillers. Word of mouth is how stories like this survive.

Thank you for reading.

— A. G. Soares

If you enjoyed The Silent Directorate, discover where Tom Harrington's story began.

Before the warlords.
Before the interrogations.
Before he understood how power really works.

It's the summer of 1999.

Tom Harrington is an American college student backpacking through Europe, chasing cheap hostels, train timetables, and the promise of adventure. But when a shadowy network of former intelligence operatives known as Phoenix becomes convinced that Tom possesses a stolen microchip containing highly classified secrets, his trip turns into a hunt.

What he doesn't know can get him killed.

Pulled into a covert struggle between governments and rogue intelligence factions, Tom is forced into an uneasy alliance with Harry Fletcher, a seasoned British operative running an off-the-books intelligence unit. Together, they race across Europe — from the rugged Highlands of Scotland to the streets of Paris, the canals of Venice, and the peaks of Switzerland — pursued by men who don't ask questions before they pull triggers.

But this isn't just a chase.

As Tom begins to understand what's encoded on the microchip, he realizes the stakes extend far beyond his own survival. The information in the wrong hands could destabilize alliances, ignite old rivalries, and shift the balance of power across Europe.

The Phoenix Gambit is a fast-paced international thriller about innocence colliding with espionage, about trust forged under fire, and about the moment an ordinary young man takes his first step into a world he will never fully escape.

This is where it all starts.

Please enjoy an exclusive preview of The Phoenix Gambit:

THE PHOENIX GAMBIT

Prologue

—June, 1999

The sun draped its warm fingers over the historic cemetery, a haven of peace amidst the bustling city of Edinburgh. On a bench nestled between ancient headstones, an elderly gentleman in tweed savored the solitude, his lunch spread neatly before him on wax paper. He bit into his sandwich, relishing the sharp cheddar that complemented the crusty bread. His eyes, hidden behind spectacles with lenses as thick as old bottle glass, roved the landscape with an air of contentment—as though he were merely another mourner paying respects to long-gone ancestors.

Every so often, he paused, tilting his head as if listening to the whispers of the dead. As he delicately wiped crumbs from his meticulously manicured mustache, a figure caught his attention—a middle-aged woman ambling languidly down the cobblestone path. Her pleated skirt swished at her calves, and she carried herself with an aristocratic air.

Sunglasses obscured her eyes, and a colorful silk scarf was artfully wrapped around her hair. In her hands, she cradled a bouquet of flowers, their hues a stark contrast to the greys and greens of the weathered gravestones.

She paused by the statue of loyal Greyfriars Bobby, bent down, and reverently placed the flowers at the weathered base. The vibrant petals rested against the cold stone, a silent tribute to the undying loyalty of the little dog commemorated in bronze. With the task complete, she straightened and resumed her tour of the cemetery.

The elderly gentleman folded his empty sandwich wrapper and slipped it into his leather satchel. His lunch now concluded, he rose from the bench, bones creaking slightly. With measured steps, he made his way toward the same statue that housed the woman's offering.

The old man stopped before the faithful hound's likeness, his gaze falling upon the bouquet.

The old man's fingers, gnarled yet deft, reached out to the cluster of petals with a deliberate tenderness. Quickly, with the skill of an experienced pickpocket, he palmed a tiny microchip hidden among the petals. The motion was fluid, practiced, a maneuver perfected over countless such exchanges. He casually turned to continue his stroll when a muffled crack rolled softly off the gothic mausoleums and whispered through the rows of headstones.

The old man jolted, a puppet wrenched by unseen strings, as a searing pain exploded across his torso. With a grunt, his lips curled back over teeth that gritted instinctively; his eyes quickly identified his unknown adversary, and a growl rumbled from deep within his chest, "You bastard..." The words were barely audible, a guttural accusation cast into the wind as his body began to betray him, his knees buckling.

Another crack rang out, almost delicately, and as it reverberated off the stone angels and Celtic crosses, a bullet found its mark with gruesome efficiency. The bullet ripped through the old man's throat, sending a fountain of blood raining across the headstones. He crumpled, with the abrupt finality of a story ending mid-sentence, leaving the old man in an inelegant heap at the foot of Greyfriars Bobby.

The sharp report of the first gunshot had barely finished echoing when the woman in the pleated skirt sprang into action. Her movements were fluid, trained, and precise. Even in her haste, there was a balletic quality to her steps. A small automatic pistol emerged from the depths of her bag, glinting dully against the muted light filtering through the cemetery's aged trees.

She ran toward the statue, legs pumping, her eyes scanning for signs of the assailant. The old man lay motionless, an unreadable epilogue written across his still face.

The air was thick with the acrid scent of gunpowder and freshly turned earth as she wove between the headstones. She crouched low, using the gravestones as cover, firing off carefully placed rounds in the direction she suspected the assailant was hiding.

The cemetery was eerily silent, the assassin's location masked within the stillness of the graves. With each movement, she felt the cold gaze of death upon her, and her breath came in measured gasps, condensing in the chill air as she reached an ornate gravestone, its angelic figure standing guard over the deceased. She paused for a fraction of a second, considering her next move. Then, gun at the ready, she carefully peered around the headstone, searching for her target.

A muffled crack sliced through the air—swift, precise, final. A bullet pierced the center of her forehead and exited in a haze of red mist. Her body slumped against the cold gray stone, her vibrant scarf fluttering to the ground as her pistol slipped from lifeless fingers.

The assassin's hands expertly rifled through the old man's pockets, quickly locating the microchip, no larger than a fingernail, hidden within the waistcoat's intricate folds.

He spared not a second more, moving swiftly away from Bobby's eternal gaze, slipping through the cemetery's wrought iron gates just as the distant sound of a policeman's shrill whistle cut through the afternoon air.

The assassin glanced back at the chaos he'd left behind one last time. The bodies of the old man and the woman lay motionless, a stark contrast against the serene backdrop of the historic graveyard where Bobby continued his vigil.

He melded into the shadows, his footsteps echoing faintly on the ancient stones. Unseen, the assassin blended with the ebb and flow of city life, another faceless figure on the streets of Edinburgh as he disappeared into the heart of the city.

www.ingramcontent.com/pod-product-compliance
Lightning Source LLC
LaVergne TN
LVHW030918080826

845145LV00013B/2944

* 9 7 8 1 9 6 6 7 8 5 0 3 3 *